BREAKING COUNTRY

Crooked Brook Book One

E.J. Nickson

Boroughs Publishing Group

www.BOROUGHSPUBLISHINGGROUP.com

PUBLISHER'S NOTE: This is a work of fiction. Names, characters, places and incidents either are the product of the author's imagination or are used fictitiously. Any resemblance to actual events, locales, business establishments or persons, living or dead, is coincidental. Boroughs Publishing Group does not have any control over and does not assume responsibility for author or third-party websites, blogs or critiques or their content.

BREAKING COUNTRY
Copyright © 2020 E.J. Nickson

All rights reserved. Unless specifically noted, no part of this publication may be reproduced, scanned, stored in a retrieval system or transmitted in any form or by any means, electronic, mechanical, photocopying, recording, or otherwise, known or hereinafter invented, without the express written permission of Boroughs Publishing Group. The scanning, uploading and distribution of this book via the Internet or by any other means without the permission of Boroughs Publishing Group is illegal and punishable by law. Participation in the piracy of copyrighted materials violates the author's rights.

ISBN: 978-1-951055-65-3

For Nicholas – do what you love even if it doesn't always love you back

ACKNOWLEDGMENTS

Thank you to my husband who keeps the place from burning down while I'm on a wine induced writing tear. Knowing you and building a life with you has made me a better human, and that's something for which I'll never be able to express enough gratitude. Thank you to my son for creating the need to go on wine induced writing tears, but also for showing me that genuine awe for the little things is possible and necessary.

I'd also like to thank my mother for showing me how strong a woman really can be, and for enthusiastically reading anything I've written in a way that encouraged me to write more, even when the first draft was crap. Big thank you to M for welcoming me back into the horse business after my ill-advised dalliance with cubicles and human resource departments. You generously brought me back home.

My heart is full of sincere appreciation for all of my dear friends who had excitement for this process even when I wouldn't allow myself to feel the same. You know who you are: H, Double A and L. A1, thank you for all the wino nights that gave me the liquid courage to move forward, and for your wizard skills once I was started on this path.

I am so thankful to Boroughs Publishing Group for taking a chance on an untested, not so young, author and to my editor who I'm sure died a little inside every time she found that same dialogue punctuation error I make. I owe this journey to you and the leap of faith you were willing to take.

BREAKING COUNTRY

Chapter 1

This was what regret felt like, Alex thought. Bile blooming up from her gut and an aching, soon-to-be black eye.

Picking a ridiculous fight with Sean for the third weekend in a row was merely a symptom of how absurd her life had become. That realization hit her as hard as Sean's right hand had. Years of wrong turns and stubborn denial had brought her to this exact paralyzing moment where rock bottom had come up to meet her.

Exhibit A: the redness and swelling already forming around her eye. Her reflection in the bathroom mirror startled her, appearing so far removed from who she used to be. Her dyed black hair, cut long and choppy, fell sharply across her face like blades. She'd always been fair, but the bloodless look of shock she saw reflected was that of a stranger. Her blue eyes stared back, dull and flat.

Alex brought a tentative hand up to test the now tender area at the top of her cheek, wondering if her eye would swell shut. She'd never been struck like that. It suited her though. *Busted.* Mentally she'd been crashing against the rocks for months. A black eye made her physical appearance match her crumbling insides. *Stupid girl*, she told herself. *Stupid girl, what now?*

The first knock at the door was timid but jerked her back to reality. She looked down at her hands gripping the sides of the sink so hard her knuckles were white. She needed to decide what to do, and the second knock told her it had to be soon.

Alex wasn't sure why she'd pushed Sean, but knew that as always, she'd been compelled to break something or someone. The talk of their future (one they'd had many times before) had escalated when Alex twisted his words to create a full-on argument. The last straw had been when she'd told Sean the significant age difference between them was nothing more than a perverted side quest in his mid-life crisis.

She'd finally found his breaking point. The guilt in his voice spoke to her now as he called to her through the door. It had been reflected in his eyes the second his fist had found her face. She'd been *surprised* by the blow. But Sean? Sean had been *shocked* by it. Wide-eyed and mouth open, all of the anger had disappeared.

Mere moments before, he'd been animated, face red from screaming, then in a flash, his expression showed nothing but disbelief. No doubt now he felt remorse. She wondered if that had been her motive all along.

Now, she had a bruised face, but Sean had to live with the knowledge that he was weak enough to break from reason and resort to violence. He had to live with that burden. It scared her that this pleased her a little. Toying with another human being because it was in her nature to take anything good and soil it.

Her fingers closed around the doorknob, and carefully she opened the door.

Sean sat on the arm of the couch, hunched over crying, pitiful and childlike. The hands that had struck her now hung awkwardly at his sides. He seemed unsure what to do with them. He caught her eye and winced, glancing away from the evidence of his brutality.

At forty-seven, Sean was twenty-five years her senior and a walking, talking representation of her daddy issues. He looked his age now as she examined him through the lens of righteous annoyance.

His hair, still thick and boyishly mussed, was almost entirely grey. Fine lines creased his forehead and the edges of his mouth. Despite the trendy blocky glasses he wore, the crinkled skin above his green eyes betrayed his good looks, aging him.

His clothes, better suited for someone half his age, had been her choice. Although his body was respectable for someone in their late forties, the round slant of his shoulders gave his age away.

Alex studied him as he waited, red-eyed and sniffling for her reaction. He was old enough to be her father, but at that moment, she felt superior. She moved about gathering her things, refusing to speak, fearing the twinge of self-doubt that could find a way to betray her through her voice. She walked straight-backed to the door and turned to take one last look at the broken version of the man.

"You're weak," she spat over her shoulder as the door was closing behind her. She knew him well enough to know her earlier words—and the punch that had stopped them—would eat at him.

The cool Chicago spring air hit her lungs as she left his building, a bizarre combination of guilt and empowerment making her head spin. There was still a part of her that recoiled from her behavior.

Depressed but still feeling oddly strong, she drove home. As she undid the deadbolt to her apartment, her dog, Holden, greeted her excitedly. Even at six years old, he had enough puppy in him to still act like one. He jumped and licked her as she bent down and rubbed his big, black Shepherd-like head and snapped a leash to his collar.

After walking Holden, Alex went to the bathroom to clean up for bed, but then changed her mind, not wanting to spend any more time in front of a mirror. As she lay down, she drifted away into sleep, only to jolt out of it periodically to chastise herself for not tossing and turning over the night's events. However, finally, the guilt vanished again, and sleep came.

The next morning the tightness around her eye socket made itself known even before she tried to open her eyes. Quickly, the fog of sleep was blown off by the winds of recollection. She tried lifting her lids but found that the left one stuck at halfway.

"It's not completely swollen shut," she announced to the dog curled up next to her.

Holden roused and shook off the night, stretched, and hopped off the bed. He seemed unimpressed with her new black eye. Alex padded to the bathroom, strangely excited to see what the full extent of Sean's wrath had done to her face. The transformation was complete, she thought, glaring at herself in the mirror. *Even you can't see that person anymore.*

Her eye at half-mast was an extraordinary shade of purple, and her lid looked so full of fluid she thought it would pop. She donned an oversized pair of sunglasses before venturing out for the dog's morning walk.

It was official, she mused while she walked. The person she was supposed to be by now was gone, but to her dismay, not forgotten. The What-Have-You-Done-To-Your-Life? monologue was still, as always, pounding at the front of her brain.

She actively worked to fight back any introspection. Her attention was drawn to Holden as he bounded joyously from tree to tree down her little street. He seemed to be trying to find anything out of place that hadn't been there the last thirty times they'd taken this walk. For a moment, she forgot her troubles and smiled at his antics.

As she returned to the apartment, she contemplated calling Sean to make their breakup official. After a minute, she decided against it. He was too practical to expect anything other than their relationship's end.

A pang of guilt began to grow as the knowledge she'd hurt him sunk in. Not only last night but over the entire course of their relatively short relationship.

Sean had been a pointless exercise from start to finish. Never being genuinely interested in him, Alex had allowed an entire relationship to spring from what he felt for her. She'd had no reason to let it start or last, and no right to create the ending she had.

She shook her head to clear the depressing thoughts. What she needed was coffee, and the one person who'd offer no judgment about her altered morality. Alex needed her best friend. Emily was great at pointing out how unimportant everything in life really was and had an uncanny ability to make Alex feel as though her moral compass wasn't as broken as she feared.

She called Emily several times, impatient to get in touch. Finally, Emily picked up on the third try, her English accent polluted and groggy, no doubt from a well-spent night doing god knows what.

"Even if someone has bloody died, it is eight o'clock in the fecking morning, call back at noon." A beep signaled that the call had ended, and then silence. Alex smiled as she redialed and listened to the latest outgoing message targeting Emily's most recent smitten admirer.

I'm obviously busy, Jake. Don't leave a message. Beep.

Alex laughed and said, "I'm on my way over you lazy British bitch. Be ready in ten."

As promised, Alex was at Emily's door within ten minutes. She knocked and called out to the dragging footsteps she heard inside. "It hasn't been eight in the morning for hours."

"You're the worst," was the terse greeting after Emily finally opened the door.

Without looking at Alex, Emily turned to shuffle her way back to the couch and curled up into the fetal position. Her hair was pulled up in a haggard tiny ponytail that bounced when she walked. The pinkish color she'd dyed it was beginning to fade into a less shocking shade of fuchsia. She was petite and took up less than half the couch at five foot nothing and a hundred pounds. Her dark brown eyes studied Alex through her retro cat-eyed glasses.

"What's with the sunglasses? Hung over?"

"Sort of. Coffee?"

Emily perked up a bit and she grinned. "I would kick somebody in the face for a latte right now."

"Amen. Get dressed."

Emily pulled on a stank-looking hoodie from the floor and turned to Alex for inspection. "Good." It wasn't a question. Emily always went out in pajamas and slippers, and today was no exception.

In their neighborhood, Saturday morning (read: eleven a.m. to two p.m.) was full of the walking dead. Twenty-somethings wandering around trying to remember how many drinks, which pills, and who had occupied their night and ruined their morning.

Some of these young zombies had never made it home and still wore battered clothes from the day before. Alex and Emily made an unkempt pair, but they wouldn't stand out. Unkempt was the majority.

Emily tried performing an angelic halleluiah as she opened the door to the coffee shop, but the hoarseness in her voice had it coming out demonic, so she abandoned it quickly. Tommy, their thoroughly pierced and tattooed friend, welcomed them from behind the counter.

"Afternoon, girlies. Enjoying the beautiful day?" Stressing the "u" in beautiful, Tommy always made his voice match the ideals forced upon him by the sunshine image of the corporate coffee house. Typically, he amped it up a wee bit for the benefit of his friends.

"Stop with the espresso enema and wipe that foolish grin off your face," Emily shot back.

"What's the matter, Em? Wake up on the wrong side of the one-night stand?"

"More coffee, less banter."

"Ah, love. One day you're going to marry me, my feisty English psychopath." Tommy winked at Alex.

Emily responded by snatching her drink off the counter and flipping him off over her shoulder as she walked away. Alex caught the twitch at the corner of Emily's mouth and gave Tommy an encouraging smile as she grabbed her coffee.

"One of these days, Alex, she's gonna fold," he said, bringing another pitcher of milk up to be steamed without taking his eyes off Emily's back.

"Yeah, or crack and blow up the place," Alex noted.

"I know." His eyes popped, and he flashed a bright, excited smile. "Maybe both."

With drinks in hand, Emily and Alex fell into an overstuffed couch in the café.

"Okay. Dare I ask?" Emily ventured. "What's with the Jackie O glasses? Are we in mourning?"

"Alas, we are. As you spent your night drinking and cavorting, I spent mine burying another relationship."

"Ahh, Sean?"

"He's no longer with us."

"I don't have to feign surprise or sympathy, do I? It's too early in the morning for exercises in futility."

"No. We're not pretending to be shocked or sad."

Seemingly pleased with that answer, Emily nodded and took a long pull from her coffee, then looked back at her friend. She narrowed one eye. "What else?"

"Well, there was one *slightly* surprising turn of events." Alex quickly pushed up the glasses, taking care not to let anyone else see. She replaced them as quickly as they'd come off.

"Jesus Christ, Alex." Emily sat bolt upright, and her hand shot out and hovered a few inches above her best friend's swollen face. All of the dry cynicism and humor that usually colored Emily's vocabulary seemed to have left her. After a few rare silent moments, she sank back into her side of the couch.

"He did this when you broke up with him?" Emily asked.

"Smack-down came before the breaking-up part," Alex corrected, attempting to bring back the humor. She needed to laugh about this, not dwell on it.

Emily didn't take the bait. Her mouth remained set in a sullen line. "I am *not* implying that any of this was your fault because it's absolutely not. But what in the actual hell? That pathetic excuse for a human completely lacked emotion. I don't get this at all. Was he drunk? Drugs?" Emily was more rattled than Alex had expected.

"Oh, I'm pretty sure I poked him with a stick. You know how I get. But, no, he was sober, and I didn't hit him first, which I think is the next most likely scenario. Whatever. What's done is done. I don't want to dwell on Sean any longer."

"Alex, seriously, this is a big deal. I want to know what happened. I'm not saying you have to dwell on Sean, but this seems like, I don't know, it's worth talking about."

Alex started to get annoyed. This wasn't the reaction she was hoping for. She'd expected a brief flash of rage and a plan of retribution, or some dry, morbid comical comment to lighten the load. Delving into serious topics was not something Emily and Alex often did, and they certainly did not do it well. This detour into reality was not welcome. They were the ones who laughed at themselves and other people. They partied, made bad choices, and then laughed some more.

"What happened? Well, we were talking, we were sober, I picked a fight, it escalated, and he ended it by cracking me one. I left. The end. I'm not sure what else there is to say about it."

After a long, tense moment during which Emily's face was hard to read, she finally appeared to relent. "Well, he's a bastard, that one. Surprised he could muster the *cojones* for a right cross. What's the protocol on this? Do we slash his tires?"

Alex let out the breath she hadn't realized she was holding. Skeptical of the sudden change in her friend, she broke into an uneasy smile.

"Unnecessary. Thanks though."

A familiar silence fell between them, both lost in thought as they worked on downing their respective espresso blessings. Alex was starting to realize that things were different now between them. Their friendship and their way of life had been morphing whether they wanted it to or not. Real life was coming for them, and that meant real consequences and real decisions.

Perhaps.

But not today.

After a few moments, Alex caught a strong whiff of something emanating from her friend. "Is that rum? Are you serious? You're actually sweating rum."

"Guilty as charged," Emily admitted, putting her hands up in surrender.

Both finally let out nervous, but relieved laughs.

"Good god, Emily, we may have to leave soon. It's got to be permeating into this chair by now."

"*El Capitán* is the most reliable man in my life," Emily quipped.

A voice from over her shoulder broke in. "You know I would love to change that." Tommy was bent over the table behind them, wiping crumbs.

Emily rolled her eyes. "Something unfavorable *is* in the air. It may it be time to leave, eh Alex?"

"Indeed it may," Alex echoed in her best upper crust imitation of Emily's accent, while at the same time sending Tommy an approving smile. They stood and made their way to the door.

Alex called out over her shoulder, "Take care, Tommy."

"You too, hun. See you ladies tonight," Tommy called, reminding them of their standing Saturday night tradition. Despite his rejected efforts to leave Emily's friend zone, Tommy was always a welcome guest at movie night, mostly due to his ability to run a hysterical commentary through any flick, and his creative cocktail-making skills.

Emily turned once she reached the door. "Oh, Tommy, I almost forgot." She tossed him a super seductive half-smile. "I had a sexy dream about you last night."

Tommy's right eyebrow shot up. "Oh yeah?" He returned the grin.

"Yeah. But you were shite." She blew him a kiss, turned and walked out the door. The regulars at the coffee house chuckled at his expense.

"You should give me another shot. I'm better in real life," he called out loud enough for them to hear.

Chapter 2

That evening Alex went over to Emily's for takeout and movies. Alex was tense because she knew Tommy had yet to see her eye. She didn't feel like rehashing her lack of explanation again, and although Emily had reluctantly played the role of a carefree friend, Alex had a feeling she was still itching to pick at the issue.

Alex approached the door and heard voices inside. Deciding that she may as well go for it and get it over with, she pulled off her glasses and knocked.

Tommy opened the door. His face fell, shock written all over it. "Alex, my God. What happened?"

"Long story and I would rather not get into it."

He watched her for a long moment and then stepped to the side, allowing her to walk past him into Emily's apartment. Emily sat on the couch, feet tucked under her, intently watching the two of them.

"Are you…are you okay though?" he stuttered, seeming to gather himself a little.

"I think so. I mean I've never had a black eye before, but it doesn't hurt more than I think it should," she replied lightly.

Tommy brought a brightly colored tattooed arm up to rub his mouth. "Not exactly what I meant, honey, but I guess that's good. Should I get you some ice?"

Emily made a sarcastic tsking sound. "Nah, icing it would mean we acknowledge it actually exists, right Alex?"

So it was going to be like that? Alex thought as she pulled off her shoes, desperately trying to go through the motions of normalcy in an attempt to make this like any other Saturday evening.

"I'm not in denial. I'm saying that talking about it won't make the swelling go down. Thanks though, Tommy. I think I'm past the point of ice."

He watched her wordlessly, obviously uncomfortable and unsure of what to do next. Alex figured she should take the lead if she wanted to avoid some ridiculous Dr. Phil session. "I could use a drink though, and a mindless night of bad cinema."

"Yes," Emily chirped in a suspiciously upbeat tone. "But to answer your question Tommy, Sean happened. Sean did that to her face."

Tommy's eyes hardened, and he turned to Alex for confirmation.

Alex sighed. "Like I said, it's a long story, but yes, the story ends with Sean wrapping up a fight in a spectacularly shitty way. We're broken up. There's nothing to do about it now, so please, for the love of God, can we please move on?"

"This feels…I mean, this feels big. Like this is…" Tommy stuttered, obviously still clueless as to how to move beyond this.

"What about your job?" Emily asked. "How are they going to take their receptionist looking like she's joined a fight club?"

"I'll tell them I fell down the stairs or something."

"Jesus, Alex, could you be any more cliché? Your lack of being bothered by this is starting to piss me off," Emily said as she finally stood.

"I'm bothered, but what do you expect me to do about it? It was a bad relationship, and now it's over. It's not like I'm going back to him or something stupid like that."

"There's no part of you that thinks this might be a symptom?" Emily asked, her voice rising. "A sign that your hot mess express is getting a little too far off the rails?"

"Like I'm the only one on a slippery slope right now," Alex shot back, planting her hands on her hips.

"Actually, Alex, you are. You've not looked up from your own mess for long enough to see that we're not all on the same path anymore. Most of us are working our stuff out. You don't care about other people, so you haven't noticed we're changing. The rest of us are growing up."

Alex actually gasped at the harsh words and the accusation they leveled. Tommy stepped in to keep things from getting even more heated. "Hey, all right now, let's take a breath here."

Alex shot him a nasty glare. "Stay out of this. It's none of your business."

Tommy looked hurt. "Alex, I care about you too, we both do, we…"

She cut him off. "I'm sorry man, but you're the barista, you don't get to weigh in on this."

Emily puffed up. "What is wrong with you, Alex? Don't speak to him like that."

"Oh I'm sorry, is he only *your* punching bag?"

"You're unbelievable. You're so averse to actually talking about anything real that you'd change the conversation any way you can, including going after a guy who has been nothing but a good friend to you for years."

"I'm not sure I know what a good friend is anymore," Alex snapped, and started putting on her shoes, abandoning all hope that the evening could be salvaged. "You guys have a lovely night of dissecting all of my life choices. I'm not going to hang around here for all that judgment." She bolted for the door.

"Look, if you're going to run away pissed off I may as well say exactly what I think," Emily called, her voice low and serious. "You've got your shit, Alex, everyone does, but it's time to get a grip. You had a loss, a terrible loss, and I'm sorry. Your dad dying was truly awful, but it's been years, and you continuing to screw up your life because of it, and it's getting hard to watch."

"Whoa." Tommy again put both hands up. "Jesus, Em."

Alex whirled around on her, completely shocked. "How dare you?"

"It needed to be said, and you're already bouncing out of here like you hate me, so what is there to lose? You've got to find a different way to pack that baggage or you're going to be here bouncing from terrible man to terrible man, and from bar to bar when we're all long gone. I love you. I don't want that for you. But I'm done sitting in the front row while you're doing it."

Alex couldn't breathe. Emily had never spoken to her like this. *Who does she think she is?* Alex couldn't form words to defend herself or refute Emily's accusations, so she went with the only thought her brain could conjure.

"Screw you." Alex managed to get through the door, fighting back the tears, and stormed into the dark night, her frustration building to rage-filled despair.

Everything in my life is garbage. I can't even count on my closest friends to stick by me. Screw this place, this life and these people. I need to get out.

Alex busted into her apartment and went into the bathroom, haphazardly throwing random toiletries into a travel bag. She grabbed several things from the closet and tossed them into a bag, unsure if she'd even grabbed complete outfits. She snagged a bag of dog food from the pantry and clipped a leash to Holden. They were going to drive until all of her crappy obligations and crappy relationships were firmly in the rearview.

She pulled out her phone on the way to the car and shot off a quick email to her boss. *Due to a family emergency, I will not be able to work for the foreseeable future. Please consider this my resignation.*

Feeling almost manic, Alex threw her bag in the trunk and let the dog into the passenger seat. She climbed into the driver's side, jammed the key in the ignition, turned and…nothing. Goddamn it. The universe can fuck right off.

I won't be deterred.

She jumped out, grabbed the dog and pulled her bag from the trunk.

I need to get to Mom's. Her car will start.

She walked to the corner and hailed a cab. When she opened the door, she leaned in and asked, "You okay with the dog?"

The cabbie nodded. Alex threw the bag in and encouraged the now confused and worried Holden to jump in with her.

"Damen and Howard," Alex barked out the intersection.

Alex's knee bounced rapidly as she stared out the window of the cab making its way north through the city. When the cab stopped, she shoved a wad of cash through the window. It'd started to rain, but Alex hardly noticed as she walked the half block to her mother's house and let herself in, confident her mother would be working the night shift. The spare car key was in the junk drawer as expected. Back outside, she clicked the fob to locate the little Honda. A quarter block down, lights flashed, and the peppy horn chirped. Alex climbed in, cajoled Holden out of the rain and turned the key in the ignition. Luckily it started right up.

Okay. Now what?

Alex took a deep breath, aware that she was drenched and freezing. She looked at Holden who was also soaked and shivering. Feeling panicky and guilty, she started crying. Trembling hands fussed with the knobs for the heater, desperately trying to get warm air to blow directly on the dog.

Alex slammed her eyes shut hard for a long moment willing the frustrated tears to stop flowing. She threw the car into drive and pulled out. West, she needed to get to the highway. *It's all such a mess. Go. Just go.*

She drove away, eyes blurry. When the light turned red, she stared at the brightness reflecting off the dark, wet pavement but didn't stop. It simply didn't register. Too late, a horn blared and she looked up in panic. A car came at the passenger side, and she threw the wheel left to avoid a collision, skidding on the wet road. The vehicle bounced over the curb and hit the traffic light post before coming to a stop. The accident, even at a slow speed, had knocked Holden off the front seat and onto the floor. Alex cried harder and reached out to pull the dog into her lap. He was trembling and she knew that her erratic behavior scared him more than anything else. She sobbed into his collar, unable to will herself to move, even after the blue lights arrived and bounced off her rearview mirror.

"Ma'am?" A cop knocked on the window. "Ma'am, are you okay? Can you turn off the car please?" Alex roused herself enough to look up and follow his direction.

Her interactions with the cops were foggy, and it had taken some doing to convince them that she wasn't drunk or high. The black eye was tough to explain away, given her decision to not complicate things by bringing up what she finally realized was indeed an assault in the eyes of the law.

At some point, the cop quipped to her, "Being sad is not a good enough reason to steal a car and damage city property." She'd tried to argue because it looked like the pole wasn't even damaged, but it seemed futile. Finally, they ended up calling her mother, who took a cab to bring Alex and the slightly damaged Honda home. Alex received a few tickets, but going to jail would have been preferable to heading back with her furious mother, who also found the black eye alarming to say the least.

The resulting fight was plain mean. Alex and her mother were past the point of being civil to one another. For years they had been struggling to find a family dynamic that worked without Alex's father. They were still failing miserably at that objective. After almost an hour of trading barbs and emotionally packed low blows, her mother seemed to break a little. She slid both palms up her face and then rubbed her eyes.

Sighing, Alex's mom said, "Enough. It's two in the morning. I can't go another round with you, Alexandra. Maybe in the morning, we'll be able to speak to one another. This…this thing you're doing with your life needs to stop. You need to make a change, and if you won't, maybe I will."

The words were ominous, and Alex wasn't sure what to make of them. Reluctantly, she headed off to lie down in her mother's guest room, her mother's threat bouncing around in Alex's head through a short night of uneasy sleep.

Chapter 3

Three days later her mother's words still echoed in Alex's head as she drove, staring blankly out of the windshield.

"Alexandra, I've decided you can either agree to go to the ranch, or I will sue you for damages to the car. I hate to put it to you in an ultimatum like this, but you need something big to change your life, and I know in my heart that this is going to be good for you."

You've never known what would be good for me.

She couldn't believe her mother had resorted to this. Threatening to take her to court if she didn't agree to live with some backcountry relatives? But her mother had won. Here she was, too afraid of staying in the rut her life had become to put up much of a fight. She watched the desert fly by, all of it dried and desolate nothingness. Not too different from Chicago, she thought. Mostly dead.

The irony of being forced to leave when she'd been trying to leave in the first place was not lost on Alex. She caught a glimpse of herself in the rearview mirror. The bruise had faded to a sickly greenish-yellow and was easier to cover up with makeup now. She'd also taken the time to wash out the black hair dye, revealing her natural red. An unwelcome sight—it reminded her too much of her father.

Alex gripped the steering wheel tightly until the plastic began to creak under her palms as her frustration began to build again. How did everyone have more power over her than she had over herself? Emily had managed to ruin Alex's most important friendships in two sentences. Her mother had orchestrated both subletting her apartment to Alex's brother and her immediate departure to parts unknown in less than three days. And here she was following orders.

"Can't imagine you would have made me do this, Dad," Alex said, briefly looking up at the oversized sky. She didn't allow herself these pretend conversations with her deceased father very often. It felt foolish and almost a little like denial, but on the rare occasion when Alex granted herself this silly thing, it sometimes made her feel better.

"I wonder what you would have said about my attempt to bail out of the city without a plan. First, I'm sure you would have laughed your ass off, maybe told me I was a ridiculous human. I would have had to give that to you. But I know there would have been a part of you that understood. No offense, but escape was kind of your thing."

Alex popped a half smile at her own impudence. *Not like he's saying much about it these days.* It was almost impossible to keep her anger at him from creeping into these little one-sided chats. After all, escaping via prescription pills and booze had been her dad's preferred method of dealing with his own life until those same things took that life from them all.

"At least we can add grand theft auto to our list of family vices." Alex sighed and allowed the quietness of the car to seep into her brain, locking on the faintest sound of the dog's breathing to keep her mind from going back into the painful memories of her father. Nope, here was deep enough, any deeper and she'd have to cry in the car. Again.

Shaking her head, Alex dropped the windows down and turned up the radio. It was brain-off time. Nothingness stretched out before her, and she refused her mind's attempts to panic over what may be in store ahead.

After another hour she came into a small town, the cheery signs welcoming her to Hobson, Montana. This was where she was supposed to meet her ride.

Alex pulled into the small parking lot of an even smaller country store. A few minutes of complete silence passed, and she turned off the ignition, feeling the warmth of the late afternoon sun beginning to heat the car. Holden perked up an ear, seeming to quickly decide stopping didn't warrant rising from his sprawled-out position. After ten minutes of seeing nothing and no one, Alex pulled out her cell phone, unsure of who to call. It was then that an old beat-up orange pickup pulled into the lot.

"Dear God," she mumbled to herself.

The truck pulled into a spot behind her and Alex watched in the rearview mirror as a man slowly pulled himself from the driver's-side door. She frowned, but since the temperature was steadily climbing in the enclosed automobile, she reluctantly opened the door and slid from the seat. Unsure of what to do, she remained standing in the opened door in case there was a need for a quick getaway. The man made his way to her across the parking lot.

"You'd be Alexandra then?" he asked, squinting at her.

She lifted her sunglasses up to get a good look at her escort, who'd stopped ten feet from the back of her car, his hands stuffed in his front pockets. He was tall with a muscular build that looked as though it had begun to get soft around the edges. Faded jeans and a blue work shirt were clean but had seen better days. His boots were ratty, and he wore a mangy straw hat. His thick corrective glasses seemed out of place on his tan face sitting above the scraggly beginnings of a beard. He looked much younger than she'd expected. She couldn't fathom how it was that this man supposedly shared a childhood with her mother. Perhaps the infamous Matt had sent someone in his place.

Instead of responding to his question, she asked, "Are you Matt?"

"Yes, ma'am," he responded with a cautious tone, seeming uncomfortable after her obvious perusal.

"*You* are Matt?" she asked again. "The one that grew up with my mother?"

He nodded.

"You look too young to have grown up with my mother." One of her eyebrows hiked up.

"It's true, your mama is a couple of years older than me, but we grew up together nonetheless."

"That would make you almost forty." Alex said with no attempt at veiling her skepticism.

"Uh, thirty-eight," he mumbled.

***

Matt took some time to size her up. The girl had her father's hair—thick, mostly red, with a touch of blonde when the sun caught it. The cut was odd. Like a madman had done it with a camp knife. Large chunks fell around her face and it was stick straight, making the look severe. But the rest, he thought, the rest of her was pure Becky. She had the same bright blue eyes with a fleck of green that reflected the light, and her features were delicate and pretty, set in a fair skin tone you didn't see too often out in the middle of the country.

It was a shame she was grimacing. Her expression was currently nothing like the warm, inviting features he remembered from spending time with her mother. He missed Becky's smile, the one that he was sure the girl was hiding somewhere. Alex glanced over and caught him looking at her. She scowled, and his eyes jumped to the sky in a silent plea for patience.

"Sure are a lot of folks around here that miss seeing your mama," he ventured. "She was a thing to behold. Never a dull moment at the ranch when Becky was around."

Again Alex raised an eyebrow. "No one calls her Becky. Everyone calls her Rebecca," she corrected.

He sucked the inside of his cheek in response. Then slowly, "Yeah, I imagine that's the truth. Your daddy always called her Rebecca."

He saw a quick flash in her eye, something he couldn't identify, before it disappeared.

"We best be getting to it then," he said.

"I'll follow you."

"Ranch is about forty-five minutes from here. You got enough fuel to make it?"

She nodded and climbed back into her car. Matt watched her settle herself at the wheel and sighed.

Mae is going to have a field day with this little lost one, he thought to himself and smiled.

***

Alex followed Matt back onto what she could only guess was the main road, and then they took a right at the single stop sign and headed out of town.

This is real, she told herself. Her nails went to her mouth and her left foot tapped anxiously. It was going to be a long car ride. She thought about the man in the truck and the informal way he talked about the tired and frazzled woman she'd always known as her mother. It was as if they knew two different people who shared the same name and nothing else.

And what was with the way he spoke?

There was something about the way his words came out that didn't seem quite right to her. She couldn't put her finger on it. It was more than an accent or a drawl. There seemed to be an uncertainty before every word almost as if he were working harder to talk than most.

What was she walking into?

She looked back to Holden, who had picked up on her nervousness, and was sitting upright watching out the front window. "No turning back now," she muttered to him.

It only took a few minutes for her to realize why Matt had driven to meet her. There were several turns, all on roads with no signs. She likely wouldn't ever be able to find her own way back. Surrounded by strangers, she would be hundreds of miles away from any semblance of civilization.

Alex made no attempt to extinguish her anger toward her mother as it crept insidiously into her chest. How could Alex ever forgive her for giving up on her and dropping her into this? Whatever *this* was.

Again she brought her eyes to the dog. "You got my back, right?"

His tongue lolled out of his mouth, which she took as an affirmative.

"And who are these people? I know Mom used to visit Mae in the summers when she was young, but I had no idea that these people would remember or care about her. She hasn't been back in over twenty years, so they couldn't be that great then, right? But now she's granting *them* permission to be my wardens?"

The dog watched her unblinking.

"Right? Total madness."

Again Alex tried to table the ever-present anger and resentment in her gut, turning her attention out the window. Slowly the scenery began to change as more and more green bushes and grass began to appear. By the time they turned off the latest nameless blacktop road onto a gravel one, the landscape could almost be described as lush. She glanced up at a wood and metal sign, announcing her arrival at *Crooked Brook Ranch*.

Finally, the house came into view. While she hated to admit it, the place was amazing. For the first time in her adult life, Alex was in awe.

She pulled into a large circular drive and parked facing what she assumed was the main house, a large two-story home with cedar siding and a huge wrapping front porch that disappeared around both corners. It looked old but classically so, the enormous logs that served as railings on the porch uneven and more weathered than the siding. The entire front of the house was filled with large windows with all of the curtains drawn, the glass panes reflecting the orange sunlight. The backdrop of the perfectly blue sky and the green pastures below made Alex feel silly for thinking places like this only existed on the silver screen.

Lost in thought, Alex hadn't noticed that Matt had arrived at her car door until he knocked and startled her out of her unabashed admiration of the property.

"You 'bout ready to get out of the car now?" he asked through the window.

Embarrassed, Alex nodded, fumbled with the door handle and stood to stretch the ache from her legs. She opened the back door to allow for the dog to do the same.

Matt's face brightened as he bent to scratch Holden's eager head. "Who's this one now?"

"Oh, this is Holden, my baby. He's a mutt."

"I imagine he is—all of the good ones are." He smiled what appeared to be a genuine smile at her.

"Yeah I guess. So um..." Alex finally tore her eyes away from the house. "I had meant to ask you earlier, but you're not like my Uncle Matt or something are you?"

"Well things get a bit confusing, but no, I'm no relation to you, so plain Matt will work." He smiled the easy smile she was beginning to recognize as his baseline expression as he added, "I think when we get inside and you meet everyone, we can try to get all of the stories straight. Most of us are only blood by ranchin' if you know what I mean."

Alex did not know what he meant, and his expression scrunched up as if he recognized her confusion. "Sometimes I can blunder up details pretty good then you won't never be able to understand it."

Alex tried to make her face impassive at his answer while she internally panicked at how he'd said, "meet everyone." It sounded like there would be a lot more people than she'd hoped. *How many country bumpkins does one need to run a ranch? Does this ranch actually run?*

Alex thought working ranches had gone out of style since, well since the invention of the Twinkie and all things processed.

Alex looked at the several wide steps that led up to the porch and finally resolved to step up. At that moment, the screen door flew open and a pack of dogs burst through followed by an older woman. Instantly Holden was pulled into a sniffing, tail-wagging frenzy that he seemed to mind very little. The woman that had followed the dogs met them at the porch, and she chuckled along with Matt.

Alex knew that this must be Mae, the woman who was to be her babysitter this summer, but no one seemed to think introductions were necessary. Mae wore very broken-in jeans, a flowered short-sleeved blouse, a busted-up pair of cowboy boots, and a grin that Alex wouldn't necessarily categorize as friendly. Her eyes didn't look a day over forty, but her gray hair and the extensive wrinkling in her face and hands put her closer to seventy. Alex noticed that the woman was sizing her up as well. Her gaze was unrelenting in its mission to take stock of Alex.

Alex began to squirm under the woman's scrutiny, and she looked briefly down at her feet, her submission surprising her. After what seemed like forever, the woman's hard face softened a tick.

"Listen," Mae finally spoke. "I know that you don't want to be here. But you can't spend the entire summer looking as if you're on your way to a funeral."

Alex's eyes narrowed.

Mae crossed her arms over her chest and continued, "So I'm going to make you a deal. If you give being here a God's-honest try—I mean you try to fit in, you try to enjoy yourself—and if you still want to leave, then I'll call your momma and convince her that this summer was a bad idea and you'll be free to go home."

Alex's eyebrow shot up. She could play that role if the light at the end of the tunnel was going back to Chicago early.

"Okay?" Mae asked.

"Deal," Alex answered, resisting the urge to reach out and shake Mae's hand to make it official.

"Good." Mae nodded. "Matt will take your bags to your room—second floor, last room on the left. Dinner is in thirty minutes. I'm sure you're starving so we'll save the pleasantries for later."

The slight sarcasm in Mae's politeness was obvious, and Alex wondered if the woman also disliked the idea of this impromptu use of her ranch as a summer camp for delinquents. Alex was thrilled, however, that the woman seemed willing to commute her sentence.

Alex watched Mae's back disappear into the house again and turned to try to put eyes on Holden. Her mutt was still running circles around the driveway with his new friends. When she whistled, Holden reluctantly came away from the party to join her.

"He's part of the pack now," Matt chuckled as he joined her in watching the other dogs.

"I don't think I should leave him out here," Alex worried aloud.

"S'up to you. This little herd spends most of the day tearing around the property and only seems to come find us when they need food or a bed."

"Don't they get lost?"

Matt laughed and lifted his arm to gesture across the fields. "Where are they gonna go? This is about as lost as you can get."

"You said it, not me." Alex allowed herself to chuckle when she met Matt's eyes.

Holden was such a good boy. He sat quietly at her side, but she could feel his excitement as his eyes stayed laser-focused on the others.

"Okay!" she said, releasing him from the stay. The dog tore off to join the pack antics again.

It's only a couple of days and he could use the fresh air. Alex was already planning on going home within the week.

Alex turned her attention back to Matt who simply said, "Ready?" as he tipped his head toward the house.

Alex nodded before following him through the front door.

Chapter 4

Matt left her alone in her room. She surveyed the place that hopefully would only house her for the next few days. Dark hardwood floors looked well-worn but shone lightly from a recent coat of wax. The Cherokee-patterned bedspread was deep burgundy with navy and green accents which matched the curtains and the woven throw rug next to the bed. Pulling the drapes open, Alex caught her breath as the entire expanse of the ranch lay out in front of her.

Directly behind the house were five large buildings. Barns, she guessed. Each was painted a cliché red, two attached to large, fenced-in dirt yards. Beyond the buildings, the ground rose gently, and the landscape reached for the sky. Trees lined the left side of her field of view, and it was impossible to tell what was behind the trees or how far the forest went. To the right, there were more fenced-in fields, a few random smaller buildings, and then as far as the eye could see, something green grew. A voice at the door startled Alex out of her astonishment at the surprising beauty before her. She spun to see Matt once again in the doorway. His quick return made her question if he'd ever left.

"We've had rain here the last few days. A lot of the animals were brought in or moved to higher ground to protect the young grass," Matt said, as if he wasn't talking to someone who only knew livestock in a petting zoo setting.

"Oh," she said dumbly. She hadn't expected to see animals.

"You've got one of the best views in the house."

Alex knew that he expected a response, but she couldn't muster one.

His glance directed her to look out across the ranch once again. "Up that hill there, if you're willing to walk a bit, is the remnants of the old ranch house and some of the farm buildings. Your momma and I used to hang out up there all the time." In response to her continued silence, Matt added, "Well, it's best not to get all sentimental, but if you want a tour later I'd be glad to find a way to get you out and about. There's a lot more to this place than you can see from the house."

Alex wasn't sure how to respond. Again, annoyance nagged at the back of her brain at the casual way in which he spoke of her mother.

You need to make small talk to fulfill the role you agreed to play, self-preservation reminded her.

"How many people work on the ranch?" Alex asked, attempting to interject sincere interest into her tone.

"Oh, let's see now. I guess there's twenty of us. Right now seven of the ranch hands are part-timers, they drive in from family homes closer to town. Only thirteen live on the ranch here."

"Thirteen people live here!? Where?" She looked out the window again. "I didn't see a farmhand house or whatever it's called…servants' quarters?"

"Oh no, there's not another house. This one's big enough for all of us—eight rooms, four bathrooms. Most of us are doubled or tripled up and it works out fine. We all have meals together in the main room. Which reminds me, you've got about five minutes until dinner. Your bathroom is two doors down."

With that, he walked out of the room and left Alex checking her watch. Dinner exactly at five p.m. *So the senior special, huh?*

She wandered to the bathroom to wash her hands, Mae's words echoing in her mind. The hard truth was she needed to plaster a smile on her face to make Mae believe.

Play nice with the yokels then it's back to home not-so-sweet home.

Alex took a long look in the mirror. The last four years she'd worked to convince everyone things were okay, even when that was not the case. How hard could it be to fake it for a couple more days?

Immediately her eyes were drawn to the shadow of the remaining bruise around her eye, a screaming reminder of how screwed up things were. With a deep breath, Alex decided that her new "happy" look required more makeup, so she jogged back to the room to rummage through her bags.

Once back in the bathroom Alex splashed cold water on her face, ran a brush over her hair and added a quick layer of powder, taking special care to bring her eye back to a normal skin tone. Trying on her best fake smile, she declared that it was time to meet "everyone."

Coming down the stairs, Alex heard the sound of loud voices bubbling up from the first level, and it ate away at her feigned confidence. As Alex rounded the corner, the room came into view, and several independent conversations slowly died out. The room was swallowed up by the silence of unapologetic and curious stares. She surveyed the room as the room surveyed her. A pack of ranch hands was more intimidating than she ever could have imagined, and God, was it crowded. Cloaking anxiety behind a rehearsed smile, Alex frantically looked for a familiar face. Across the room, she found Matt and abandoned any attempt to hide her angst as she walked hurriedly, eyes trained on the floor.

A moment later, Mae bustled in carrying a large, steaming pot and was followed by two men each with their own hands full of bowls and baskets. The men started to take their seats around the gigantic wooden table.

Mae appeared to notice the awkward quiet in the room and said, "I want everyone to meet Alexandra. She's Becky's daughter."

A murmur moved around the table as the men nodded. Alex was surprised that most of them seemed to at least know of her mother. She tried to force herself to look up and to acknowledge the eye contact from the men at the table.

"Hi," Alex said dumbly.

"I don't suspect you'll be able to remember this, but here's everyone's names." Mae looked to her left and moved her gaze quickly around the table. "Jacob, Christopher, Sam, Ben, Matt of course, then there's Eli, Nick Bishop, Nick O'Reilly, his brother Jeff, then there's Phillip, Matt's brother Winn, and finally this old man here is James."

While Mae rattled off the names, Alex tried her best to keep up and store the information. Most of the ranchers had shyly smiled when being introduced, and each mumbled something resembling a *hello* or a *ma'am*.

All of them were well built in the way people who work outside tend to be. The majority of them looked like they were in their late twenties, early thirties, with a few exceptions. The man called Sam was older, maybe closer to Mae's age, and the gentleman seated to

Mae's right, who she had called James, looked as though he could be ninety.

The one who most caught Alex's attention was the guy Mae had called Matt's brother. He was younger than most at the table and was shockingly good looking.

No way this guy is related to Matt. Even though he hadn't looked up when being introduced—he hadn't acknowledged Alex in any way—she could see the square line of his jaw, the fuzz of a dark five o'clock shadow. The strong width of his shoulders pulled the t-shirt he wore snugly across his muscled chest. Like all of them, his hair looked like a hat had been worn all day and had recently removed. His messy light brown waves had somehow found a way to keep some life and flicked out around the base of his neck and his ears.

Alex found it hard to look away from him, and perhaps sensing this, he finally looked up. She sucked in her breath. His amber eyes were such a light brown they were almost golden. It wasn't the color that startled her though. It was the pure disdain they held.

"How long will she be here?" he asked Mae, without taking his harsh stare off Alex.

Alex narrowed her eyes at the rude question.

"Well, Winn," Mae said with a slight edge in her voice, "Alexandra will be here for as long as she wants to be."

"What will she be doing here?" he asked accusingly, obviously not fazed by Mae's tone.

Others at the table shuffled slightly and began to fidget with their food. Winn had not stopped staring at Alex, and something in her wouldn't allow her to cave and break eye contact first.

"I'm not sure of that yet. But I'm sure it's not one bit your concern." This time the disapproval in Mae's voice was anything but subtle.

Thankfully, her answer seemed stern enough that he finally broke his stare to turn to Mae, opening his mouth to speak again.

Mae spoke over him with a firm, even tone. "Winn, enough of this."

At that he finally dropped his eyes to his plate and people at the table released their breath. Alex followed suit, finding it much easier to find the air now that he was no longer staring at her. Slowly movement and life came back to the table, and in a matter of moments, the noise of conversation, clinking plates, and men eating filled the room.

Matt leaned over to her, speaking quietly. "No mind that. He's a little rough around the edges, and he's been pretty stressed lately. Nothing personal, okay?"

"Yeah, sure," Alex mumbled, more for his benefit than out of any sense of forgiveness.

"Everyone here really is nice. It's a great group of guys." Matt lightly carried on. "Trouble is, pretty much everyone has a nickname or two, but we'll let you try to get real names down before we throw too much at you." He winked at her when he said this, and Alex found it awkward but slightly endearing.

Alex brought her eyes to the top of the table. "Mae, Jacob, Christopher, Sam, Ben, you, Eli, Nick Bishop, Nick O'Reilly, Jeff, Phillip, *Winn*," her gaze narrowed as it briefly skimmed over him, "and James," she finished triumphantly.

Matt laughed, drawing some short-lived unwanted attention their way. "Not too shabby, kiddo, you are a chip off the old block. Your momma always was quick as a whip."

Alex rolled her eyes, hating the comparison to her mother, and she could tell that was going to happen a lot with Matt. He was right, though. Her mother did have an uncanny knack with names and faces.

Too bad she wasted her talent waiting tables, Alex thought bitterly, before she could check the impulse.

"Try this one on for size." Matt looked back to the top of the table, and starting with Jacob, nodded at each man in turn again. "Trix and Tiny. Sam, we call Capitan or Becker—he's Mae's brother-in-law. Next is Bud, then Griz, Bishop, and O'Reilly. Those are easy except sometimes O'Reilly is called Junior, since he's the younger O'Reilly. Then there's Harley, Casper, and Winn, who everyone calls The Kid, which he hates, and finally the Goat, or Sarge, or sometimes Old Man." He looked at her playfully waiting to see what she would do with the challenge.

Alex shrugged and smiled sheepishly. "You're right. The nicknames complicate things."

Matt laughed again. She was starting to like him despite herself.

"What's Mae's nickname?" Alex ventured.

"Ah, Mae? Most of us call her Moms, but when we're in trouble it's always Mrs. Becker." Matt looked pleased with himself and he watched Mae with a look of love and respect before continuing. "It's funny, none of us are Mae's children, but we feel like we are. She always says that she should have run a kennel because lost puppies eat less than lost men. I'm not sure if it's a joke."

Alex decided it was nice to hear about Mae through Matt's eyes. "And you?" she asked, "What's your nickname?"

Matt's cheeks blushed slightly. "Most of the guys call me Slick, but Winn calls me Mattie."

Alex allowed her eyes to flick across the table over to Winn, who was staring at them, appearing to disapprove of his brother's friendliness toward her. Quickly her eyes darted away and she felt foolish for letting this pompous ass get under her skin.

"So he really is your brother, huh?" Alex finally had built up the nerve to ask. She hoped he would assume it was the age difference and not the contrast in their appearance that made her question.

"Yeah—same father, that is. I was almost out of high school when Winn was born."

"Oh," was all Alex could get out. She wanted to know more details but didn't understand why she cared. "Why won't he call you Slick?"

"Well, he's protective of me and thinks the other guys say it to be mean. I'm not really very slick you see." He let out a chuckle with his slightly self-deprecating remark, and again her attention was brought to how sometimes it seemed hard for him to get words out.

At her skeptical look, he continued, "Winn thinks everyone needs protecting, especially me." He smiled slightly. "The Kid has always been like that though. He's twenty-three going on fifty. Mae calls him her old soul."

Matt was talking lovingly of his brother, but Alex wasn't buying it. If you asked her, Winn was the hillbilly version of a handsome frat-boy jackass. She shot a look his way again, but he was talking to James, elbow on the table. A hunk of bread held loosely in his hand swung along as he conveyed some point with the flick of his wrist. The old man simply nodded. Alex was disappointed with her failed attempt at showing him a menacing glare.

As dinner was wrapping up, Mae stood and nodded toward some of the guys. "Bud, Griz, Casper, y'all are on clean up. I'm taking Alexandra for a tour."

Alex started at the use of her name and then looked up to Mae, whose facial expression wasn't one you'd argue with. The men she'd addressed were already rising and reaching for plates, which were being passed toward the front of the table. Mae walked toward the front door and Alex followed obediently, catching Matt's eye as he winked at her again. The wink was weird, but she decided she liked it.

At the base of the stairs Mae turned and said, "Go grab a jacket. I'll meet you out front," and then walked out the door.

What is it about this woman that makes me feel like a reprimanded kindergartener?

Perhaps being the only woman on the property had sharpened the drill sergeant aspects of Mae's personality. Alex tried to conjure an image of Mae at her own age but failed. That one for sure came out of the womb grizzled and a bit scary.

Chapter 5

Mae pulled up to the base of the porch in what appeared to be a golf cart on steroids. Alex jogged down the steps, climbed into the passenger seat and they drove off around the house in silence. The sun was now below the horizon and the sepia effect on the surroundings gave an old-timey feel about the property. Alex felt like she was watching an artificially colorized version of reality as they got farther away from the house.

Abruptly Mae stopped the cart and turned to face Alex before starting in on what felt like prepared remarks. "This ranch has been in my husband's family for generations. He's been gone ten years now, so his brother Sam and I co-own it. We primarily keep cattle here. Beef. But Winn and Matt also have a horse-training business they run out of this main horse barn here." Her arm raised to point at one of the large red barns Alex had seen from the window. "We also have a foaling/calving barn." She gestured to a smaller barn off in the distance that was behind the large one. The two barns were separated by what appeared to be two different sand enclosures.

Mae continued, "We do a lot of babies each season, some from our own stock, some from people around here that send their mares and cows over when it gets close to time."

Motioning toward the center of the property, she said, "Over here in the middle is the vegetable garden, greenhouse, and a handful of fruit trees. If you're ever looking for me during the day, you'll probably find me around here or in the office of the main cattle barn, which is over there." She motioned toward her right at the immense red building on the other side of the property.

"We also have a few fields we grow hay in for our own use. The hay fields are the ones you drove past on your way up the drive. Most of the property is north of what we see here. It goes for a few miles, and it's all broken up into pasture land for the cattle." She paused and glanced at Alex, perhaps to see if she had questions, but of course, why would she? Mae could have been describing the surface of Mars for all Alex knew.

Appearing disappointed with Alex's silence, Mae kept talking. "This is a busy place and it would be best for you to see if there's anything useful you can do while you're here. Even though I didn't appreciate Winn's tone, he's right that no one here cares for freeloaders. Even though you don't know anything, if you're willing to learn, there will be someone willing to teach you."

"Okay," Alex said simply, noticing that her "tour" really wasn't very extensive as they had only driven about fifty feet from the house. Mae had vaguely pointed at some of the buildings and didn't even address several others that were in view.

So, what was the real point of this?

From everything Alex could tell about this woman, direct was the best way to go. "Why did you drive me out here?"

"Here's the thing. I'm not without empathy for your situation. You've had tough times, I know. Everyone here has too. We've all lost people and lost ourselves, some of us more than once. You have an opportunity to find some of what you've lost while you're here, but if you don't decide to look for it, then you're wasting my time and my people's time. I'm not going to tolerate that. The people here are family, and they look out for their own. You can either be a part of that or be on the outside of that, it's up to you."

Alex tried to take in and unpack everything Mae had told her but found it overwhelming. "I feel like you've already decided you don't like me," Alex worried aloud.

"Not the case. I'm withholding judgment, for now. I guess I'm asking you to do the same."

"Fair enough."

"I thought so." Mae nodded sharply.

There was an uncomfortable pause. Alex thought about the disapproval she sensed earlier when she couldn't come up with any questions. In the lightest tone she could muster she asked, "So, are most of you related?"

Mae's gaze snapped back to Alex. "You and I are blood, didn't your momma tell you that?"

"No." Alex could tell this surprised Mae, who recovered quickly.

"Your Grandmother Elizabeth was my sister. I'm your momma's aunt."

Now it was Alex's turn to be surprised. She rarely heard her mother speak of her own parents, who had died before Rebecca had turned twenty.

All this time I've had family on my mother's side who I've never met or hardly even heard of.

Alex sputtered past her disbelief. "I'm actually related to the people here?"

Mae laughed. "Not by a long shot. Sam is my husband's brother, so I guess he's technically related to you. Everyone else came from somewhere else before they put down roots. We're all brought together by this place and we love each other unconditionally. That's better than blood for most of us."

Alex waited for more details, but they didn't seem to be forthcoming. "Some of those guys don't look old enough to have put down roots," she mused aloud.

"There are men here who showed up as boys and some of them haven't been here long, but a bond like that forms pretty quick, or it doesn't form at all."

Alex nodded, although she'd never been a part of something like that, so it didn't sound possible.

Mae went on, "We've got a handful of rules here that we abide by to keep ourselves sane and this place running smoothly. I won't bore you by running through them all, but the first one is that the animals come first, they need to. Technically they're our boss, and they pay us. But the second one is that we always have each other's backs, and that's non-negotiable. This group is tight-knit for a reason. If you do what I'm asking they'll welcome you into that protection with open arms."

Alex thought of Winn and his snap judgment of her but decided against bringing him up to contradict what Mae said.

When it became apparent that Alex wasn't going to contribute further, Mae patted the steering wheel and said, "Okay, back to the house, I'll give you the lay of the land in there, so you don't accidentally catch an eye full of a rancher's bright white ass."

"So an actual tour?" Alex couldn't stop the touch of sarcasm that crept into her tone.

Mae chuckled. "Yup."

Mae drove a small circle and took them back to the house, this time parking on the back side. They walked up the steps and through a small door that brought Alex into one of the largest kitchens she'd ever seen outside of a restaurant. She'd caught a glimpse of it earlier but hadn't comprehended its size. There was an industrial-size fridge, a stove with eight burners, two ovens, a large wood-topped island and counters for days. If they were feeding more than a dozen people at every meal, it made sense that all this was necessary. Tucked in one corner was a small four-person table and on the other side, under what Alex guessed must have been the main staircase, was a large walk-in pantry.

The rancher named Eli was still standing at the sink, drying the last of the dishes by hand. His friends appeared to have already completed their tasks and were nowhere to be found. When they walked in, he looked up from his job and gave her a quick nod and a tiny polite smile.

Mae spoke first. "As you can imagine, this is my domain. I love it in here, and I'm not afraid to say that keeping these boys fed is one of my favorite jobs on the ranch. Isn't that right, Griz?"

Alex tried to mentally tie the nickname to the face. This rancher was seriously tall and wide. The part of his face not covered in a beard was tan making his green eyes pretty piercing. Easy to tell where the grizzly nickname originated. This guy could probably fight a bear.

"Best damn cook in the state," Griz replied.

Alex felt a pang of guilt. She hadn't even noticed the food she'd wolfed down during dinner. *Did I eat anything? I can't remember.*

"That's not to say I won't go round-up with the best of them," Mae said. Griz chuckled and nodded before Mae added, "But that garden out there and these bellies are my priority." Mae patted on Griz's gut as she spoke, and he leaned over and pecked a kiss on her cheek.

"About finished here, Moms, need anything else?"

"Nope, thanks hun, see you in the morning." Mae turned her attention back to Alex. "Right, let's keep going."

They walked through the opening into the dining room. "You already saw the dining room, out through here is the sitting area."

Alex followed Mae out past the front door and the staircase that led upstairs. The sitting room had an enormous stone fireplace and several weathered leather chairs. To the right was a hallway that Mae waved toward. "Down the hall is a bathroom and the room that Trix,

Tiny, and Bishop share. I wouldn't recommend using that bathroom unless you're desperate. The men are in charge of their own cleaning, and that one doesn't get a lot of attention."

As if to punctuate the sentiment, the sound of a toilet flushing made its way down the hall and Jacob appeared out of the bathroom.

"Rule number three," he said, obviously having heard part of their conversation. "Moms doesn't clean up piss."

His bright blue eyes were laughing as he approached them and started to reach out his hand then thought better of it and waved. "I'm Jacob, but everyone calls me Trix."

Alex appreciated his change of heart on the handshake and allowed herself to laugh a little. Again she tried to store his nickname while her eyes logged his features. Trix had the same sun-darkened skin as the others along with closely cropped dark hair, and a matching five o'clock shadow below sharp cheekbones. The longer she looked at him, the more she noticed that his eyes were really a remarkable shade of light blue.

Why is Winn's image still bouncing around in my skull when this guy is actually pretty hot?

Chalking the issue up as another example of her terrible instincts, Alex tried to stay in the moment and kick Winn's intense eyes out of her mind. Regardless it seemed she was going to like Trix and his inviting but mischievous grin.

"I'm Alex."

"You guys headed downstairs?" Trix asked.

"Why don't you show her?" Mae said, then looking at Alex, "I've got some food prep to work on, so I'll see you in the morning. If you eat breakfast, it's at six a.m."

Alex grimaced. *No wonder they ate dinner at five.*

Trix caught her look and laughed again. "You'll get the hang of the early-to-bed, early-to-rise schedule, I promise."

He leaned over and gave Mae a kiss on the cheek before opening a door in the hallway that led down a set of stairs. "Come on down, Red, if you dare."

Alex cocked her eyebrow at the nickname. His eyes danced and despite herself Alex found his easy-going lighthearted nature genuine and believable.

"Sorry, *Red*, I'm the name assigner around here. You don't get a say in this one. No one else did." With that he turned and headed down the stairs.

Voices floated up from the basement and Alex became nervous again. As they reached the bottom, a large finished basement came into view. Matt and two other guys stood around a pool table and two ranchers sat on a couch playing what looked like an X-Box racing game on a large-screen TV. Alex was relieved Winn was not among them.

"This is where we hang out the most," Trix said. "Also, down here is where Slick and The Kid sleep, their bathroom should also be considered off limits." He gestured toward a hallway leading to two closed doors.

"Guys, you remember Red?" He flashed her a teasing smile while the guys at the TV paused the game and turned around.

"I'm Harley and this is my brother Junior," one of them said.

Matt smiled at her and pointed at his two pool buddies. "Casper and Tiny."

"Hi again." Alex smiled and nodded all the while chanting in her head, *Give it a try, give it a try. I have to convince Mae that I'm giving this a try.*

"You play pool, Red?" the one they called Tiny asked.

Like almost everyone on the property, he appeared to be mid to late twenties, tan, well built. He had dark hair, dark eyes. He was, as his name suggested, on the shorter side, maybe five foot four. The smile he gave her was easy and natural. Alex began to feel calmer.

These men are nice, she tried to convince her brain.

They were being welcoming without being fake, which struck her as odd but a good odd.

"I've played before, but rain check? I'm feeling a little tired from the drive." Alex tried to make her tone match their low-key disposition, but more importantly Alex wanted to get out of there before Winn made an appearance.

"Understandable," Matt said. "I'll walk you upstairs."

"Night everyone," Alex called over her shoulder.

"Night," was the chorused response.

When they returned to the first floor, she found that the free-range dog pack had, as promised, returned to the house in search of food and somewhere to sleep. She knelt down as a very tired but satisfied looking Holden found her. Scrubbing his ears and briefly clutching his head to her chest she whispered, "Missed you."

Alex and Holden followed Matt up the stairs and he turned to her when they hit the second-floor landing. "You and Mae along with James and Sam each have a room up here. You share a bathroom with Mae, so I suggest you stay tidy." He smiled and brought his eyes to the stairs that turned and went up to another level. "Next floor is where Bud, Griz, Casper, Junior, and Harley share a couple of rooms along with another bathroom. Sounds like you've already heard about Rule Three, so you know, beware. Not sure you should ever go up there. They're pretty rowdy and, well—not always great about wearing pants if I'm honest."

Alex smiled. "Thanks, Matt."

She registered but ignored her strange urge to give him a hug and said, "Goodnight."

"Goodnight, Alex. I'm glad you're here."

To that, she nodded, unable to agree. Alex went into her room and poured some food into Holden's dish, which he ignored, instead opting to curl up and instantly crash out on the foot of her bed.

She smiled at the exhausted dog. "At least one of us is fitting right in. When we get home I promise we'll go to the park more."

Holden's only response was a deep snore.

Chapter 6

Alex was an outsider. Despite most everyone being nice, it was clear that in their world, she was without any relevant skills, without use, and thus, in her mind, without importance. After missing the ridiculously early breakfast and still lacking the guts to ask someone flat-out to show her how to do something, Alex spent her first morning walking.

Throughout the morning, Alex had chosen several different directions. So far, this methodical meandering had kept her off everyone's radar, and perhaps most luckily, it had kept her path from crossing Winn's. There had been a few brief glimpses of the others going about their day, but she never stopped moving long enough to speak more than a few passing pleasantries. Alex also decided to skip lunch to keep from repeating last night's uncomfortable dinner scene until she had more allies.

Avoiding the horse areas was a straightforward rule. Mae had told her Winn and Matt ran their business from those two barns. However, in her exploration, she'd discovered a third stable on the property. She'd gone west from the house and taken a path through the woods. The path made a quick turn into a clearing, and she'd glimpsed Winn. By some divine intervention, Alex ducked quickly out of sight before he saw her.

Her heart hammered at the back of her ribs, making her feel foolish.

What is he doing so far away from where he is supposed to be?

Curiosity forced her to sidetrack a few feet into the woods and approach the clearing where she felt hidden enough to go unnoticed.

Winn stood in a pen that was fenced on three sides and closed on the fourth edge by butting up against the small old barn. He neared the large open door of the barn and peered into the darkness. Alex held her breath, afraid of what could come busting out at any second, but nothing happened. Winn whistled lowly to himself, then backtracked on a slight angle toward the other side of the pen. He climbed up to the top rail, turned and sat facing the black open door.

Alex studied him as he sat with his heels hooked on the middle fence slat, elbows resting on his knees as he casually interlaced his fingers and hung his hands. He bent over at the waist while he stared down.

It was hard not to notice the striking parts of him. The contrast of the white t-shirt against the dark tan of his bicep, the tint from a few days of growth on his squared jaw, the ends of his unruly hair creeping out from under a tattered baseball cap. It was unnerving how quickly she noticed and admired the man in him. Their initial hateful interaction had led to her categorize him as a child throwing a tantrum. Watching him in secret, not having to deal with his self-righteous mouth, it was hard to not see him for what he was: a damn near perfect specimen.

A few minutes turned into fifteen. Winn sat unmoving while nothing happened. The curiosity was killing her.

For all of his harping on what I would do here, he's doing a pretty good job of blowing off actual work.

After another five minutes passed, Alex's feet were falling asleep from the way she was resting on them, but if she left now, and so did Winn, he may catch up to her on the path. He would know his thinking spot had been compromised.

Mercifully, Winn finally moved. Unhooking his boots from the fence, he slowly lowered himself back to the ground with enviable grace. The hem of his shirt pulled slightly away from the waist of his jeans, revealing a few inches of tan flat abdomen. Despite her mouth going dry, Alex had to roll her eyes.

You're not so hard up that a flash of a six-pack makes you forget someone's personality sucks.

Winn walked back to the barn door, again making a low noise, so soft and quiet it was almost a coo. Then he turned and started in her direction, ducking easily through the pen fence. Alex backed farther into the brush to remain undetected as he walked past her.

After a half day of wandering, it was time for Alex to commit to the mission. She needed to show Mae that the sentence should be commuted, and Alex should be able to return to Chicago early.

Plus, if I don't make any friends who will I tattle on Winn to?

It seemed like a good bet that Winn would be going back over to the main horse barns now, which presumably left Matt off the table. Which meant Trix and his easygoing personality was the next best bet. Perhaps he could be found in one of the other buildings.

Leaving the woods, Alex crossed behind the house to the large building that, thanks to her earlier wandering, she knew was a large garage that housed a bunch of machinery. Poking her head in the large open roll-up door, Alex listened for the sound of movement. She was rewarded with a metallic thunk and a *"Son of a bitch!"* It sounded like the curse could have been Trix.

Be brave, Alex ordered herself as she walked through the door.

In the middle of the building a pair of Levi-clad legs stuck out from under a cliché-looking green tractor.

"Hey," Alex ventured.

The boots jerked, followed by another metallic crash and more swearing. The legs shuffled and scooted and, much to Alex's relief, revealed themselves to be attached to Trix who inched out from under the machine.

"Hey, Red!" Trix seemed happy to see her despite the frustrating tractor debacle he was experiencing. "You making the rounds?"

"I guess so. Do you…need any help?" she asked.

"Uhhh…" He looked genuinely concerned about what to say next. "I hope it's not rude to guess that you lack familiarity with tractor hydraulics?"

"Um, no, that's a pretty solid assumption." Then with Mae's face flashing in front of her eyes, Alex added, "but I'm stronger than I look, and I can usually follow directions."

Trix shrugged. "Okay, seems like a shame to get you dirty, plus I need a break from this P.O.S. How about I show you one that's working to start off and we can call that lesson one?"

"Great." Alex was instantly relieved.

Trix walked her over toward another smaller but equally green tractor and patted the yellow seat. "Climb on up, Red, feel her out. This here is your run-of-the-mill John Deere 5E Utility tractor. It's kind of the little brother to the one we were at before."

Alex nodded at his nonsense words then climbed up the two steps to sit in the chair and was surprised when it bounced a little as she sat. Not knowing what child spirit possessed her, Alex grabbed the steering wheel and gave it a few good old-fashioned wobbles.

"Wanna take her for a spin?"

"What? Don't be insane, I can't drive a tractor," Alex scoffed.

"You can drive a car?"

She nodded.

"Ever driven a stick shift?"

Alex nodded again and then rolled her eyes at his obvious surprise.

Trix laughed and said, "Then you can drive a tractor. Hang on."

Jumping down from his perch next to her, Trix jogged over and opened the large roll-up door directly in front of them. Returning to his stance beside her, he pointed down to a pedal on her left—"Clutch"—then he pointed at a bent bar coming out of the floor by her right foot—"Gas"—and then at the pedal by her right foot—"Brake."

Trix turned to see her eyebrows raised. She nodded and he nodded back.

"Steering wheel," he teased and then grinned at her second eye roll. Next he pointed to the lever to her right. "There's your gears. You're in park right now so it can start up without worrying about any pedals, everything else you let me worry about." He motioned toward several levers coming out on the other side.

Trix bent over the steering wheel to turn the key that was already in the ignition. The engine jumped to life and was significantly louder than Alex had anticipated. He had to yell over the sound of it, saying, "Hang on, let me pull up the front loader."

Trix pulled back on a lever that picked the bucket up off the ground a few feet then looked at her expectantly.

"Oh. You want me to go now?" Alex asked.

Trix tipped his head. "That's the point, unless you want to run it long enough to build up fumes in here."

"Oh," she said again, feeling instantly flustered.

The volume of the machine's noise made it feel like she could accidentally drive it through a building before stopping it. Alex peered down at all of the controls, fortifying her nerve.

Okay, it's go or die from diesel fumes.

Alex pushed in the clutch, pulled it into first, and started to press on the gas while slowly letting up on the clutch. The tractor jumped and Trix was almost thrown off the side. She panicked and pulled all feet from all things causing the engine to choke and die.

Trix belly laughed next to her as she tried to catch her breath. "Okay, try again," he said between chuckles.

Alex allowed herself a nervous half laugh, admitting, "I about crapped my pants."

Trix laughed harder before directing her to put in the clutch and start it again. The second attempt to get rolling was equally abrupt but she kept on the gas and the tractor rolled forward after its initial jump. Alex applied a little more gas, and they were rolling out of the garage and onto the gravel path. With a slow turn of the wheel, they were on their way, and Alex laughed despite herself.

What would my friends in Chicago think of me driving an actual tractor?

Trix leaned in and yelled, "Any plans on picking it up a little here, Red?"

Alex felt like they were flying given that the large machine could flatten anything in its path, but she put in the clutch and bump it into second gear.

Trix laughed his easy laugh. "Guess that's a little better. If we ever get there, you should take the left up ahead to go toward the equipment barn."

Alex nodded and tried to follow his direction.

***

Winn walked out of the foaling barn after checking on a few of the mares and caught sight of Trix hanging off the side of a creeping tractor driven by the Chicago girl.

Of course. That didn't take long.

When they caught sight of him, Trix bent over to give instructions. She put her foot on the brake without taking it out of gear and the engine died. Winn let out an exasperated breath.

"Hey, Kid," Trix called. "Look who's acing Farm Hand 101."

Winn turned a hard stare on the girl and when her eyes instantly narrowed he didn't even address her.

"This mean that the post-hole digger is working?" Winn asked Trix.

"Well no, not yet, ran into a roadblock with that one. As luck would have it, Red came by to give me some assistance."

"More like a distraction. We're scheduled to start repairs on the north fencing soon, need the digger for that, Trix. Plus, I thought you were going to try to get some time in at the stable between now and then?" Winn could hear that his own tone was scolding and obnoxious but couldn't keep the frustration out of his voice. Even Trix seemed a little taken aback at his rudeness.

Trix recovered quickly, however. "I know that, Winn. I was hitching a ride over to grab a few more tools from the equipment barn. If she can drive a tractor, we can put her to work." Trix looked down and gave Alex a reassuring crooked smile and a little bump with his elbow.

"Not likely," Winn said gruffly under his breath.

That appeared to be enough for Alex. "Seriously, what's your problem with me?" she demanded.

"You mean other than that you're on the property less than twenty-four hours and work has already stopped?" Winn replied.

Trix started, "Not really fair—" but Alex interrupted.

"I didn't get the memo that you're everyone's boss, but if you're dead set on being a hard-ass let me make this easier for you." She jumped down off the tractor and headed in the direction of the house.

"Seemed a little harsh, Kid," Trix said, watching Alex's back storm off.

"What are you thinking, man? She won't last here more than a few days. Any time spent with her is a total waste." Winn had to make himself stop before he allowed his stress to say even harsher words.

"We were having a laugh, dude. What's up with you today?"

Winn pulled off his hat and ran a hand through his hair. "Nothing's up with me, trying to get a little work done is all." Then softening his tone, he added, "Frank Powers is going to be bringing a few horses for training this week. If you want to hang out, we can work on them together."

Trix accepted the olive branch. "Would be great, thanks, Winn."

An awkward moment passed, and Winn finally broke and cocked a half smile, waving his hand at the tractor, "You going to put your toys away?"

Trix laughed, slapped Winn on the shoulder and said, "Not until I go get those tools."

Trix left him standing there alone, and Winn couldn't keep his mind from revisiting his frustration about this newest development being piled onto his already full life.

Crooked Brook was in serious trouble. Winn's training business was in serious trouble. They were already struggling. What was Mae thinking when she agreed to let some spoiled city girl use the ranch to work through whatever her silly imagined problems may be? The timing couldn't be worse considering this season was going to be so critical to the survival of the business. Winn knew people thought he was dramatic, but the problems with the ranch threatened his way of life as he knew it.

Plus, what kind of twenty-something has no responsibilities and can screw off for an entire summer vacation whenever they felt like it?

Winn had more responsibilities than he could breathe through most of the time, and this girl has nothing? No one counting on her, expecting anything from her? Nothing riding on her actions?

Must be nice, he thought bitterly.

***

Alex fumed in her room until it was time for dinner. Since blowing up at Winn would ruin her chances of convincing Mae that she was trying to fit in, the next best option seemed to be an easy friendship with Trix. When she finally went down for dinner, Alex was confident in her plan to make Trix an ally.

Alex was engaged in surprisingly easy small talk with Trix and Tiny when Winn came in the room. The weight of his presence was stifling, and it seemed that it was not only for her. Others in the room quieted as he arrived.

Trix was the only one who seemed to neither notice nor care. "So Red helped work on the post-hole digger," he announced to Tiny loudly enough for everyone to hear.

"That so?" Tiny laughed. "Well thanks, Red, but that was supposed to be Trix's job since he broke it."

Trix let out a playful, annoyed sigh, "First of all, that rule doesn't apply. I wasn't the only one who broke that piece of crap." Then leaning over to Alex, he added, "Rule Eleven is if you break it, you fix it."

"How many rules are there?" she asked, desperately clinging to his good humor, despite feeling Winn's glare on the side of her face.

"Fourteen," Trix said.

"Nope, fifteen now, remember?" Tiny corrected and several guys joined in chuckling.

"Right, right, forgot about that most recent one." Trix rubbed his jaw.

Tiny screeched in an angry, high-pitched impression of Mae's voice, "Rule Fifteen: read a goddamn book once in a while!"

As Tiny was mocking her, Mae came around the corner followed by helpers with arms full of platters and bowls. She gave him a fake stern look and received a faux apologetic look in return.

"I don't sound like that, and let's not forget there used only to be two rules until you idiots came along and made reason for more." Mae insisted.

Alex joined them in the laughter that followed. The ease with which they all interacted reminded Alex of a large family—an unruly, smelly one, but a family nonetheless.

"For that, Alex, Trix, and Tiny, you're on clean up tonight," Mae added for good measure. The three nodded, accepting their fair punishment.

Trix leaned over to her and whispered, "Rule Fourteen: if you don't do dishes you don't eat."

Alex couldn't help but stifle a giggle. "I'm going to have to start writing these down."

He shrugged. "Nah, they'll be burned in your brain soon enough."

Alex returned his easy smile before her eyes were drawn to Winn, who sat stone-faced unapologetically staring her down until she broke and looked away.

Thank God my release from this place isn't dependent on gaining his approval.

Chapter 7

Alex discovered Winn had returned to the little barn in the woods the next day around the same time, which was confusing because out of all the things she disliked about him, slacking off work or avoiding his people didn't seem like something he was guilty of. This then raised the question: what in the hell was he doing, and why?

During this second day of hovering in the woods and spying on Winn, Alex got a glimpse of his purpose. Same as the day before, he entered the pen walked to the open barn door, made some soft murmurings she couldn't quite make out, and then made his way back to perch on the fence. All the while he was quietly humming or whistling to himself. But today after the first ten minutes there was movement from the open doorway. From the blackness a brown nose appeared, followed by a low-hanging, extremely hairy horse head.

There was mud caked on the side of its face and the woolly ears appeared to have knotted mats of hair growing between them. Alex couldn't look away from the animal's eyes. They were so deep and dark—and terrified. The poor horse never took its eyes away from Winn, watching him with an unwavering caution that was so tense even Alex could identify it as fear.

Alex spared a glance at Winn to see how he was reacting and was shocked to see that he wasn't. He didn't even appear to have looked up from his hands.

Does he not see?

Alex held her breath and an inexplicable lump began to form in her throat. As tentatively as it had appeared, the horse shrunk back into the shadows of the dark barn and the moment was gone.

Again, Alex's eyes bounced to Winn, who, as he had the day before, slowly slid down from his perch. He walked toward the door, humming again, but this time he reached into his pocket, pulled out a single sugar cube and placed it in the opening of the door. Alex caught herself smiling at the first and only kind gesture she'd seen from this man.

Alex returned to the little barn the next day, hours before she knew Winn would arrive. Not fully understanding her own motivation, Alex did recognize that the plight of the sad horse had somehow touched her, and she felt compelled to be near it. There was something broken, and she could empathize.

It took all of the bravery Alex could muster to step through the wide rails of the paddock. Cautiously, she shuffled toward the open door and placed a shaking hand on the doorway. It was foolish to assume anything would happen. She'd seen Winn do the same for two days and nothing ever came barreling out of the darkness.

"Hey there, um…little guy," Alex murmured into the nothingness, attempting to keep the nerves from showing up in her tone.

"I'm, uh," she said, backing away slowly. "I'm going to sit right here if that's okay with you?"

She squatted about fifteen feet from the opening and then with a sigh lowered herself to sit cross-legged in the dirt in the middle of the paddock. If today was the day she died a terrible death by stampeding horse, then so be it.

You haven't had a good "man up and get it done" moment since you arrived.

"And now what?" she asked the empty open door. Alex started humming but quickly learned that she very much lacked the creativity to come up with a melody a sad horse might be drawn to. Instead she spoke, yammering into the abyss with any words that popped into her head.

"So you're alone out here, huh? Believe me when I say I know what that feels like." Alex bit the inside of her cheek for a second, surprised at the emotion she felt after such a simple statement.

"Do you have a family somewhere missing you? I used to have a family. But in what seemed like an instant everything changed and it kind of broke. Nothing was ever the same. Not for any of us. It would be great and healthy for me to say I was angry, but if I'm honest, I didn't feel anything, I guess, and that's maybe the problem." Tears stung the back of her eyes and threatened to fall.

Wow, the shrink Mom made you see after Dad died would have a stroke if he found out it took a shadowy open door to make you say that out loud.

"Do you feel angry that you're alone? Or are you numb too?"

Around the corner of the door, a nose appeared. Alex couldn't move, didn't know if she should. Glossy, deep-brown eyes peered at her from the doorway.

Alex held her breath. The horse leaned toward her, sticking out one tentative foot and then another. In addition to the filthy and matted hair, there were marks down the horse's neck. Wounds, she realized. So many swollen sores.

What did this? A whip? Could a person have done this to an animal?

The thought of someone beating this horse was more than she could bear.

One sob caught in her throat and then Alex refused to fight her tears any longer. She broke. Burying her face in her hands, she sobbed. She cried for the horse, for herself, for all of it. It was not a pretty cry. Her eyes hurt, her head hurt, and still she couldn't stop. There was no telling how much time had passed before Alex was pulled from her essential breakdown by a soft warm breath that puffed across the back of her head.

She froze.

The horse had walked all the way to her and now stood directly over her pathetic pity party. Looking up into the watery depths of the horse's eyes, she saw so much there, such knowing, such sadness, its almost human emotions. Without thinking, Alex brought her hand up to rest in the middle of his head. Not petting or scratching—she lay her hand flat, and let out a long, ragged breath, and then, so did he. A moment passed, perhaps both waiting for something terrible. Then nothing happened, and the nothingness settled them both.

In a flash the moment ended.

The horse threw its head up. Eyes trained on the trees, he backed up a step and turned to bolt back into the barn. Alex was shocked and confused before understanding hit. Winn must be coming. Not knowing what to do, Alex got up and bolted for the trees on the opposite side of the paddock. Winn cleared the trees as she turned and settled out of sight in the brush, all the while her heart drumming against the back of her ribs. She watched as he repeated his routine from the day before. Her pulse was nearing normal by the time he left again.

The next morning, Alex rose early and went to find Matt. She was relieved to find him in the equipment barn tinkering with a huge mass of twisted metal attached to the back of yet another tractor. She'd made up her mind about what she wanted to accomplish and felt lighter now having a purpose.

"Matt? I need to ask for a favor."

He put down the tool in his hand, and in typical Matt fashion, slowly wiped off his hands before he responded. "What's that I can be doing for you, Alex?"

"I want to learn about horses. That is, I want to learn to work with them." If he was surprised by this, he didn't let it show.

"Winn's really the one that works the horses." There was the slightest twitch at the corner of his mouth.

Alex rolled her eyes. "I know that, Mattie, but he and I don't really…mesh. I was hoping you'd find a few minutes here and there to show me some things. I promise not to be a pain and I plan on reading everything I can find. I need a little hands-on experience." She could tell he was starting to cave. "I don't even want to ride them or anything, you know…hang out with them…?" Alex winced. She was pretty sure "hang out" with horses was not the correct terminology.

Matt didn't seem to mind her vocabulary. "Ok then. When do you propose we have these lessons?"

Resisting the urge to bounce and give a little clap, Alex tried to keep the overzealous excitement out of her voice. "Right after lunch maybe, you know, if you have time?" She wanted to ensure that Winn would be nowhere around, and it was looking like after lunch he always went to see the little horse.

Matt nodded.

"Today?" she asked.

He simply nodded again, and Alex moved to leave. When she looked over her shoulder at the door she found him grinning at her back.

She returned his smile. "Thank you, Matt."

As promised, Matt started Alex's horse lessons later that day. Of course he began by showing her how to clean a horse stall properly.

Is he trying to scare me off this endeavor by showing me a crappy job first?

Alex would not be deterred, however, and found it easy to fall into a rhythm with the work.

"So, how's your time been treating you so far, Alex?" Matt ventured, calling out to her over the stall wall that separated them.

"Well, being here is weird, you know, I don't really belong, but almost everyone has been nice." Alex wondered if he would think of Winn's face as the exception like she had.

"Yeah, this group, they're the best group I can remember."

"Have you always lived here, Matt?" She could picture him nodding in the silence even though she couldn't see him. "How did that come to be? Winn is your only family here, right?"

"My dad and Mae's son were best friends. When Mae's son died in the war, my dad moved in with Mae and John. Well, for a while at least."

Alex was taken aback. She didn't know Mae had a son that had passed away. She grew sad thinking of Mae and the way she'd basically adopted all of the crew.

"Only for a while?" Alex asked when he didn't continue.

"My dad was—well, is I guess—a bit of a drifter. Living here he met my mom, had me and then took off to follow the rodeo circuit for a while."

"Where is your mom?" Alex wasn't sure if she was skating on thin ice because she couldn't see his face, but if he was willing to talk she wanted to know.

"Gone," was Matt's simple reply.

"Dead?"

"I don't think so."

Alex waited for more, but when it didn't come she put down the pitchfork and made her way out of the stall opening so she could see him in the neighboring stall. He was still picking through the wood shavings methodically, but she could tell his mind was elsewhere.

"When was the last time you saw her?" Alex asked quietly.

Matt jumped a little, obviously unaware that she'd moved to outside his stall.

"Not since I was young—eight, maybe nine years old." His expression was hard to read, and she waited to see if he would keep talking to fill the silence. He did. "I uh, I was diagnosed with diabetes as a kid, when I was about seven I had an episode. It was pretty bad, guess it scared her. I was never really the same, you know, a little slower than the other kids, trouble in school, stuff like that. It was too much for her to handle. She was young, too young to be able to stick that out. No one's heard from her since she left."

"I'm sorry." Alex felt guilty for prying and struggled to understand a mother that would leave her young son, no matter how hard things got. The story did, however, fill in some blanks. It explained Matt's trouble speaking and the parts of him that seemed off, but also the closeness he felt toward Mae.

Matt looked up at her and gave her a shallow smile. "It's okay, doesn't hurt for you to know. I barely remember her anyways. Mae has been my mother in all the ways that matter, and I wouldn't change that." He looked sure but a little sad and Alex decided she needed to give him a break and let him talk about something else, something he liked talking about.

"So how does Winn fit into all this family drama?" she asked, trying to keep her tone light. Matt's expression immediately lifted. She didn't fully understand the bond between the two brothers, but it was impossible to deny its strength.

"Winn's mom met my dad on one of his trips back through town. I was maybe a junior in high school. Our dad stayed that time for almost a year. All of a sudden, I had this whole little family and this tiny baby, someone who I would get to love and take care of. I knew the moment I put eyes on him that he was going to be the most important person in my life, and I wasn't wrong."

Alex smiled. Despite her own dislike of Winn, seeing Matt talk about him was heartwarming. "What happened after that?" she asked.

"Well, Winn's mom couldn't really put up with our dad—he was pretty in the bottle in those days—so she split. She was young too, guess Dad had a type. I think Mae might keep tabs on her, but I don't know where she is. Then Dad gave into his need to wander again not long after. For us though, we had each other, and we had Mae and John. Didn't really need anything other than that. We had a happy life." Matt eyed her before adding, "Which included your mother for a time."

Alex's face scrunched up before she could police it. She'd almost forgotten that her mother actually spent substantial time here before Alex was born, but for some reason she'd come back and hardly ever talked about it.

"Your momma was something else," Matt went on. "Brave, funny. So quick with her words. Everyone loved when she was here. You know, she got to meet Winn when he was a little tiny thing. It was right before she went back to Chicago for the last time."

Alex tried to conjure a version of her mother with those characteristics and failed. Doing the math, it appeared her mother must have been here months before she met Alex's father if she overlapped with a baby version of Winn.

"If she loved it so much, why didn't she ever come back? Why did she send me here to punish me?" Alex asked, incapable of containing the frustration and sense of betrayal in her voice.

Matt's face got soft, and she could tell that he was a little stuck and unsure of what to say. "Well, I don't know about everything, but your mom went back to Chicago and met your pops. I guess her life got busy, they had you not too long after. I do know she loved it here and I think sharing it with you isn't supposed to be a punishment. Being here helped her for a time, maybe she hoped it would help you."

"He's dead, you know," Alex blurted, completely shocking herself with her blunt words.

Matt nodded in that methodical way of his and said, "Yup, I did know that, and I am sorry. There's never a good time to lose your father, but when it's that young, it seems worse. You were in high school then?"

She nodded silently but couldn't really hold down her feelings of annoyance.

Why do these people know so much about me when I hadn't even known their names?

"Yeah," he continued. "That's really tough."

Alex looked up into his face and couldn't tell what he was expecting of her, but if Matt was still willing to talk she was going to get some answers. "Why didn't she come back, Matt?"

"You'd have to ask her."

"I'm asking you." Then she came out with the question she actually had been too embarrassed to even really let herself think before. "I guess I'm asking if you and Mom had something that she needed to stay away from after she met my dad."

Now it was his turn for his face to crinkle in confusion. "I don't know what you mean."

"Did you date my mom? So, like when she got a new man she couldn't bring him around here?"

"Oh! Good lord, no." Matt's face went beet red. "Nothing like that. Your mom was like my sister." He was flustered now, and Alex was counting on the words to keep spewing. They did. "After Becky met your dad they didn't come around because the life he wanted, the life they were building, it was too different from here, too different from us. I think your mom was embarrassed, either of us or…I don't know, maybe of him."

Alex could see him flinch at his accidental admission.

What Matt said hurt, but it wasn't all that surprising. To some extent Alex must have already known that who her father was wouldn't have fit in here with these people. He wouldn't have approved of them and they wouldn't have approved of him. Pretty boy, college grad, business suit and the pressing drive to prove himself and his worth through nicer cars, bigger houses, better offices. That drive had eventually led to her father's own undoing, and so Alex couldn't say at this point that it had been any kind of right.

Matt took her silence as anger, and maybe it was. "Like I said Alex, I don't know. You have to ask Becky if you want to know, or maybe Mae can help you. I never knew all the details and even if I did my brain doesn't recall the past like I wish it would."

She took in a deep breath and felt that she'd heard enough. She needed to cut him and herself a break or she'd lose one of the only allies she'd made so far.

"I guess you're right. Water under the bridge and all. What's next?'

He eyed her suspiciously but seemed relieved at the abrupt shift. "Okay, let's talk hay."

They continued through the rest of the afternoon with banal small talk and Matt teaching her the routine for feeding the horses, which was thankfully relatively straightforward.

Chapter 8

For two more days Alex continued her visits with the little horse in the woods, noticing he was quicker to leave his stall each time she arrived. Gradually the horse became brave enough to approach her while she was standing, and on her last visit she'd been able to reach up and lightly run her hand down his neck, cautiously feeling around the bumps and ridges his neck wounds made.

I'm going to help this horse, even though it means my visits will no longer fly under the radar.

The next day Alex came prepared. Thanks to her reading and the sessions with Matt, she was ready to administer more minor vet care and perhaps as importantly a little beauty TLC. Alex had lifted a wound salve from the other barn, because while she knew the open wounds were too old for stitching, they were still begging for an infection. The little horse approached her and the tote cautiously. She repeated their interaction from the days before, speaking in low tones, saying nothing really, gibberish and anything that came to her mind.

"So maybe you'll meet Emily someday. We're not speaking right now but that feels less permanent than it did a while ago. She's secretly in love with this barista, Tommy, who's not so secretly in love with her back…"

The horse dropped his head to smell the disinfectant she'd cracked open while speaking. Alex continued her steady flow of conversation while slowly rubbing the antiseptic into one of the larger wounds. He twitched but his feet stayed planted, which seemed like a good sign. Alex began scrubbing a little harder all the while chatting about anything and everything.

"Emily is from England, and she's very trendy and she's constantly, well…mussed, but she manages to have a job that allows for that. She's in club promoting and she's got everyone, including me for a while, convinced that she's some party girl, always looking for the next good time. But she's not that way. She's driven and sharp as hell. You'd never know what was going on inside if she didn't periodically let you see it." Alex paused to change sides and cracked a new pad. Starting on a different laceration she continued her confessional.

"God, I miss her. I can't even really tell you why, but I miss her more than I thought I would. Kills me, because there's really no reason for her to miss me back. Remember I said we were not on the best terms when I left to come here."

Alex stepped back to survey her work, then rinsed and dried the newly cleaned wounds. She cautiously waited for the little horse to tell her that he'd had enough, but as he watched her he didn't look ready to run. Alex bent to retrieve the jar of salve and allowed him to softly blow into the little tub as he investigated it. He seemed unimpressed, so she took a gob out and began to spread it into the openings in his neck. Stepping back to review work, Alex was met with a strong sense of pride.

"Now for the fun part," she promised him as she bent to retrieve her own bottle of leave-in-conditioner. It seemed silly, but really, was there a better option? The knots at the top of his head had to be pulling on his skin by this point and she didn't have access to a horse detangler, if it even existed.

Alex squeezed out a healthy helping into the palm of her hands and rubbed them together before she began to work the product into his mane. Again he seemed not to object, so she continued with her babbling, while pulling a large-toothed comb out of her back pocket.

"So it dawned on me you don't have a name, which is sad, everyone should have a name. I wish I was clever enough to come up with something witty and epic to call you, but I'm at a loss." Her hands started the work of combing out the snarled hair.

"Maybe I'll call you Tommy, because that guy always seemed to come back stronger after being knocked down." She chuckled thinking about what her friend would think of naming a horse after him.

Halfway through the mess at the top of his head, the little horse twitched, turned abruptly to run back into the barn.

Oh no, it's Winn. I've been here too long.

This time Alex wasn't quick enough. She and Tommy had been too wrapped up in their interaction to notice Winn's approach until he broke through the trees in time to see the back end of the horse darting through the stall door.

Shit. I'm about to get busted with a women's comb in my hand and a bottle of hair product at my feet. Alex's eyes met Winn's, and by the anger in them, she knew he was not going to hear an ounce of explanation from her.

His fist tensed around the halter and lead rope he held at his side. As he approached the fence, he quietly said through clenched teeth. "Alexandra, I don't know what in the hell you're doing in there, but you need to come out immediately."

The stillness in his tone was terrifying. Alex couldn't wrap her mind around a scenario in which she didn't instantly obey. She started to bend to retrieve the tote.

"Leave it." The command was quiet but harsh, and she snapped back up, afraid to meet his stare.

Winn waited for her to awkwardly climb through the rails of the paddock. Once she was through the railing, he stormed off down the path, making it very clear she was to follow. Alex rushed to keep up with his angry strides. The longer they walked, the more she felt like a scolded child and she didn't care for it. By the time they reached the equipment barn, Alex was mostly recovered and was gearing up for the fight she knew was coming.

Winn plowed through the door and wheeled around to face her. His expression hadn't softened, and his eyes narrowed to harsh, glowing lines. Her bravado extinguished.

"Who in the hell do you think you are?" Winn demanded.

Alex pulled in breath to respond but he wasn't finished. "This is an actual working ranch here, princess. You do understand that, right? Up to now you've been a nuisance, but this has gone too far. Do you even understand what you've done?"

"I was trying to help," Alex stammered. She was angry and confused, but even more, she was embarrassed.

"You silly little girl. It's a horse." Winn's voice rose as his frustration peaked. "It doesn't need a spa day!" They both glanced down at the comb still held in her clenched fist. Alex wanted to throw it at him.

"I don't know the first thing about any of this and even I could see that poor animal needed help. Why didn't you help him?" she demanded as her fear was getting replaced by her own frustration.

"We can't catch him without traumatizing him," Winn yelled, and she could see having to admit that to her upset him even more. He continued, "Do you know how much time and effort has gone toward earning his trust? Your little beauty salon experiment undid all of it."

"As far as I know, *you* were the one who put those marks on him in the first place!" As Alex said the words, she instantly regretted them. She knew it wasn't true, but it was too late to take them back. She was powerless to do anything other than watch the rage fill his face.

When his frustration apparently boiled over, Winn threw the halter he was still holding against a shelving unit, knocking a mason jar to the ground in the process. More out of instinct than anything, Alex brought her hand up to protect her face. Immediately, she saw Winn's reaction change from one of shock to a hard, speculative stare. She opened her mouth to speak and couldn't find words.

Winn's eyes narrowed as he growled, "You thought...you thought I was going to hit you?"

The line of his mouth thinned. He was upset, but his eyes showed a fatigue older than this fight.

"So that's what you think of me? That I'm some crazed animal that rules by brute force? I beat my horses? I take aggression out on women?" The volume of his voice had quieted. Now it was low and slow but still deeply menacing. "Don't pretend that you know who I am or what I'm capable of." As he turned to go, he looked at the glass scattered on the floor and swore under his breath.

"No," Alex said quietly.

He stopped but didn't turn to face her.

"That's not what I think," she said to his back, silently willing him to turn around so she could explain, but after a brief pause, he kept walking.

***

Winn made his way back toward the little quarantine barn in the woods, his heart rate still unrecovered from finding the city girl in the pen with the abused gelding.

She thought you were going to hit her, his mind scolded him.

She deserved to be throttled for putting herself at risk like that, his ego scolded back.

His head hung as frustration began to ebb and a more familiar overwhelming weariness crept into his body. Coming around the bend, his eyes landed on the tote the *princess* had brought into the middle of the paddock. His irritation tried to claw its way back up but failed. The gelding's head poked out but after seeing Winn, he sunk back into the dark doorway.

"No, I'm not her," Winn called to him, gritting his teeth against the taste of begrudging envy. "I've been taking care of you for over a week and you never let me see you like that," he admitted to the hiding horse and to himself.

"It's not like I don't care. You've been taking the antibiotics and I'm trying to do right by you." Winn continued as he bent to duck between the fence slats. His eyes narrowed at the pile of discarded veterinary supplies alongside some women's hair products.

"She's ridiculous, you know that right?" he said softly into the doorway and the gelding's leery face appeared. Winn stood, hands on his hips, watching the horse watching him. "She doesn't know a thing about any of this. She could have seriously hurt herself. She could have further damaged your opinion of humans."

She didn't.

The horse stood statue-still, and Winn bent to gather the supplies. He should feel grateful that someone was trusted enough by the horse to allow the medical care, but he couldn't get himself over the threshold of his own pride.

"She doesn't belong here and she's not staying. You're going to have to get used to me," Winn told the horse who retreated back in the doorway as he approached to leave a mint.

I don't have time for a nosy, wannabe cowgirl and her baseless accusations, he thought bitterly before heading back toward the main stables with her gear in hand.

***

Still raw from her exchange with Winn, Alex was surprised that her strongest desire wasn't to hide alone and stew in her room until dinner. She felt like company would do her good. Standing in the doorway of the house, she contemplated heading to the kitchen, positive Mae would find a task to keep her busy. However, Alex wondered if somehow Mae would manage to see right into Alex's brain and sense she'd had a fight with Winn. Even stranger still, she was afraid Mae might force her to go home because of it, a thought that inexplicably made her panicky.

Instead Alex turned to wander down into the basement. Her bravery was rewarded when she saw it was only Matt and Bishop together downstairs. They were both on the couch staring at a video game on the split-screen TV.

Without looking over his shoulder, Bishop called out, "It's our day off, which means it's not your day off, which means you still have work to do, jackass."

"Do I?" Alex asked with a smile on her lips.

They both whirled around, Bishop sputtering words as he rose, controller still in hand. "Aw…jeeze, Red, sorry about that…I thought, uh, I assumed you were one of the guys."

Alex couldn't help but laugh at his discomfort. If she'd learned anything about ranching boys in the last week it was that being rude didn't suit them—unless it was to each other.

"Don't worry about it, Bishop, seriously. I've never trespassed down here unaccompanied, so it was a fair assumption." Then with mock horror on her face Alex added, "But what if I had been Mae?"

His face blanched. "Don't even joke about that." Then with a laugh, "That would have earned me a head slap for sure."

Matt and Alex chuckled at the visual.

"Mind if I join you guys?" she asked.

"Not at all. You wanna play?" Bishop asked, pointing at her with the controller.

She put her palms up to refuse. "I'm not great at these kinds of games." She looked at the screen. "Is that a zombie Nazi?"

Matt laughed. "Yup."

"Then yes, I'd like to shoot something. I'll need a tutorial though."

"You got it," Bishop said as he walked to grab another controller from the shelf.

The late afternoon passed easily, and Alex reaffirmed that she was quite bad at first-person shooter games but did find her mood much improved after blasting multiple Third Reich undead.

At a quarter to five a herd of rumbling footsteps sounded overhead, and then they split up, some coming down the basement stairs, others heading up to the second and third floors. For a moment, her gut twisted knowing that the boots heading her way were probably Winn's. When he appeared and saw her, he looked briefly surprised before he covered it with a glare of annoyance.

Alex narrowed her eyes, challenging him to call her out on being down there, but Winn wordlessly walked past the three of them and down toward his room. Bishop rose from the couch, patting his thighs as he stood.

"Gonna go wash up. Thanks for the games, Red."

"Thanks for letting me play—it was fun," she said, a little shocked at how much she meant it. "I'll walk up with you."

Back in her bathroom upstairs, she washed her hands and threw her hair up into a ponytail. Alex looked at her expression in the mirror.

"You look…calm," she said quietly to herself.

Her mind wandered to the interaction with Winn and she decided then and there to ignore him. Alex felt a pull toward the little abused horse and needed to see him healed. The other guys here were great, as evidenced by her gaming afternoon. If she was home, she'd have to be dealing with finding a new job, temporarily sharing the apartment with her brother and deciding if her relationships with Emily, Tommy, or her mother were salvageable. That felt too big, too scary—scarier than some sanctimonious redneck blowhard.

"It's settled," she said to the determined face staring back.

She was going to serve out her whole summer-long sentence. Alex nodded at her reflection and ran down the steps to join everyone for dinner.

After dinner she found Mae in the front room with a book, looking relaxed knowing all her minions would be tidying the kitchen.

"Mae?" Alex ventured.

"Hmmm?" Mae said, looking up from her book after a brief pause.

"I've decided, if the offer still stands, I'd like to stay a little longer."

"I know."

Alex's eyebrow shot up. "How could you know? I only decided an hour ago."

"If you say so." Mae chuckled and returned her gaze to the book.

Still a little confused, Alex asked, "So, like until August first?"

"Sure."

"Ok…" Alex warily watched Mae turn a page and it became obvious their conversation was over, so she added, "Good night then."

"Night."

Chapter 9

Alex worked to keep herself busy, keeping her horse education going, and most importantly, staying off Winn's radar. Earlier in the week, she'd discovered that if she arrived early enough, she could sit in the hayloft of the main barn and keep tabs on the goings-on without being noticed.

A trailer came down the gravel path toward the paddock, and when the driver stepped out, Winn and Trix wandered out of the barn to meet him. The men shook hands and then moved to offload a couple of horses that they set loose in the arena.

Winn turned to the older man from the truck. "What's the story with these, Frank?" he asked, then brought his attention back to the horses as they explored the enclosure.

"Well, the little bay there's always been a little ornery. Lately, though, he's been getting pretty sour, doesn't want to work anymore. Seeing as how he's eight, that doesn't work for me. Figured I'd bring him over for a bit of a tune-up since I was bringing you the new one. The paint is new, and he's a piece of work. Seems to be 'fraid of its own shadow. Won't work in the rain, doesn't seem to want to put a foot in the water. Also got a pretty big shy when it comes to working around the machines, tractors, trucks, whatever. Thought you'd be the best man to bring him around."

"All right then. I'd say you can come get that bay next week and I'll know better then how much longer for the new one."

"Sounds good, Winn, I 'preciate it." The gentleman nodded and hopped back in his truck.

Soon after Frank drove away, Bishop and Matt came out of the equipment barn to meet up with Winn and Trix. The four of them stood surveying the new horses, each with one boot up on the lower rail, both elbows resting on the top rail.

They look like a cowboy postcard.

Alex laughed at herself then continued on her spy mission to observe without being detected.

"What's your plan, Kid?" Matt asked.

Without taking his eyes off the two horses, Winn responded, "Well, Trix here's been making noise like he wants to be a horse trainer, so I figured I'll work with him on the bay and then depending on how rough that paint is, maybe you and I will work on that one."

Winn popped a little smirk and looked over at Trix, who took the ribbing with a smile and a nod. The men split up. Matt and Bishop went into the paddock and haltered the horses. Bishop held the little bay in the middle of the ring and Matt left with the paint. Trix came out of the barn with a bridle slung over one shoulder and a saddle over the other. Winn climbed up to the top rail and sat as Trix walked up and took hold of the bay horse.

"Want to know what I think?" Winn asked with a half-smile.

Over his shoulder, Trix shot him a sarcastic glance. "All right there, horse whisperer, no one's even been on it yet. You want to give me a minute so I can form an opinion?"

"Suit yourself." Winn shrugged and leaned back like he was ready to take in the show.

Seeming wary of Winn's response, Trix looked back at him. "You're screwing with my head?"

"I'm saying normally I like to watch them go around a bit before I sit on them, is all."

"Well, Wonderboy, I already did that. Been watching this one since it stepped off the trailer." Then after a pause, he pumped his fist in the air and yelled, "Rule Eight!"

Winn laughed and then said, "Roger that, carry on."

Trix bridled the little horse and threw on a pad and the saddle. After cinching up the girth, he put a foot in the stirrup and swung up and on. When nothing happened, Trix tossed Winn a triumphant look.

Winn responded with a nod and prompted, "All right, then let's see him do some work."

Trix started putting the little horse through some basic exercises, looking like he met some resistance from the horse right away. Winn opened his mouth and then shut it again.

"Does seem to be pretty crabby about moving forward. Think he needs a bit of a strong ride to remind him we've all got a job to do," Trix reported right before giving the little bay a quick, strong kick on the sides.

As quickly as the horse kicked out, it spun right out from under him. Before anyone could blink, Trix was in the dirt looking up at the horse that had unseated him.

Winn hopped off the fence and started toward them. As Trix began to get up, he looked down at his elbow. It bled through the torn fabric of his shirt.

"Goddamn, look at my arm," he hollered as he rose.

Quickly Trix reached out to snatch the rein dangling from the side of the horse's bit, but Winn put a hand up, and Trix stopped mid-motion watching and waiting. Winn reached out and slowly grabbed hold of the rein.

"You can be mad you came off. You can be mad you didn't know any better, but you don't get to be mad at him. Even if it was his fault, getting up out of the dirt with anger in your voice and movements doesn't help. Ever," Winn warned him coolly.

Trix handled the quiet but stern reprimand well and nodded.

"Okay," Winn continued, the ice now out of his voice. "Now this horse has always been ornery. Frank's right about that. I know because I broke it, which means I also have the luxury of knowing when this horse is difficult, it's nervous. It doesn't get slow. It gets too quick and doesn't turn well."

Cupping his elbow to shore up some of the bleeding, Trix cocked his head. "You broke this horse, so you had an unfair advantage."

"True, but do you think you'll have a full and honest history on every horse someone's going to pay you to fix?" Winn asked.

"No, fine, all right, get to the part where you knew I was gonna fall off that horse before I saddled it." Trix sighed.

"That horse hurts. That's why it doesn't want to work right now."

Trix's eyebrows shot up. "Now that's a pile of B.S. I'm newer, but I know a lame horse when I see one. This one doesn't have a limp, Kid."

"Nope, this one's got a gut ache. If I had to guess I'd say ulcers." Winn said, scrutinizing the horse's side.

"A gut ache…" Trix scratched his neck. "Explains why he handled me giving him a strong boot so badly. Not colic?"

"Frank's a good man, and for the most part, a competent horseman. Don't think he would have brought me a colicky horse. Plus, Frank doesn't like to pay me to fix what he thinks he can."

"Well all right, I'll talk to Matt about treating him for ulcers for a couple of days. But I get to be the one back on it when it's feeling better." Trix wagged a finger at Winn.

"Fair enough. Go wash up. I'll take care of him." Winn nodded toward the house and while he watched Trix climb out of the pen, Alex watched Winn. He turned to the little bay and ran a hand up his neck working his way to the saddle. He murmured a bit as he loosened the girth and pulled the saddle from his back. "Won't he be surprised when you turn into a little spitfire soon as your stomach's off the injured reserve?" Winn chuckled to himself. He pulled the bridle from the horse's head, gave him a little scratch, and turned to walk into the barn. The horse followed like a puppy, a step behind all the way out of sight.

"Learn anything?" Matt asked from behind her and Alex jumped about a foot in the air.

"Jesus, Matt, you scared the crap out of me. How long have you been there?" Alex asked, trying to catch her breath.

"Long enough to watch you watch that whole thing. Winn's taught Trix a lot these last few months. What did you think?"

She eyed him, unsure of how to respond, so she punted asking, "What's rule number eight?"

Matt laughed. "Rule Eight: wear your big boy panties."

She smiled, remembering Trix yelling it to the sky right before getting on. She then thought of Winn. "Looks like Winn knows his stuff. It's impressive really. But if he knew Trix could get hurt, he should have said something. That was mean."

Matt shrugged. "Winn knew that Trix wasn't really in danger, a slow fall off a slow horse never really did anyone damage. He knew that same as he knew that horse had a bellyache by looking at him."

"How though? How could he possibly tell that?" Alex asked incredulously.

"Ah, I'd say he noticed the horse looked a little ribby, like maybe it's dropped weight recently. A few little kicks or glances toward his belly. Winn's got a good eye. Sometimes that boy doesn't have much sense when it comes to people, but he's rarely wrong about a horse."

"Where did he learn all of this?" she asked.

"I taught him everything I knew, but he's way beyond that now. The rest, well, he'd say the horses taught him. Winn says horses are always talking. But we're not always listening. And Winn? He's a good listener."

Alex snorted. "He didn't seem like such a great listener when he tore into me out at the little barn."

Matt's eyebrows shot up, and Alex grimaced as she realized her mistake.

"What's this now? The quarantine barn in the woods?" Matt asked.

Alex knew she was busted, so she spilled the story, including the embarrassing bits about hiding in the bushes to avoid Winn. She did, however, leave out the part about her cruel accusation and Winn throwing the halter.

Alex could see the discomfort on his face as she told the story.

"Best to listen to Winn about these things, Alex," Matt said, fixing a hard look on her.

"Tommy likes me, Mattie," she confessed.

"Who?"

"I named the little horse Tommy. At least that's what I'm going to call him."

She could see the dilemma he was facing. She was asking him for permission to disobey Winn, a prospect she imagined made him very uncomfortable.

"What I don't know can't hurt us I guess..." Matt murmured.

She adored him for his capitulation and gave him a quick hug. "Agreed, thanks, Matt."

Later in the day Alex was late coming to lunch and caught herself pausing on the steps to listen to the bustle of the dining room, taking unfamiliar pleasure from the chaos of a large family sitting down to a meal.

"Frank brought over some horses today?" Alex heard Mae ask.

"Yeah, a little bay terror," Trix replied. "Put me on the ground in a heartbeat and tore up my elbow something fierce."

"Aye," Winn chimed in. "Rodeo pony in the making for sure."

There was a round of laughter from the table.

"Sure," Trix replied, milking it for all it was worth, "Eyes wild and rolling like a rabid dog." He paused for another round of laughter. "And your golden boy here offered me up for sacrifice, Moms."

Alex rounded the corner in time to see Trix put on his saddest face before sending a little triumphant grin toward Winn, who had his back to the staircase.

"Is that so?" Mae added with a teasing tone. "How's the elbow now, my poor boy?"

"It's hard to say, Moms. It's been touch and go all afternoon." Trix was milking it now.

"Well, Rule Four—" Mae started.

"I know, I know, 'No bleeding in the house.' I was careful."

They all laughed, and Mae reached forward and gave both Winn and Trix a squeeze on the shoulder. "I'm sure everything's going to be all right."

Winn surprised the hell out of Alex when he softly sang, "No woman, no cry." He got up and started serenading Trix in a terrible attempt at a Jamaican accent.

The table blew up as Winn knelt in front of Trix, gently cradling his bandaged elbow and continued to sing, then the table joined in for the chorus.

Winn glanced up to see Alex at the base of the stairs, and his carefree grin immediately melted from his face. He replaced it with a stone mask as he rose and returned to his seat. The table grew quiet, picking up on the ever-present tension. Alex took her seat next to Matt and tried her best to avoid eye contact with Winn.

Alex leaned over Matt to give Trix's hand a reassuring squeeze. He looked up and gave a guilty grin, saying, "You feel like playing nurse, Red?"

The whole table erupted in laughter, and the heaviness in the room lifted.

"Maybe later," she teased, laughing with everyone but Winn.

That evening Alex made a trip out to see Tommy after dinner. She'd thought twice about directly contradicting Winn's orders, especially so soon after their blowup. However, she'd come to a few conclusions. One, screw that guy, and two, if he wanted to rage at her again next time, she would be ready to rage back.

Matt and horse Tommy are the only two beings on the property I'm completely bonding with, and I am flat-out unwilling to give either of them up.

Alex decided she'd go for a chat. Weirdly, it felt like a reasonable temporary substitute for her ruined friendship with Emily. However, after letting time get away from her again, Alex saw she'd been out longer than she planned, and the sky was getting quite dark by the time she was making her way out of the woods. Walking across the back of the property, Alex noticed the floodlights over the horse rings were on and went to investigate.

Winn was in the round pen with a horse she hadn't seen before. She smiled. Being able to tell them apart was a new skill recently helped along by her lessons with Matt. This new horse was black and larger than most of the little quarter horses on the property.

The horse eyed Winn cautiously as he slowly began to tack it. Every move he made the horse twitched or snorted, never actually moving its feet but never being still either. Winn continuously mumbled a stream of quiet, unintelligible murmurings. The horse had one ear turned back listening intently. With the girth tightened Winn walked forward, the rein resting over an open palm. The horse started forward and stopped abruptly. Winn's hand came up soothingly, and he never stopped the slow-talking. The horse started forward again and instantly reacted violently, standing up on its hind feet and lashing out with his front. Winn quickly stepped to the side to avoid the flailing hooves and stood, patiently waiting for the horse to land and again. "Sorry friend, that's not okay. It's rude to stand up like that. Settle, settle." Winn kept a string of hushed words coming continuously.

Once the horse was back on the ground, Winn started forward again. The horse went to follow, again rearing up, and this time Winn kept tension on the rein and the horse pulled back against the pressure. Winn mumbled, "So rude, settle, settle." The horse landed again. This little scenario played out a few more times, with each attempt resulting in a shorter tantrum from the horse.

Finally, the horse was following Winn around the paddock without incident. Winn's voice was soft, but full of praise. "So much better with all four feet on the ground…quiet …sorry, this next part is gonna upset you."

He walked to the side of the horse and put a foot in the stirrup. Alex's jaw dropped. She couldn't really believe someone, anyone, would try to sit on that horse after all of that drama. The horse snorted, trying to shy away from Winn, who by now had placed most of his weight in the one stirrup. He took a few hops with the foot still on the ground to stay with the prancing horse. "I know, I know…you'll make it, you're going to be okay." In a fluid movement, he was fully seated on the horse, and Alex held her breath to the point where her chest hurt.

It almost seemed as though nothing was going to happen, and then in a blink, the horse stood up on his hind feet, spun to the side and the second his front feet hit the ground he took off at a bucking run around the paddock. Alex's hands flew to her mouth to silence the cry of alarm bubbling in her throat.

Winn's upper body appeared to be flailing out of control. However, he never seemed to come away from the saddle. To Alex's amazement, he still managed to keep his un-panicked words coming, punctuated by the air being forced from his lungs each time the horse landed.

"Whoa…whoa…all right…settle…whoa." He pulled up on the reins as he spoke. The entire episode took an eternity in Alex's mind. Such is the way things work when you believe you're watching someone die.

Finally, the flurry of movement stopped, and the horse stood in cloud of dust in the center of paddock, chest heaving.

"Okay, all right…see…we're okay." Winn leaned forward to run his hand up the horse's neck, when in a split second, the horse stood up again, throwing the top of his head into Winn's face. There was a sickening thud as Winn's head cracked back. The horse landed, seeming to have startled itself by connecting so solidly. Winn's baseball cap was skewed from the collision and a small trickle of blood appeared from a cut right above his eyebrow.

"Well…ouch," he said calmly as he raised his hand to right his hat. "You okay?" he asked the horse as he dropped his hand to once again rub the horse's neck. He blinked as the small stream of blood made its way into his eye. He brushed his fingers through the blood and brought them, bright red, back down for inspection.

"Awww….damn," he breathed softly. "I like this hat."

Winn reached to pull a handkerchief from his back pocket and the horse jumped a little with Winn's shift in weight. He responded evenly, "Hold on dude, seriously, I need a minute."

Winn was so conversational that Alex half expected the horse to respond. He wiped the blood from his head with the cloth and then stuffed it up in between his forehead and the hat to staunch the flow of blood. Alex had to admit, he did have composure. He hadn't been preaching earlier when he chastised Trix for getting heated with the bay horse. With this one, things had literally come to blows and he remained steady without a trace of anger. There was a patience here that she'd yet to see from him at any other time. Despite her dislike of this man, in this he was not a hypocrite.

"All right…game on." He gave a soft little cluck and the horse took a tentative step forward. They both seemed cautious and unwilling to repeat the head butt. The horse took one more step and then tried to take off at a buck again. This time Winn pulled him up short into a halt. "Nope, time to play nice, my friend." The horse stopped bucking but began prancing side to side.

"Hush, settle…"

Finally, the horse stopped his anxious moving, and Winn softened his hold so the horse could walk forward again. This time, after an entire lap around the paddock, Winn pulled the reins again. "Whoa…okay, good man."

After the horse stopped and remained still, Winn swung his leg over the saddle and hopped down. "That's enough for us tonight, huh? Not being a psycho is what ends this for you. Remember that tomorrow." He reached up and rubbed the horse between the ears. "Don't forget my head is as hard as yours." He smiled to himself and turned toward the barn. The horse followed.

Chapter 10

The next day Alex repeated what was becoming her morning routine. She was in the hayloft in time to see Matt and Winn pull the paint horse into the paddock. Winn was sporting a shiner below the little cut on his forehead, and someone had put on a few butterfly bandages to help keep it closed. Neither Matt nor Winn acknowledged his injury. She wondered if being this banged up was par for the course, and then remembered that Matt and Winn roomed together. Matt was probably the one who had doctored his brother's head. She smiled to herself thinking of Matt's kind demeanor and also at Winn having to admit he let himself get clocked in the face. Something she imagined his ego didn't care for.

"What's Frank got to say about this one again?" Matt asked.

"Says he's too afraid of everything to work—machines and water mostly." Winn answered while idly scratching the paint behind the ears.

"So, what'd you want to do first?"

"I want to see what he's like without anything scaring the crap out of him, then I guess we'll add distractions until we get a reaction. Go from there."

"Fair enough." Matt started back to the barn to grab tack and Winn stood with the paint. Slowly Winn worked his way around the horse, running his hands around the horse's back muscles and then down each leg. She guessed he was looking for any reactions from the pressure.

Alex had to admit when it came to the horses, Winn genuinely seemed to care for them and their health, both mental and physical. The paint didn't react to Winn's handling of him. It stood there quietly keeping an ear trained on the soft murmurings Alex now recognized as Winn's habit of always soothing and comforting them. When Matt returned, the men tacked the horse, and Winn easily hoisted himself up. He paused and gave Matt a sheepish grin as he took his baseball hat and spun it around, putting the bill to the back.

Matt chuckled. "Learned a lesson last night, eh?"

Winn laughed back. "Wasn't one of my brighter moments."

He nudged the horse into a walk toward the fence. As he worked the horse, he commented here and there, looking quite at home in the saddle and not at all like someone who had taken a beating the night before.

"Nice horse," Matt threw out.

"Yeah someone took some time with this one, put in some cool buttons," Winn replied, sending the horse quickly and then pulling him up in a sliding stop. Next he asked the horse to spin clockwise on its backend.

"Really cool buttons," he added. He stopped the spin and sat facing Matt, arms crossed casually over the horn of the saddle.

"All right," Winn postured. "So I'm training a horse and I'm good enough to put in some sharp reining skills. Why don't I train him to handle the everyday things? Puddles? Tractors? Whatever? Why don't I teach that?"

"Well either you're an idiot, or you did train him right, but something happened," Matt ventured.

"Exactly."

"I don't think Frank's in the habit of buying from idiot trainers," Matt said with a grin.

"Well, he buys from me quite a bit." Winn sent back a grin. "This one must have had one hell of a scare to override the kind of training he's had."

Matt nodded, and Winn continued speaking quietly to himself. "No scars. Whatever happened didn't leave a mark. Also means we have no way of knowing when he got this scare. Is it ongoing? A one-time thing?" he asked again, more to himself.

"So what's next, boss?" Matt asked with a touch of sarcasm.

"I'm going to untack him. Let's work him on a line and start with water, easier to keep small."

Matt nodded and disappeared into the barn to retrieve the long line. Winn hopped off and pulled off the saddle and bridle. Rubbing his hands up the horse's neck, he leaned in and was softly speaking into the horse's ear.

"You're fancy, I get it. We'll work on it. It's all right to get scared once in a while. I've got you though. A'right?" On and on he mumbled little comments to the horse until Matt reappeared.

Alex noticed that Winn only spoke directly to the horses when he thought he was alone. When others were near, he murmured and made little soft noises. She let a twinge of guilt creep into her chest, feeling voyeuristic seeing Winn in his element this way. He was an easygoing brother, a compassionate and patient animal lover. She knew it wasn't the part of himself that he would ever willingly show her. What confused her was why? What was it about her that made him hide this man under gruff and open hostility? He must be able to tell that she couldn't be trusted with something as pure as his relationship with Matt or the horses. She felt sick knowing how right he probably was.

Matt handed a halter and lunge line to Winn. "I'll go grab the hose."

Winn nodded, pulling the halter over the horse's head and attaching the clasp of the long line. With a small step to the side and an almost imperceptible twist in his upper body, he sent the horse away from him and started it walking a circle. Matt opened up the gate, left it swinging open as he worked to bring the hose through.

Alex heard the tractor coming before she saw it, and the next series of events happened so quickly she was unable to get out a word of warning. As Matt wrestled with the heavy hose, he caught himself by the feet and stumbled to his knees as the large piece of farm equipment made its way around the side of the barn. The horse immediately began to panic, thrashing against the line in Winn's hands. Matt looked up from the ground, fear in his eyes, his body blocking the only exit for the frightened horse.

"Get up, Mattie!" Winn yelled.

Winn fought against the frightened horse as it took off at a run toward the open gate, the line zipped through his hands before he was able to stop it.

"Get up!" Winn yelled again.

Alex took off down the ladder and came busting out of the barn door in time to see Winn leaning against the tension he held on the rope as the horse reared against the pressure. It was desperately trying to get farther away from the machinery, its hooves pounding frantically only feet from where Matt sat on the ground tangled in the hose.

She was at Matt's side in seconds, pulling the loops of the hose from his feet and helping him to stand. She freed him and rushed to the gate to shut it. By this time, Trix, who had been driving the tractor, turned off the engine and was running toward the yelling.

"Shit, shit. What happened?" Trix called out.

Winn was able to let out enough slack on the line to let the horse run to the fence line where it seemed content to anxiously circle the round pen, snorting, and cutting short the side of the circle nearest the now silent machine.

Winn shot a glance over his shoulder. "Trix, check on Matt."

As Trix made his way over, Alex watched Winn. He visibly checked his breathing and watched the horse as it continued to move around him anxiously. He was softly mumbling, "Whoa…easy…it's okay now," and slowly taking in slack to decrease the circle, moving the horse incrementally closer to him.

It was then Alex noticed Winn's shaking hands. At first, she chalked it up to nerves, and the high-adrenaline moment, but on closer inspection, it was clear that it was more than that.

As the horse finally came to stand at rest in front of him, Winn immediately dropped the rope and brought a trembling hand to the horse's neck.

Alex looked to Matt. "You okay?" she asked. He nodded, and she looked up at Trix. "Could you go get that horse, please?" she requested.

At the unsolicited instruction, Trix looked at her and then at Winn. Seeming confused, but happy to oblige, Trix stood and went over to the horse. Alex followed Trix into the pen and when Winn handed off the horse, he looked down at his own trembling hands, yanked off the shredded gloves and grimaced.

Alex ignored the warning look he shot her. She walked up to him and gave him an expectant look, when he lightly balled up his hands, refusing to show them to her, she turned her back to him.

"Come with me," she ordered.

Surprising them both, he followed. She walked toward the garage where some first aid supplies were located. Once inside, she turned to him again.

"Let me see." There was no question in her tone, and he responded, raising both hands, palm up, between them. "Jesus, Winn." She couldn't help but gasp.

Both hands were still trembling, and she was surprised by the damage to them. They were bright red, with lines of rope-burn blisters already forming from fingertip to the base of his palms.

Winn pulled in a deep breath and exhaled slowly. "Yeah, not good."

Alex cocked an eyebrow at him. "They still burning?"

He nodded.

"We've got to get ice on that," she told him.

Alex turned to the deep freeze to pull out two ice packs and went to the cabinet to find some gauze. She wrapped his hands with a thin layer of gauze and got a pack of ice on both hands. As she worked, she could feel his eyes on her.

※※※

Winn watched Alex's small hands as they gingerly worked around his own. The look of concentration on her face was…compassion? While she worked, Alex pulled a corner of her lower lip into her mouth to run her teeth over. His gut dropped.

I need to get out more.

"Any better?" she asked.

Her huge blue-eyed gaze traveled from his arm to his face, and his gut clenched again. He cleared his throat. "They'll be okay," he lied as the throbbing was working its way to his elbow.

"Once the burning stops, you'll need them cleaned and bandaged for real," Alex told him.

Winn nodded. "Mae will take care of it."

She watched him.

He squirmed under her scrutiny. "Um, thank you…for keeping Matt safe."

She narrowed her eyes, he assumed in an attempt to read him for signs of sarcasm. Trix and Matt burst into the barn, cutting off any response she was working up to.

"Crap, Kid, you okay?" Trix rushed over.

Matt was behind Trix, and his questioning eyes found Alex. Winn was annoyed that Matt's trusting nature was already wrapped around this girl's finger. Matt had more faith in her and her motives than she deserved.

Alex smiled at Matt, maybe in an attempt to reassure him. "Pretty bad rope burn, but he's all right," she said.

Winn shot her a look. "He speaks for himself too," he ground out, getting his back up again.

Alex rolled her eyes. "And speaking about yourself in the third person is obnoxious."

Matt put both hands up, opening his mouth to try to keep the peace, but Alex spun on her heels and headed for the door.

"No woman, no cry," she hollered over her shoulder and Trix snorted back a laugh before the door slammed behind her.

***

Over the next few days, Alex was curious about how Winn would spend his time while his hands were bandaged up. She knew he couldn't help with most of the labor around the ranch and she was pretty confident he wouldn't be able to ride. She wasn't surprised to find that in the mornings he spent more of his time out at the little barn with Tommy. He was making slow progress, and she felt a little childish for being pleased that she and Tommy got along better.

In the afternoon she'd caught a glimpse of Winn in the kitchen with Mae, who had put him to work at the island gingerly husking a comically large pile of corn.

"Bit of a rough week for you, Winn," Mae said, no doubt referencing his still healing face and his bandaged hands.

"I've had better," he said casually.

"You doing all right?" Mae pressed.

He looked up, perhaps hearing in her tone that she meant more than his injuries.

"I'm doing fine," he said with a cautious tone.

"Liar," Mae stated simply.

This was followed by a long but strangely comfortable pause. After a long time, Winn looked up to meet Mae's gaze.

"Feels different around here, Moms." He looked back down at the table and quietly added, "Like change is coming, and I've got no say, no option but to hang on for the ride."

"Oh kiddo, things are always changing. It's not now, it's always. For you, maybe different wouldn't be so bad."

Winn responded with an agreeable murmur.

"You've always got a say, Winn. Letting yourself feel helpless is going to make it upsetting."

"A say in what, Moms?" he said with a little heat. "A say in the cattle prices going down while the cost of diesel doubles? A say in losing training clients left and right? A say in hosting visitors like we're a damn Girl Scout camp?"

Mae made a tsking noise, but Winn talked over her. "I'm serious, Mae. Things are already teetering at the brink and *she's* not here for two weeks before things go even further down the shitter. Hell, Matt'd rather spend all day tucking her under his wing than doing his damn job. The guys are distracted and seem to think teaching the princess how to drive a tractor is good use of their time."

Alex had to bite her tongue to keep from giving away her spying position.

How dare he speak about me this way? He doesn't even know me, that arrogant, rude, judgmental asshole.

"I suppose it's Alex's fault you got your bell rung breaking that warm-blood? And she must be pretty talented to orchestrate that accident with the paint horse," Mae said. Alex felt slightly vindicated that someone was defending her when she couldn't defend herself.

"Of course I'm not saying that, but this string of bad luck is one more drop in the bucket already filled to the brim. I don't have time for any of this. I can't afford to be taking time off training. Maybe if everyone wasn't so intent on babysitting, I'd have a little more help."

"Oh you'll be back on by tomorrow, and if you'd asked, any of the guys would've helped you. But you're incapable of saying the words, Winn. Maybe you're the one that's distracted by Alex because she makes an easy scapegoat?"

"Ridiculous. I'm the only one willing to carry on business as usual," Winn huffed.

"You're the only one with this strong of a reaction to her."

"I've got enough sense to be pissed."

"Well I think you're being a petulant child," Mae firmly said.

"Nice, Moms. Thanks for the pep talk. Really appreciate you checking in on me and taking the time to point out my character flaws."

"It wouldn't be very loving for me to kiss your ass."

"Sure." He stood, dropping an ear of corn to the table. "I'll finish these in a bit. I need some air."

Mae let out a long sigh but didn't argue as he took off from the kitchen and went out the back door, letting it slam behind him. Alex could barely see past her anger about Winn's hateful words enough to wonder which one of them was correct about the state of the ranch.

Mae seems calm and it's her ranch, and she would know better, wouldn't she? This is probably Winn being overly dramatic and self-pitying, Alex told herself, but a sense of nagging worry didn't quite go away. She remained on the steps for a few minutes, to ensure she'd left enough of a buffer between her and wherever Winn was storming off to.

By the time the late afternoon rolled around, Alex was working with Matt in the equipment barn, talking to her about the machinery he was tinkering with. She listened as Matt went on explaining and remembered Winn's comment about Matt being more interested in babysitting her than doing his job. She inwardly huffed.

Well here he is doing his job and I'm not hindering him at all.

"The whole point to this is that it takes the cut hay and forms it into bales," Matt was explaining while he leaned into the equipment. "But it won't work if this part right here won't create enough force to lift.

"Can you hand me a five-eighths socket?" he asked. "Then come hold this. This is the part that rotates like so."

Alex watched as he spun a gear to show her its movement and then she turned to the rolling tool cabinet trying to pick out what he was asking for. At that moment Winn came plowing through the door. The panic emanated from him in waves as his still bandaged hand frantically pointed toward the foaling barn.

"It's Rosie," he stammered. "She's in labor, but it's bad. Mattie, I need you."

Matt dropped everything in his hands and headed to the door. His head gave a slight incline in response to Alex's questioning look.

She followed them out the door, rushing to keep up with their frantic footsteps.

"What's going on?" Matt asked Winn as they jogged across the lawn.

"Water broke forty-five minutes ago, but the foal won't come. I don't know…it's…she's dying, Mattie, I think she's dying…" Winn's rambling faded into nothing, his eyes briefly passed over her, unseeing in his distress.

"Doc Meyers?" Matt asked.

"Can't—he's hours away on a call up north. He can't get anyone to us. She's bad, Mattie. She won't make it until he gets here." The fear and utter grief in Winn's voice was palpable. Alex followed into the foaling barn and walked into the most gut-wrenching hours of her life.

Chapter 11

Alex pulled herself back to reality. She looked around at Matt and Winn. Their vacant, exhausted, grief-stricken faces reflected what she felt. She'd no concept of what time it could be or how long they had been at the barn trying to save the life of the little mare. After an eternity, the vet had arrived and the foal had finally been delivered, but the tired little mother had continued to bleed and eventually had taken her last breath. They all had slumped to the floor, the weight of what had happened weakening them further.

The cold wall against Alex's back supported her exhausted body, and through swollen, sore eyes, she looked up and registered that it was already dark outside.

When did the vet leave? How long has it been?

Before, when she'd been incapable of stopping her tears, Matt had tried to console her but she inexplicably felt like she couldn't allow him to. As she met his eyes now, he shook his head and finally spoke. "It's a sad day." He turned his gaze to his brother. "Winn, I'm sorry we couldn't do more for her."

Alex too turned to take in Winn's face. It was ashen, and his teeth were clenched making his skin seem tight against the sharp line of his jaw. His eyes slowly stirred and began to focus. He looked at her and her heart ached a little more with the sadness she saw, before he seemed to catch himself and brought his eyes to Matt's.

"Me too. She was a good mare and would have been a great mother." His voice caught there—almost imperceptibly, he covered it so well. "I should go check on the foal." Back to business. Winn began to stand, and Matt put his hand out.

"Winn, Sam's got him, he's working with the surrogate now. It's taken care of, leave it alone."

Winn opened his mouth perhaps to argue more, but no words came out.

"Let's go back to the house," Matt coaxed, looking at Alex next. She stood and refused his outstretched helping hand more out of habit than a conscious decision.

"You go on, I'll be up in a bit," Winn said softly. Then he turned to Alex and looked like he was about to say something else before changing his mind. With a slight nod he simply stated, "Alexandra."

"Winn," was her quiet answer.

He turned from them, and headed down the far side of the aisle, out of the barn and into the darkness.

"It's a sad day," Matt repeated, watching his brother's back disappear out of sight.

Matt and Alex walked the hundred yards back to the main house in sullen silence. Mae greeted them at the front door and read their mood instantly. She dropped her eyes and in a small sad voice said, "Oh no."

"There was nothing more we could do," Matt stated again. "We tried our best, but she's at peace now."

"Winn?" was Mae's next question.

"Walking." The one-word answer seemed to convey more to Mae than Alex heard.

"The poor kid can't even tell when he could use a good hug anymore." She turned her sights on Alex. "Oh, honey, how are you holding up? Can I fix you something to eat? You've all been down there since four."

"What time is it?" Alex asked, more to avoid the food question, than to put a time reference on her evening.

"It's past nine," Mae stated with obvious concern in her voice.

"No thank you, I'd rather go to bed. I'm so tired, I can't think." It was a lie, she could think, but didn't want to. Alex needed to be away from them, away from their sadness and away from them noticing her own.

"Night," Matt and Mae said in unison, sharing a look before they walked toward the kitchen.

"Night," Alex responded as she walked up the stairs to her room.

Alex crumpled onto the bed without even kicking off her shoes, sawdust falling from her jeans onto the bed spread. Turning over, Alex curled into a ball on her side. She wanted more than anything to fall asleep but knew it wouldn't happen. Images from the evening passed through her mind, and she relived it through the tension in her body. There was a strain in her chest from when the horse's labored breathing had caused Alex to hold her own.

And Winn's face. She couldn't stop seeing it over and over again, his worry and fear so tangible that even now it reached out and grabbed her. She slammed her eyes shut, trying to block out how closely his pain was now her own.

Alex tortured herself for nearly half an hour, but sleep would not come. She made a quick and easy decision.

"I need a drink," she said out loud as she jumped off the bed. Holden perked his head up and watched her go, opting for staying in bed.

Sneaking down the hallway, Alex stopped at the top of the stairs to listen for movement. Silence surrounded her as she slinked down the stairs and into the kitchen. The light above the stove cast elongated shadows atop the counter and floor. She stopped at the fridge and snagged the wine Mae had opened at dinner the other night. Once out of the house and onto the large lawn, Alex let herself deeply exhale. It felt so good, she wondered if she'd done it all night.

The plan was flawed, however. A chilly nighttime wind was picking up, and once she'd gotten out of the house, she hadn't thought about where she would go to go to stay warm. Looking at the foaling barn, she shuddered and knew she wouldn't be able to return there for a while, let alone tonight. Her eyes traced the blackened horizon and landed on the main stable. It seemed as good a place as any to revert to her roots and drown her sorrows.

Alex jogged to the side of the stable with the wind at her back. She whipped open the door and her hair blew up from behind her, the cold following her in.

Her breath caught in her throat. She was not alone.

Winn was sitting on a wooden trunk in the entryway to the aisle. His apparent surprise to see her was short-lived and for a second she almost thought he looked relieved.

"Oh, I—err...I'm sorry. I didn't think anyone would be in here," Alex stuttered, trying to regain composure and her breath.

Winn's eyes stayed with hers longer than she was comfortable with and then slowly made their way down to the bottle in her hand. She thought she saw the corner of his mouth pull up the slightest bit. He didn't speak.

"I can go. Looks like you want to be alone." Alex reached a hand for the door.

"Did you come in here to be alone?" he asked quietly, stilling her movement.

"Yes."

"Then you can come and be alone…over there." Winn motioned to some hay bales on the other side of the room.

Confusion furrowed Alex's brow, but her feet followed his direction and she made her way over to sit across from him. Winn made a small motion with his hand toward her confiscated wine bottle, and this time she knew she saw him smirk.

"Interesting," was all he said.

Out of habit Alex bristled. "I needed a drink."

"It was a good idea," he quickly responded, "But I'm way ahead of you." He produced a half-empty bottle of Jack Daniel's from the far side of the trunk. "At least I was civilized enough to find a glass." He pulled a clear Solo cup from his hiding spot, tossing back the last little bit of golden liquid still in the bottom while his eyes laughed at her a little.

She quickly returned his little condescending smirk, and without breaking his piercing eye contact, she threw back a huge swallow directly from the bottle. He tossed up a lone eyebrow and the half-broken smile retuned. A moment passed and then to her surprise, he laughed. Not loud or hard, but it was a laugh.

"All right, forget civilized," he said and drew a long swig from his bottle. She was unsure of what to do next.

"Are you drunk?" she asked.

He laughed again, this time shorter, terser. "No, that was my plan though, and then I got interrupted."

She narrowed her gaze and eyed the half-empty bottle. He followed her stare. "This was like this when I went to get it. In typical *you* fashion, you barged in and ruined my first drink. I thought you were Matt, so I stashed it."

In response to her raised brow he added, "I don't have to explain myself to you, Alexandra."

The last bit made him sound childish and he grimaced as if he heard the immaturity of it too.

"Then don't, Winn, you're an adult. Let's drink." Alex challenged him now, taking another gulp of her wine.

"Alone," he added, with a nod, accepting her unspoken contest.

"Alone," she agreed, leaning her back against the wall, trying to mirror his relaxed posture.

Alex noticed that the bandages he'd discarded during the birth had not been replaced. His palms were still a little pink but would soon be fully healed. Relief rose unbidden in her chest. Maybe some of his sense of normalcy would return when he was fully back to work. She tried to conjure anger about his earlier mean-spirited words when talking with Mae, but after the evening they shared, she knew she was incapable.

A moment of silence stretched into five and then fifteen. They both took turns drinking from their respective bottles, never quite making eye contact again. Even though the plan had been to forget the day, Alex was discouraged by how quickly the wine bounced off her empty stomach and went to her head. Winn seemed rock solid, of course.

Alex allowed herself to look at him, remembering how panicked he'd looked when he came running for Matt this afternoon, and then seeing the inconsolable defeat in his eyes when they had lost the fight for the mare's life. Again, confusion came when she thought about how much it had hurt her to see him like that. Winn was the asshole, the granite and uncompromising asshole. It was strange how challenging it was to see him desperate and unnerved. Alex finally looked away, searching her now fuzzy mind for something to say to him.

**

Winn watched Alex. She looked tired. He wanted to be angry with her for being there, but as he had earlier in the day, he found a confounding comfort in her presence. He couldn't reconcile his regular knee-jerk frustration with her with how he was feeling at the moment.

Earlier when Alex had come blasting through that door his heart had jumped. He wanted to blame it on being startled, but deep down knew that her wild windblown red hair and the flush in her face had had something to do with it. Admitting the effect she had on him was dangerous ground that shouldn't be attempted given the current circumstances. He felt like he owed her something though.

"Thank you for your help today," he said.

As he spoke, Alex jolted a little, maybe because he broke their silence, maybe because grateful words weren't what she was expecting. She met his gaze, no doubt searching for some sign of sarcasm. He held her stare, hoping she could see he was speaking genuinely.

"Winn, I'm sorry about the mare." She too was being sincere. He could sense it.

"Rosie," he softly corrected, almost whispering her name.

"Yes, Rosie," she repeated. "Are you going to be okay?"

"I'll be okay," he lied.

A few more minutes of "alone" time passed.

"Why would you hide your booze from Matt?" she finally asked.

"Cause it's not my booze." He let a small grin escape, and she giggled a little. He wondered if the wine wasn't playing a factor in her apparent thawing toward him.

"Oh, I thought it would be some disapproving older brother thing," she said.

"Nah, it's his whiskey. Well that, and I don't think he would approve of drinking alone, especially after a day like today. It's not a good precedent to set."

"Ah, I see. Well, you'll have to tell him it won't become a habit."

He flashed his half-committed smile but could feel it didn't reach his eyes. He raised his bottle and said, "To drinking alone."

She raised hers. "To drinking alone," she repeated, and they both ceremoniously drank. Their lightheartedness died out as quickly as it had started.

As he watched her he could tell there was something brewing close to the surface. He decided to cut her off and go straight at it.

"Listen, about the other day. I, uh, I'm sorry if I scared you," Winn said to his feet before looking up at her again.

Her eyes bounced to his quickly, looking stunned by his admission, but Winn was confident she knew he was referencing their fight about the abused gelding. He remembered that day and the staggering shock he felt when he found her in the paddock at the little barn in the woods.

Winn forced himself to hold her gaze now and watched her face as she appeared to struggle with what to say next. Strangely he was able to quickly identify her dilemma. To accept his apology, Alex would have to admit that she was scared, something that he imagined wouldn't come easy to her.

"I wasn't…scared." She took a deep breath. "I was out of line to insinuate what I did."

Interesting, Winn thought. He took a moment to consider his next move, and against every bit of self-preservation, he spoke his mind. "You're frustrating, Princess, Matt would say 'stubborn as the damn day is long.'"

"What?"

"You would rather turn my apology into yours so that you don't have to admit you were afraid."

Alex opened her mouth for some quick retort and then slammed it shut again. Perhaps insight was the last thing that she'd anticipated.

"You think I don't mean it when I say I'm sorry?" she finally challenged.

"I don't think that you're sorry for one second about butting in on my work with that gelding."

Alex visibly shifted, straightening her spine. "I don't know much, but I do know I didn't do any damage to your work with that poor horse. But I am sorry that I made you think that I thought what it looked like I thought."

After getting out the convoluted sentence, he watched as she glared accusatorily at the wine bottle before setting it down on the ground.

"What's that now?" His smile and tone were triumphant.

Winn felt a change in her when she relaxed her posture and looked over his shoulder, causing him to regret the over the top "I win" grin.

"Look, again." He let out a slow breath, holding her eye contact. "I'm trying to say *I'm sorry*. Okay? I felt out of line and even though I didn't mean to scare you, I know I did."

She opened her mouth to counter, and he spoke over her. "I know I did, I could see it in your face. You were scared of me…and it wrenched my gut." Now it was his turn to feel off balance.

Did I really say all of that out loud? To her?

Next time, he vowed, drinking alone really needed to be drinking alone. He looked down at the bottle of Jack that he'd put a serious dent in and decided to set it down before he dug himself into a bigger hole.

***

Alex was at a loss, startled by how vulnerable Winn had made her feel with one sentence and one intense but honest stare.

He did scare you that day, and he's trying here. Don't you owe him something back? Ugh, the wine, what a good idea gone so terribly wrong.

She lowered her eyes to the floor and in a quiet voice that she barely recognized she mumbled, "Fine. You did scare me."

After a moment she looked up and registered how upset her admission made him. His eyes were intense now, stormy, but different than the fire she'd seen in them the day he smashed the glass.

"I want to explain something to you," Alex paused, and he nodded. "I wasn't scared of you because I think you're capable of that. It all happened so fast, I was startled, that's all. I don't think that you're a bad person. I've never seen you cruelly lay your hands on anyone or any living thing for that matter. I watch you with the horses, and you're so patient, and..." She was rambling and caught herself. Did she admit that she watched him? She pressed on. "I'm sorry if I made you feel bad...I don't think you're some 'crazed animal that rules by brute force.'"

He swallowed hard. Her words seemed to have calmed him some. "No, I'm sorry, it was stupid of me. I was so angry, and it was a tantrum. After I realized what you thought, I couldn't believe it. I should have known better, though. I could have been more considerate."

Alex looked up at him, confused.

"When you first got here, the makeup job was good, but it wasn't that good." He made a quick gesture toward his eye that still had a hint of a bruise.

Instantly, Alex flooded with embarrassment. Her mind flew back to the day she'd locked herself in Sean's bathroom. She remembered the yellowing tint under her eye when she arrived at the ranch.

How can I explain that to Winn now? I wasn't some battered woman. I had been the bully. There's no way he'd understand.

"No, that wasn't..." she struggled for the words.

While she grasped for anything to say, Winn rose, took two large steps, and was kneeling in front of her.

"That bruise"—she continued trying not to react to the sudden closeness of him—"that was my fault..."

Alex mindlessly brought her hand up to touch her cheek, remembering the feeling of the swollen skin. Looking past him now, afraid to meet his gaze, knowing what he would think of her if she told him the truth about that night with Sean.

Winn brought his hand to her face and replaced her fingers with his own. He traced across her cheek from the bridge of her nose, under her eye and then down her jawline. With the lightest touch he turned her chin, forcing her eyes to meet up with his own.

"You don't have to talk about it if you don't want. But know this, whatever you think you did, no one should get to put their hands on you."

He was so close to her now, she couldn't look away from his stare. It made her feel disoriented, confused.

"No, really. It's not like I wouldn't iron his shirt or spoke out of turn. It was mutual. I mean he..." Alex trailed off when his face hardened at her words. She realized she'd confirmed that a man had done that to her.

He was so near. She was off-balance.

How did we get to this point? This time yesterday we were fuming at each other. Winn despises me, he has made that very clear. Why is he doing this?

Alex had to blame his behavior on the whiskey, but then what was her excuse? Her mind was clear, the fog from the wine had lifted as soon as he touched her. Her pulse pounded in her ears. She was ridiculous, the disdain he felt for her hadn't gone away. The day's events subdued it. He was treating her like one of his skittish horses.

That's not who I am, she thought vehemently.

"Why are you doing this?" Her words were sharp as her eyes jumped back to his and narrowed.

"What? Doing what?" he asked, dropping his hand, defensiveness creeping into his tone.

"Why are you looking at me this way, sitting there, now, like this? Why are you doing this?"

"I wanted…I was…I don't want us to fight, not after a day like today," he stammered, obviously struggling to keep up with her flash of indignation.

"You want a truce?" she said, louder than she'd intended.

He rocked back on his heels, quickly getting to his feet, standing in front of her.

"You want a truce because you scared the little girl and now you feel bad?" She was close to yelling now and gaining steam.

She stood, trying to get as close to eye to eye as she could with him. His closeness had confused her, and she was embarrassed by her reaction to him. She pushed back against it by mustering anger.

"What?" He seemed genuinely shocked at her accusation. "You think I'm doing this because I feel sorry for you?" Winn's voice raised to match her tone.

"Guilt is a tricky thing, Winn. I wouldn't want you making any rash decisions while you were drunk on Jack and regret."

Winn opened his mouth most likely to yell at her but then quickly shut it. He stepped towards her and grabbed her roughly by the tops of her arms, pulling her up to meet him. He kissed her, hard and impatient. Shocked for only the briefest of seconds, Alex met his mouth. She kissed him back with all of the anger and frustration that had been building in her for weeks. Nothing remained of their gentle moment from minutes before. The kiss was passionate and crushing, pulling the air out of her lungs, the harsh taste of the Jack on his lips, the heat and strength of his body. She couldn't tell if she was fighting or surrendering.

She needed to gain some power, some control. She freed her arms and brought her hands to the back of his neck, filling her fists with his hair. In response, he banded his arms around her waist, jerking her up and in, holding her tightly against his chest.

Winn pushed the kiss further, deeper. Alex felt the vibration as he moaned slightly against her lips. Suddenly he pulled his mouth from hers, dropping her quickly.

As soon as her feet had found the floor, she glared up at him, panting breath rushing past her lips. For a long moment, they both stood there, staring at each other, both seeming astonished by what had happened.

Winn appeared to gather himself first. "How's that for rash?" he spat out at her and turned to go.

It took Alex a second to regain her composure, but his words required an answer. He was at the door when she yelled after him.

"You've lost your damn mind, Winn. You...you...drunken fool."

Alex didn't know what she was accusing him of. *Was he crazy for kissing her or for stopping?*

He spun on his heels, leaving a hand on the doorknob. His eyes looked like pokers pulled from the fire as his stare bore into her. "Don't worry, Princess, it won't happen again," he hissed.

"You bet your ass it won't," she answered with every false bit of ego she could conjure up. She only hoped it sounded believable. It must have, because he slammed the door hard enough to knock two bridles off of their hooks. She kicked at them angrily and fell back to the hay bale. Despite her bravado, she was going to need a minute to actually stand and walk, and a lot more time than that to wrap her head around what had happened.

***

Cold air hit Winn as he stalked up the lawn toward the house.

What in the hell was that?

His breathing had started to return to normal, but the vibration in his hands seemed to creep up his arms.

You're shaking? Really?

Against his own will, his brain, always a glutton for punishment, began replaying what had happened.

When had it all gone sideways?

It'd been when Alex had confirmed his suspicion that a man had given her that black eye. Winn had been unable to combat his screaming instincts to protect her from whatever demons she was conjuring.

When she began to withdraw from him as he sat in front of her, he'd panicked. He couldn't say why but he didn't want to lose the moment of being so close that he could smell her shampoo and the light aroma of wine on her breath, feel the warmth and softness of her skin under his fingers. Then Alex had called him on the hypocrisy of him showing her any sort of compassion. After all, Winn had been aggressively objecting to her presence since she arrived.

When Alex drew attention to the absurdity of his actions, he'd tried to keep a lid on his temper, fueled by his confused, embarrassed and demolished ego.

And then you kissed her.

God, she'd been so fierce, so firm but so soft at the same time. The kiss had made his head spin. He'd lost himself in it, in her, only coming to his senses when he'd heard his low satisfied murmur escape his lips. When he'd finally released her, she glared up at him, accusing him with vividly liquid and storming eyes. Her lips were pink and swollen from his, and she was panting. He then became aware of his crazed breathing and the sound of blood rushing past his ears. He had to fist his hands at his sides to keep himself from reaching out to yank her back to him.

She's right, I am a drunken fool.

But he searched himself for any signs of intoxication—nothing. He felt clear and sober. He had nothing to blame except his own cracked brain. She was right about one thing, though: he was insane.

Chapter 12

Three days had passed since Winn had inexplicably kissed Alex. It was obvious that they had both decided the best way to handle it was never to speak or make eye contact ever again.

Fortunately, the other guys were not following Winn's lead. They were happy to show her more projects around the ranch, and Matt's horse 101 sessions continued without missing a beat. During her evenings of downtime, she'd knocked the dust off of her pool-playing skills and also developed a slightly unhealthy addiction to the war game they all played on the X-Box.

It was time for the weekend and the guys had invited Alex to go out with them, a turn of events that made her unapologetically giddy. It sounded like they often went to town on Fridays and she'd finally earned enough respect to receive an invitation. All of the younger guys were going—Junior, Trix, Bishop, Harley, Tiny, Matt, and unfortunately Winn. It was a bit of a downer that he was going, but not problematic, given that they had already proven they could co-exist without so much as a glance. Alex knew that he must have been outvoted about her being included in boys' night out, and it made her proud of her new friends that they must have stuck up for her. She imagined there was a whirlwind of a tantrum when Winn had found out she was going.

Alex didn't want to be foolish and ask what to wear. She assumed jeans would be fine, given the fact that she hadn't seen anything but jeans since she arrived. A little button-up white blouse completed her simple outfit. Her hair was left loose and wild. It was where it always wanted to be, so she figured why fight? The look was finished with a light touch of powder and, because she was so thrilled to be leaving the property, she even dusted a tint of color over her eye and added some mascara and a touch of lip gloss.

The sound of the guys gathering at the base of the stairs floated up to the second floor. They had said seven, and of course, as she'd learned, ranchers are prompt as hell. Alex skipped a little but got a hold of herself before she rounded the corner. As she came down they all looked her over, each of them the perfect gentleman, only taking a fleeting second to notice how different she looked cleaned up.

Mattie was the only one that felt the need to speak. "Alex, you look great." Pure unabashed enthusiasm, that was what she loved about him.

"Thanks." She smiled a little shyly.

"We got you something," Matt confessed, seeming like he could hardly hold in his excitement.

"You what?" She was embarrassed but intrigued.

"Well, we think you're turning into one hell of a ranch hand." As he said it they all laughed, Alex included. "Okay, well we all think you're *trying* to be one hell of a ranch hand. So, we thought you needed one of these." Matt pulled a little straw cowboy hat out from behind his back. He was beaming, and so were the others.

"I love it," Alex gushed and meant it.

Matt walked over and plopped it on her head, her untamed red waves spilling out from all sides. She reached up and ran her fingers along the edge of the hat lovingly. "I can't tell you what this means to me, you guys. Thank you so much."

"You look good, Red," Bishop chimed in.

"Damn, Red," said Junior.

"Thank you guys, seriously. Do I look like a cowgirl?" she laughed.

"No," they all replied in unison before laughing again.

From in the back of the pack she heard an annoyed sigh. It wasn't hard to guess who it came from. Alex only let her smile fade a bit.

"Can we get out of here?" Winn said to no one.

"Yeah, let's go," Matt said, some of the wind obviously taken out of his sails.

Mac stuck her head out of the kitchen, "You take it easy on these poor boys now, Alex." Her eyes were laughing, obviously approving of the night out.

"No promises," Alex yelled back as they filed out of the house.

"Ride with us, Red," Trix called, knowingly saving everyone from the awkward conversation to keep Winn and Alex out of the same truck.

Alex hopped into the back of Trix's truck with Bishop while Junior hopped into the front seat. Harley, Tiny, and Winn piled into Matt's truck and they were off. That simply, she was free, bound and determined not to let Winn ruin her night.

***

In the other truck Winn was fuming silently, convinced the night was going to be a disaster. He tried to push the image of Alex coming down the stairs out of his mind. The way her jeans hugged her figure just right, that wild mane of red, barely tamed by her new silly hat. Her eyes were pools of electric blue when she was excited. He needed to stop noticing her. He felt ridiculous.

Winn was still horrified and embarrassed by their night in the stable. It bothered him how hard he'd needed to work to keep his memory from revisiting every detail. How she'd felt in his arms, the way his body reacted without any rational thought, the way her body had responded to him. And her furious expression and flushed cheeks when he'd finally released her. Tonight was going to be a disaster. He needed to get a grip instantly.

***

The honky-tonk bar was dark, loud, smoky, and packed. Alex loved everything about it. Everyone in the place seemed to know them, and she was whisked around, being introduced to piles of people. Finally, her little herd had made it to the bar, and when the bartender asked for her drink order first, Alex could feel all of their eyes on her.

"Whatever they usually have," she called to him.

The bartender flashed an approving smile and set up eight shot glasses, filled them all with Jack and popped the top off of eight beers.

Harley slapped her on the back. "Good thing you're little, Red. We may have to carry you out of here."

"You think so, Jeffrey?" she challenged, throwing back the whiskey shot and slamming it down on the bar. "You ain't seen nothing yet, cowboy."

Alex knew her limits and had thankfully eaten well before leaving.

Not going to make that mistake again.

She was, however, going to prove to them that she wasn't as frail as they all thought she was. All of the guys grabbed their shots off the bar and followed suit.

"I'm going to play music," Bishop said, tipping his head toward the jukebox.

Alex nodded and watched as Trix and Tiny followed him. She noticed a lone shot left on the bar as Winn snuck up next to her, cupping his hand over the shot.

"Careful, Princess, we know how you get," he murmured into her ear. He raised an eyebrow and threw up his condescending half smile before tossing back his shot.

"I'm in much better company this time, and let's keep in mind, how *I get*…wasn't the problem the other night." She drew her beer to her mouth and took a long sip, never taking her eyes off of his exceptionally gratifying reaction.

"Suit yourself," he said through his teeth and walked away from her.

Matt came up behind her asking, "You okay?"

Alex assumed that Matt had missed the gist of her interaction with Winn but read enough from the body language to be concerned. She wondered how much if anything Winn had told his brother about their night in the barn. Her eyes searched Matt's face for a clue, but if he had any idea he didn't let it show.

"Yeah." Alex perked herself up. "When do I get to learn to two-step?"

Matt eyed her suspiciously for only a beat before looking like he decided to drop it.

"Well, that would be now." He tossed out his arm, she took it and they were off to the floor.

Two-stepping was not an easy thing, but Matt was a patient, good teacher and surprisingly light on his feet. After a few songs, Alex thought she was getting a feel for it, even getting brave enough to let Matt whip her around a few turns. The guys called to them from the bar. Out of breath and laughing, she and Matt made their way back to a fresh new row of beers.

"You're getting good, Red," Bishop piped up. "When do I get my turn?"

"Ah, give it up Bishop, you know your woman will be here any minute," Trix said. "How about my turn, Red?" He gave her a cheesy smile and a bounce of his eyebrows.

"We'll see," she teased, embarrassed from the attention, but comforted by being surrounded by this group. They were all so attentive and polite, all without ever crossing the line. For all of their teasing, she never felt like she was being hit on. It was like having a half dozen adopted brothers. All of her friends eyed the next round of beers and looked to her.

"Slainté," she toasted and raised her beer. Six others came up to meet hers.

Alex looked down the bar and saw Winn leaning over the counter, one foot propped up on the rail on the ground, elbows resting on the edge. His biceps strained slightly as he tipped forward, and his hair, uncharacteristically free from the confines of a hat, was falling boyishly onto his forehead. He was flashing a brilliant smile while talking to one of the female bartenders who was leaned provocatively over the bar toward him. The bartender kept reaching out repeatedly touching Winn's hands when she laughed. God, she was eating it up.

Alex couldn't help the flash of irritation that hit her in her gut. *You don't care,* she ordered herself. She couldn't convince her hands though. Her eyes dropped to the tight wad she'd made out of a bar napkin.

Harley came up behind her. "Can I have this dance?" he asked.

Alex hoped he didn't witness her silly reaction to Winn and the bartender.

"Absolutely." She flashed a relieved smile.

The next hour went by in a similar fashion. Alex was able to dance with all of her buddies and was getting quite good at the two-step, the stationary cha-cha, and some other one that didn't even seem to have a name. She got to meet Bishop and Junior's girlfriends, who were friendly, funny, and so welcoming. Everyone appeared to be having a blast.

Alex had even managed to learn another one of Mae's rules, thanks to Trix's lamenting after meeting a particularly available blonde. Turned out Rule Seven was no one-night stands in the house, which Trix had called the No Man-Whores Rule.

Alex had tried her best to refrain from watching Winn, who had plenty of attention wherever he turned from numerous waiting females. She couldn't stop herself from wondering if he also followed Rule Seven. All night he'd managed to avoid the group almost entirely. Once in a while he sat with some of the other guys, laughing and chatting while Alex was on the dance floor. Winn always seemed to make an exit, though, before she returned for another sip of her beer.

Despite the weird energy from Winn, Alex was feeling at ease and happy. Other guys from the bar were starting to ask her to dance. At first she was cautious, but Matt seemed to approve of them and all of them had been perfectly well behaved. While out on the dance floor with an older gentleman, their song ended, and before Alex could get back to the group, a guy her age appeared asking if he could have the next dance.

The new guy was good looking in a high-school-jock kind of way, but something was off about him. Instinctively, Alex felt wary. He gruffly pulled her up against him before she'd technically even agreed to dance. As the next song started, her new partner pulled her even closer, tighter than the others had. Alex tried to make herself go with it. Causing a scene would not bode well for her attempts to shake off the high-maintenance city girl stereotype.

"I'm Blake," the new guy introduced himself once they had picked up the rhythm of the song.

"Alex," she replied curtly.

"I've been watching you tonight. You came in with the Crooked Crew, right?" Blake breathed on her then, and she caught a nauseatingly strong whiff of alcohol and tobacco.

"I guess you can call them that." Alex attempted to paste on a smile, but she was starting to grow even more uncomfortable. He was holding her much closer now, stifling even. The hand holding hers was vise-like and bordering on painful. She squirmed slightly, and he responded by dropping his hand lower and roughly grabbing her ass.

Alex opened her mouth to protest, but before she could make a sound, Winn was there dryly saying, "I'm cutting in."

A tense moment passed, and Alex could see Blake was sizing up Winn, maybe determining how much to object.

"We're not done dancing, Winn." Blake said with an out-of-place casual air.

"I think you are." There was no question.

Alex's mouth hung open but refused to make words.

Blake took a second and appeared to weigh his options before he released Alex and tipped his hat in her direction. "Thanks for the dance, Alex." He gave Winn a long look. "Winn."

"Blake."

Alex's face was hotly embarrassed. Winn stiffly put his arm around her, took her hand, and firmly pulled her along for the rest of the song. He didn't look at her and Alex didn't look at him. Neither spoke. She was so angry, for a second she'd worried about spilling tears from pure frustration. When the song finally ended, Winn immediately dropped her hand and gave her a hard stare.

"Still think you've got such a great handle on all of this?" His tone was so condescending Alex gave serious thought to giving in and screaming at him. She pinched her mouth shut to keep from embarrassing the hell out of herself.

"Go back to the group, Princess." Winn dismissed her.

"How dare you?" she finally growled. "Who in the hell do you think you are?"

"Oh, I'm sorry, were you planning on letting every guy in here paw you up and down?"

"What?! That's a ridiculous accusation. I was going to handle that." Alex continued to try to calm herself down.

"Yeah, it sure looked like it."

"What is it to you, anyway?" she pressed. That looked like it caught him off guard.

Winn's eyes flared. "It's nothing to me. Blake Martin is not a good person, Alexandra, but next time I'll let you figure that out on your own."

"I will, especially if it keeps your condescending, false sense of chivalry from butting in."

Alex spun on her heels and stalked back to the guys, still so angry she could spit. They saw her coming and handed her a shot, which she tossed back before slamming it back onto the bar while she stood there practically panting.

"Okay, maybe it's time to go," Trix hollered with a questioning eyebrow directed at Alex.

The group started making their way out, but they had to go past Blake, who had perched himself on a stool right by the door. As Alex made it past him, Blake reached out and gave her a hard slap on the ass. "Night, sweetheart."

Both Bishop and Winn spun, reaching for him, but Alex got there first with a hard right-cross, cracking him in the side of the mouth. Pain shot through her hand and up to her elbow, but Blake appeared to be so surprised he stumbled off of his stool.

"Holy shit," Bishop yelled. Junior and Harley busted out laughing, while from the floor Blake looked like he was trying to find his bearings again.

"We need to go," Winn insisted, and with his eyes scanning the room he pulled her roughly by the elbow out the door.

In the parking lot, Alex wrenched her arm free from Winn's clenched fist, the rest of their group following close behind, all of them hooting and hollering, laughing it up.

"That was awesome, Red."

"Hey, little Tyson? Where did that come from?"

"Hope I never make it to your shit list."

Only Matt and Winn were subdued. Her hand really hurt now. Alex shook it, still extremely surprised by what she'd done. Matt walked alongside her and over the yelling of everyone else asked about her hand.

"I think it's okay, it hurts though." She showed it to him and the top of her hand near her pinky finger had already turned red and started to swell.

"We can put some ice on it when we get home," Matt said quietly.

"Matt?"

"Yes?"

"Are you mad at me?"

"No, I'm not mad. Guess you could say I'm in shock."

"I'm sorry if I embarrassed you," Alex said, looking to the ground.

"My guess is, I'm not the one that's going to be embarrassed. Blake's going to have one hell of a fat lip in the morning," he said.

She smiled to herself. She hoped so, but there was a warning in Matt's tone she didn't fully understand.

The entire ride back to the ranch was filled with raucous cheers from her compatriots while they retold the moment she knocked Blake off the stool. She wanted to join in their merriment but was still feeling shaky. One thing did please her immensely: for sure she'd proven her point to Winn.

"Do you think he'll press charges?" she worried aloud to the truck of men. They roared and laughed louder.

"Oh I'm sure. Can you picture it?" Bishop snickered and then mused in a whiny voice, "Officer, I'd like to file a report against a spunky little chick that knocked my ass to the floor."

Trix answered him in a deep fake baritone. "Well son, I'd like to file a report that you should grow a pair."

Everyone laughed.

"So that's a no, I take it?" she said.

"That's a no way in hell, Red," Trix confirmed.

"Good," she sighed.

When they had gotten back to the ranch Matt was quickly at her door to help her from the truck.

"You should get some ice on that hand, Alex," he told her.

"I will, but I don't want to wake the whole house rummaging in the kitchen. I'm gonna run out to the garage and pull some ice from the deep freeze." Honestly, she needed a break from them to gather herself.

"Okay, I'll come with," Matt offered.

"Matt, it's okay. It'll take me five minutes. Go to bed, it's late." She hoped her smile would convince him.

Matt watched her for a long minute and then opted to follow her wishes. Turning, he followed the rest of the guys while they snuck through the door of the house.

Alex went around the side of the house to the garage. When she opened the door, the pitch-black room was ominous. Turning left, she fumbled down the wall for the light switch. She muttered to herself, wondering where the hell it could be.

Instantly the room lit up. Startled, Alex spun back toward the door where Winn was casually leaning on the door frame with his hand on the switch, which of course had been down the other wall.

"What're you doing here?" she hissed.

"Making sure you don't cause any more trouble," Winn said, his eyes taunting her.

"In the garage? Really? I think I can manage getting ice from the garage."

"Obviously," he said, looking down at the light switch and then back at her all the way across the wrong side of the garage.

She puffed out a breath.

Your hand cannot handle meeting the broad side of another man's head today.

Refusing to speak to him, Alex stalked over to the freezer and pulled out an ice pack.

"Let me look at your hand," he pried.

"No."

"Is it broken?"

"No," she said with force, even though she had no idea.

Winn's eyes narrowed as he walked toward her. Reaching into his back pocket, he pulled out a handkerchief, took the ice from her and wrapped it. When Winn handed back the ice, his eyes lingered on her hand for a long second before bringing his gaze back to her.

"You've stirred up some trouble for yourself now, Princess," he said.

Her eyes opened wide in disbelief. "I've stirred up trouble? It's your fault that all happened."

Now it was his turn to look shocked. "Me? You're the one that punched out a guy twice your size. You're the one that spent all night encouraging attention like that. How could any of that be my fault?"

"Encouraging attention!?" Alex had to try to keep the hurt from reaching her voice. Luckily the venom from her anger masked it. "I was dancing and having a good time with *your* friends and *your* brother. You're the one that made the rounds. I don't think a single woman in there missed your company tonight, Winn."

"There is a difference between being friendly and parading around a bar full of men, Alexandra." Despite her instant recoil, he kept after her. "What did you think was going to happen? At some point, you were going to catch the attention of someone like Blake Martin."

Despite her fury, she couldn't hide the hurt his words caused any longer.

He's telling you that you deserved to have that scumbag feel you up that way. How dare he?

"Forget you, Winn. Forget you and your antiquated double standards, you caveman. Who asked you to step in anyhow? From now on I'd appreciate if you kept your holier-than-thou opinions to yourself." Alex's voice rose sharply.

"Next time I'll let him club you over the head and drag you to his truck, you silly little girl." Winn scoffed.

"Get off your soapbox, you dick. Don't wrap me up in your white-knight complex. Not every damsel is in distress."

"You wouldn't know distress if it bit you in the ass, Princess."

"There will never be a time when I need you to swoop in to save the day. So, save us both the trouble and stay out of my damn business."

She whirled on her feet and bolted for the door. He snatched her elbow, bringing her back to face him again.

"And what is your business? Blake Martin? Is he your business?" Winn's eyes were glowing, molten.

She looked into his eyes, returning his icy glare. "Maybe he is," she challenged.

He pulled her to him hard and quick, his mouth on hers in an instant. She surprised herself at how willing her lips were to find his again. She rose up on her toes and pulled him into the kiss by the base of his neck. There was heat and anger in the kiss. They punished one another. His rough hands roamed over her body, pulling her closer to him then running up her back to her hair. Winn reached up, grabbed her hat, and tossed it aside, bringing her face closer to his. The strength of his arms contrasting the softness of his lips on hers was making Alex lose it, lose herself in the kiss, in him.

Alex caught herself going under. "No," she mumbled into his mouth.

He paused, pulling away from her slightly.

"No," she said with more force, letting her anger and hurt work its way back up.

He instantly let go of her, and she pushed off his chest, eyes seething.

"You're not allowed to kiss me whenever you're pissed off and can't use your words," she yelled, still out of breath.

That certainly stopped him in his tracks. "What?" he panted.

"At some point, you're going to have to man up and admit that you want to kiss me. Stop hiding behind the it's-the-only-thing-I-can-do-to-shut-you-up...thing you do."

"I..." He appeared to be at a loss for words, but Alex was on a roll.

"And next time, do it sober, you jackass!" Alex bolted, trying to put as much distance between them as possible. She was halfway to the house before she heard him start stalking up behind her.

"Alexandra, hold up a damn minute," Winn called out to her, and she whirled around to face him.

"What?" she said with as much hostility as she could muster.

"It won't happen again." There was contrition in his tone. "I was riled up with the Blake thing...because...he and I have history, and it was the booze. You're right. It won't happen again. I'm—I'm sorry," he said, hands on hips and eyes turned downward.

"Fine. Good. I'm not here for your amusement, Winn, and I'm not here to be caught up in some childish macho rivalry. You should leave me alone and let me have this summer in peace," Alex stated curtly, desperately trying to mask her sudden and inexplicable desire to cry.

Winn merely nodded so she turned to make her way up the porch.

**

Winn watched as she disappeared through the door of the house, hating the feeling of regret that instantly bloomed in his gut. He'd told her it wouldn't happen again, but he was unsure of how truthful it sounded. It had felt hollow as he said it.

It's not about her. She showed up when you were looking for something to get under your skin.

The night, as he predicted, had become an unmitigated disaster. No matter how hard he'd tried, Winn couldn't keep his eyes off Alex, couldn't keep himself from turning to look when he heard her laugh, couldn't help but keep tabs on her as she flowed across the dance floor.

It's not about her.

When he'd seen Blake's hands roughly grabbing and running over her, Winn's vision had gone red. He'd wanted to kill Blake and shake her for getting that close to him. All he wanted—no, needed—was to ensure that never happened again. If that meant crossing the line with horrible accusations, then so be it. But when he'd said those terrible things to her, Winn saw the hurt in her eyes, and it killed him.

It's NOT about her.

After he'd hurt her feelings, Winn had watched the anger build in Alex's eyes. His gaze had dropped to her mouth and the urgency to erase Blake from her mind became overwhelming. He needed to make her understand even though he didn't comprehend his yearning.

When he'd grabbed her, Alex had met him with all of the strength and passion he knew she would. The kiss, as the one before, had made his head spin and he'd struggled to keep up with her words after she broke away from him. It was almost impossible to slow his mind and breathing down enough after he'd felt her body under his fingers.

Fuck, maybe it is *about her.*

Chapter 13

The next morning Alex caught up to Matt in the barn. Trying to keep her tone nonchalant, she said, "No rest for the wicked, I see. What's on your agenda today, Mattie?"

He watched her from the corner of his eye as he walked through the aisle. "Going to the north field, checkin' fences. Need to make notes on what needs fixing before we put out the herd up there."

"Can I come? I make a pretty good scribe."

Matt watched her in that slow but knowing way that always made her wonder what was going on beneath his surface. He turned, and she followed him as he went into the tool room, when he grabbed a toolbox and two pairs of gloves she knew she was in. Alex rushed around the back of the pickup truck and hopped in the passenger side.

"Thanks, Matt."

He nodded as the engine rumbled and sputtered into a normal rhythm. They drove in silence through the heart of the ranch, and when they stopped at a gate on the north end, Alex hopped out to let them through. They bounced through the field at a pretty good clip, and Alex smiled despite herself as her eyes took in the endless blue sky. After about fifteen minutes, they reached the far corner of the high pasture. Matt handed her an old notebook and got out.

"We'll start on this line and walk the field. Easier to see on foot than from the truck. We're looking for broken anything—posts, wire, staples."

Alex nodded as they started off walking north. "Matt, I wanted to talk to you about something."

"You don't say, Alex."

She rolled her eyes. Of course he was on to her and wasn't going to let her get away thinking she was smooth. But she was here, and she needed information.

"What's the deal with Blake Martin and why do we hate him?" she asked.

Matt let out a long breath of air. "Why is Blake Martin a concern of yours? Other than you punching a drunk guy?"

"Okay, we can start with that. You seem to think punching Blake was a pretty bad idea."

"I think punching anyone is a bad idea."

Alex let out an exasperated sigh. "Of course, Matt, so do I...well, I did. It sounds like it's worse because it's Blake, but I don't understand why."

"Even nice guys don't take kindly to being embarrassed like that, and Blake is not a nice guy."

An uneasy feeling settled over Alex when Matt practically quoted Winn from the night before.

"But what does that mean? You think he'll come after me or something? That seems... ridiculous."

Matt stopped in his tracks and shocked her a little with his cold stare. "Alex, no one is going to let him come after you."

She was startled by his seriousness since she'd been half joking. "But he would try? That's...that seems so dramatic."

"I don't know what he would do. But I gave up on making predictions about Blake Martin's behavior a long time ago." His eyes moved over her shoulder to the fence line. "Mark that there's a split rail and the need for four new staples here."

Alex stammered trying to wrap her head around what Matt was saying. "Uhh, what? Okay one post, four staples, but how'll we know which—"

"Write 'east.'" He pointed in their direction of travel. "Post thirty-one."

She narrowed her eyes and looked back in the direction of the truck but could no longer see it over the crest of the hill.

"You've been counting?" she asked.

"Haven't you?" He turned to keep walking and she squinted at his back before jogging to catch up.

"Matt. Can we please talk more about how I may have stepped in it with some redneck psycho? I feel like maybe you're trying to scare me, but I don't understand why."

"I don't want to scare you, Alex. Blake's a wild card and there's no shortage of bad blood between his family and this one."

"Like what? Why does Winn hate him so much?" There it was. She surprised herself by coming outright and admitting this was what she wanted to know all along.

"Winn's got good reasons to feel strongly about Blake."

Alex sensed that Matt wanted to leave it there, but he turned to meet her unrelenting and expectant gaze and continued. "It's not my story to tell. You'll have to ask Winn." Then Matt picked up his pace.

"Matt, you and I both know Winn isn't going to tell me jack about anything, and now that this concerns me I have a right to know the back story, don't you think?"

Matt sighed as he pulled on some gloves and handed her a pair. He walked up to the fence line and grabbed ahold of the top wire.

"Grab this and pull," he directed. Alex obeyed. He walked to the nearest post and fiddled with the staples that locked the wire in place. He pulled the slack out from her to the post and fidgeted some more.

"East post forty-six, new staples, fifteen feet of wire."

Alex nodded and jotted it down, looking at him expectantly.

Matt sighed again. "You know Winn played baseball," he stated, and she gave him a hard stare.

"No, how would I know that, Matt? We don't chat much." Her mind briefly wandered to the two steamy kisses they'd shared and briefly reflected on how little they knew each other outside of those interactions. Feeling guilty, she was snapped back to reality by Matt's voice.

"So Winn played baseball and was good, I mean really good. Good enough that when he was a senior, Colorado State came out, watched him play and offered him a big scholarship to play ball at their school."

Alex furrowed her brows. "I didn't know Winn went to college."

"Well he didn't. I guess that's where Blake comes in. Winn was a catcher, and like I said, a damn fine one. Close to the end of the season, our guys were up against Racine, Blake's team. Winn and Blake already had a few childhood...tussles, so when Blake came in for a play at the plate and plowed into Winn, no one was surprised. But it was an illegal hit, dirty, unnecessary. The play tore up the Kid's knee real bad. He needed a couple of surgeries to fix it, spent a year rehabbing, and of course the scholarship was off the table."

Matt looked up, watched the sky for a few moments and looked like he was trying to carefully pick his next set of words. He slightly shook his head and simply said, "So the Kid and Blake have a history."

Alex bit the inside of her lip. "That's terrible, I didn't…" She watched Matt carefully. There was tension in his face, and Alex had never seen Matt even approach angry, so the hardness in his eyes was foreign and unnerving to see. "There's more though?" she ventured.

"That's all of someone else's business I'm willing to get into, Alex." There was finality to his words, and she didn't want to push a wedge between her and her friend. She knew asking Matt to betray his brother's confidence was a waste of time, and it actually felt a little mean.

Matt's face softened a bit. "Alex, you don't need to worry. You don't need to concern yourself with Blake Martin at all. You don't need to see him again, and that's for the best."

She let out the air she was holding and nodded. This was a Matt roadblock, and she knew that was as far as she would get today.

"Okay, Mattie. I guess there's a lot more fence to be looked at. How about you teach me what we're looking for?"

They continued into the late morning walking the entire perimeter of the large pasture. Matt showed her how to tell when a post was split or rotted beyond repair, what to look for in the large staples that held the wire. He spoke to her about when they would need to replace a whole stretch of wire and when they could splice wire in and only repair a section. She learned a lot, and when they got back to the house, she offered to tally up the count of what they would need and volunteered to be in charge of picking up all of the supplies. The productivity felt good, but she couldn't shake the feeling that there was more beneath the surface and that whatever it was felt ready for an explosion.

After lunch, Trix walked into the front room where she was sitting gathering her notes on the fence materials. "You got any gas left in the tank, Red?"

"Maybe," she answered carefully.

"Well, time to stack some hay. It's a tough job but it's gotta be done." His eyes were teasing and almost daring her to say yes.

"I'm in," she answered, guessing that sitting out a chore because it was hard wouldn't win her any points with Mae or the guys.

Alex walked with Trix toward the front of the property. Winn was there in the first field, climbing out of a truck attached to a large, empty wagon. He briefly looked up but then looked away as soon as he saw her. Trix motioned for her to follow him as he met up with Winn, Matt, and Bishop at the front of the truck. Even though she kept bringing her gaze back to Winn he never once looked at her.

Trix started explaining, "Okay, Red, here's how this goes. Everyone takes a turn driving the truck, everyone takes a turn on the ground, and everyone takes a turn in the wagon. Basically, you see those bales?" He pointed out at the fields where every twenty or so feet a newly baled square of hay sat. She nodded, and he continued. "We have to pick these up and put them in the wagon. Not a complicated process but we've got maybe five hundred to do today."

"Let's get to it then," she said lightly. "Where do you want me to start?"

He handed her a pair of gloves and said, "You hang with me on the ground, Matt's gonna drive, Winn and Bish will stack in the wagon."

After fifteen minutes, it was brutally apparent that she was terrible at throwing hay. For every bale she managed to get on the back of the wagon, Trix threw up five. She could tell her slowness was throwing off their rhythm and often times Winn or Bishop were standing at the back waiting on a bale she should have already put up.

"Okay, maybe a switch," Trix yelled.

She climbed into the wagon with him as Winn and Bishop hopped down. Again, the entire exchange worked without Winn ever actually looking at her. The machine-like way that these men hoisted the heavy bales was a sight to behold, but after another fifteen minutes of her poor efforts helping Trix stack the bales in the wagon, he made the executive decision that she should drive the truck and they would load the rest. Her arms were screaming and so she stuffed her ego deep down and took him up on his offer.

After two hours they had cleared the two large fields. She hopped out of the truck. Winn got in and wordlessly drove it away toward the back of the property.

"Well, seems like that's probably more than enough productivity for you today, Alex. Why don't you take a break before dinner?" Matt said as he watched the wagon drive away. She nodded and decided she needed to go sit somewhere quiet to relax and forget about her wounded pride.

During her previous wandering on the west side of the property, Alex had come across the little creek she assumed was the ranch's namesake. She found herself drawn to it frequently. When she was deep in the woods, she crossed the little footbridge and followed the creek for a while. As she came around a bend, she was surprised to see Winn sitting in the grass on the opposite bank.

"Hey," she said, knowing it was too late to retreat unnoticed.

"Hey," he replied.

"Mind if I sit? I'm exhausted."

"Go ahead. You want me to leave?" Winn watched her with a look of unease mixed with suspicion.

It seemed they were both unsure of how to proceed after last night and it appeared both were going with stiff courtesy.

"No, I don't think that's necessary. I know we've had some drama, but we're adults, right? I'm looking for a quiet moment. My arms are aching, there's hay dust in my nose and I'm pretty sure I smell terrible."

He nodded. "Throwing hay can be pretty rough."

"Tell me about it. Another instance of new respect for ranch life."

"Yeah." He allowed his surprise at her admission creep into his tone.

They watched each other for a moment before Winn broke the silence. "Hey, I feel pretty bad for…overreacting, last night. We'll figure out how to coexist until you leave. It's not good for anyone when things are so…volatile."

She wondered what part he considered the overreaction. For telling her that the Blake thing was her fault? For yelling at her? For kissing her again? It was tough to pin down what she herself regretted. There was one thing that was clearer now. What she'd said about Blake was maybe out of line. If they were going to survive her time, they needed to be able to interact without going nuclear.

She met his olive branch. "Yeah, things were a little tense. I agree we can be civil until I leave and I'm sorry I called your issue with Blake a childish rivalry. I didn't know."

"Know what?" he asked, a slight hint of alarm in his eyes.

"Matt told me about what Blake did to you when you played baseball."

He let out some air as he looked up at her. "Why did he do that?"

"I asked him."

"You asked him about Blake?" There was a hint of something in his tone, not purely the venom she'd expected but something more.

"I asked him why you hate Blake," she corrected.

"A lot of people hate him, Alexandra. It's not me holding a torch for my glory days." There it was, she thought, that solidly defensive tone.

"I get that, I can't get anyone to tell me why, but I get that." She paused and watched him, continuing, "I wouldn't blame you if hated him for that."

His eyes narrowed, "I appreciate your permission."

"Oh Christ, stop that, I'm not trying to pick a fight here."

He continued to watch her, slowly he said, "All right. Yes. I think Blake is a scumbag, for numerous reasons, one of which is that in a malicious fraction of a second, he ensured that I wouldn't play baseball again. At least not like I needed to."

She watched the grass blade in his finger twirl while she worked out what to say next, but he continued, "That's all in the past, though. I mean it was high school, feels like an eternity ago."

"You would have gone to college, though. That moment impacted your entire career, your entire life." She raised her eyes to find him staring at her again, surprise evident on his face.

"Mattie told you about Colorado?" he half asked, half spoke to himself.

She nodded, waiting for him to get angry or to lash out at her. He kept watching her for a long time. She could see the unease in his eyes. He didn't like talking about this, and she was sure he hated every moment of talking about it with her.

"It didn't change my entire life." He tried to shut the door on the conversation.

"Didn't it?" She put her foot in the jamb despite knowing better. When he decided to answer her she could tell by the slight defeated sag in his shoulder.

"Well, that injury didn't prevent me from going to school. It kept me here. Also kept me off of a horse for nine months. I learned a lot standing on the ground, things I would never have learned if I had kept trying to always train a horse from its back."

She studied his face. He was genuine. She wasn't sure how she could tell, but this wasn't a blow off from him. "You almost sound like it's what was best."

"Being here is what I want."

"So Blake did you a favor?" Instantly his face went cold again, and she regretted the step back.

"No," he said sternly.

"I'm sorry, that was glib. I didn't mean to imply that you getting hurt was a good thing." She bit at her lower lip, struggling to find the right words to dig herself out.

Again, he watched her, unapologetic in his scrutiny of her. He slightly shook his head. "No, what Blake did that day was rob me of choice. In an instant he took away decisions that were mine to make. I know that training is what I'm supposed to do now, that this is right for me, but that doesn't keep my mind from wandering. Thinking about what might have happened if I did go to school, maybe further with baseball, graduated." He looked past her. "Who knows."

"Do you think training is right because it's your only option?"

He frowned, and she could sense him withdrawing again.

"Only option?" He cocked an eyebrow at her. "No, I'm good at this. I belong here."

"Maybe." She wouldn't concede all the way but didn't want things to escalate. "What would you have studied?"

He opened his mouth then seemed to change his mind. After a long pause, he said, "I don't know."

She watched him and didn't believe him but didn't pry.

She tried to change and lighten her tone. "Well, college is overrated. Look at me. I did what I was supposed to do. I have my degree, but I'm not going anywhere with it."

He popped a small smile at her rare moment of self-deprecation. A silence fell between them, not an easy silence, but less uncomfortable than she would have been able to imagine a day ago.

The Blake issue was still sitting badly with her. If Winn was glad to stay, as he said, how could he possibly still harbor so much hatred toward Blake for something in high school? She still needed to know more but was content if not surprised that she'd been able to have a conversation with him that didn't devolve into screaming.

***

Winn watched Alex fidget with several blades of grass, all while chewing on her bottom lip. He could tell her mind was still going a mile a minute, but he wasn't in the mood to discuss any more, especially about Blake. Alex wasn't stupid and she knew that some sports rivalry wasn't the end of the story. The question was, how would she react if she heard more? She'd recently proven to be even more unpredictable than he thought.

He smiled to himself as he replayed her knocking Blake down, like he had a hundred times during the day. That sure shocked the hell out of him, and he felt strangely proud, but he thought about how the last thing he needed was her flying off all halfcocked. He surprised himself by being genuinely concerned with what would happen to her if she did.

Uncomfortable with his own line of thought, he broke into hers. "Dinner'll be soon, we should get up to the house."

She looked at him and seemed resigned to let it go. She stood and absently wiped grass from the back of her jeans.

"Okay," she smiled.

***

Alex mulled over what she'd learned as they walked parallel lines on either side of the creek to the little footbridge. She crossed over and they headed off silently. As they neared the house she watched him walk and said, "You know you don't even limp."

"Yeah, but I've got a few really cool scars." He grinned and headed up the stairs. Bishop was rounding the corner and caught the gist of their conversation.

"We talkin' about Kid's battle scars? I love this story."

Bishop kept on it as they entered the dining room. "I tell it best too, Red. You should've seen our boy. The Kid was a hell of a ballplayer, had a real good head for the game, smart-like, and he could read a pitcher so well it made him a terror when he was at bat too."

The "was" in Bishop's sentences stuck out to Alex like a crooked nail, and she wondered if it did the same for Winn. She watched him, looking for, what? Direction? His face had gone blank and it gave away nothing.

Matt was sitting at the table and raised an eyebrow first at Alex then at Winn when they came in together. Both refused to acknowledge Matt's questioning face and as soon as they hit the door, they split up. Bishop was on a roll by then and the others were getting into it. Undoubtedly, they had all heard or told this story hundreds of times before, but the enthusiasm wasn't diluted.

"So this fated day, hot as all hell, the middle of August," Bishop started, hands out, fingers splayed in a dramatic fashion.

"June," Winn said quietly. Bishop shooed him with his hand.

"Middle of June, and we're playing at home, last game of the state championship playoffs."

"Third game out of five," Winn corrected again. Bishop ignored him.

"Top of the ninth and we're up by one."

"Two." This time it was Matt who interrupted and was also completely ignored.

"Racine is up to bat. Two outs and that bastard Martin is on second. This other guy comes up to bat and drives one into left field."

"Right," said Winn, sounding bored.

"Aw, shut the hell up. Who's telling this story, Kid? So anyway, hard ground ball, almost back to the wall. Martin puts his head down and starts barreling around the bases. Strong throw from our guy out there in right. It's cut off by the first basemen. Quick turn and a throw but it's high. Martin's already rounded third like a freight train. Kid leaps up, trying to snatch this ball out of the air. That beast Martin gets there, lowers his shoulder like the lowlife he is and crashes into The Kid, not even trying to slide. He knows he's too late, that he's gonna be out so he's trying to knock the ball loose with that huge melon of his. The crowd is silent, all you can hear is this beastly growl, helmets cracking, cleats scraping and the whole thing goes up in a huge cloud of dirt."

The whole room was quiet now, enthralled in the story, watching Bishop as he grew more and more animated.

"The dust starts to settle and there's a heap of body parts at the plate. The Kid's helmet is nowhere to be seen. He sits up, slowly spits out a mouthful of blood and dirt, and…what does he do? He holds that damn ball up right in Martin's face. Ump yells, 'You're out...' The crowd goes wild. Game over. Mustangs win. Mustangs win!"

The table erupted in cheers. Bishop was still on a roll and continued with a huge grin across his face. "So, The Kid gets up, detangling himself. Martin's nose is bleeding, and it's made this little pool on the plate. The Kid reaches down, swipes the ball through the blood and tosses it to Martin who's still stunned. What did you say to him Kid? It was freaking genius."

"I don't remember," Winn said, deadpan.

O'Reilly jumped in, "Yeah, yeah…so he tosses the ball to Martin and The Kid goes, 'So you can remember today.'"

"Yeah, now ain't that some badass movie-type talk?" Bishop enthusiastically looked around, the entire table nodding in agreement before he carried on. "The Kid walks all the way to the bench, starts taking off his gear, and looks at us over his shoulder. It's me, O'Reilly, Sarge, and Slick right? The Kid looks dead at Slick and calm as can be says 'Might have caught my leg up in that one a bit.' We all look down and after he's pulled off the guard you can see the knee cap isn't even where it's supposed to be. One of the nastiest things I've ever laid eyes on. Of course, Slick being how he is, he said, 'Might have.'"

The whole dinner table laughed. Alex looked at Winn, who was watching Matt. Matt looked up and smiled, taking the gentle ribbing in good humor. Winn looked less amused, but Alex couldn't tell if it was the story or the little jab at Matt that had him looking unhappy.

Unaware, Bishop kept on. "So, The Kid makes us all hang out there until the field is empty. You know, so no witnesses. We have to almost carry him all the way to the truck on a leg that's floppy as Stretch Armstrong. We go to the ER and turns out that 'catching his leg a little bit' meant a bunch of wrenched-up shit. What was it? Torn tendons?"

"Torn ACL, MCL and meniscus," Matt said, almost to himself.

"Yada yada," Bishop continued. "Had to go all the way to Helena to find a surgeon who could put humpty dumpty back together. Bottom line? The Kid's one tough S-O-B and was a great ball player who really stuck it to that Martin kid, that day and a bunch of days after as a matter of fact." Again the table nodded in agreement. "Made us proud that day, Kid," he said whimsically, and then to Alex, "You should let him show you his scars, I can tell you The Kid looks good in his boxers." With a wink at Alex, Bishop jabbed Winn in the ribs with his elbow to drive home his less than subtle point.

Alex watched the room as the excitement from the storytelling began to die down. The conversations started to fracture and began down different paths. The joy these men felt in retelling this story was strange to her. She thought back to how surprised Winn had been that Matt had told her about the scholarship to Colorado State and it dawned on her that these men loved this story like an old war tale because they had no idea what it had truly cost Winn. They thought he missed out on the final two games of his last season and in return had gotten an epic rivalry story and a few ice-breaking scars out of the deal. They didn't know about the scholarship.

Why on earth had he kept something like that so close to the vest?

Alex looked at Mae, who was watching the table, with her concerned gaze frequently returning to Winn. The worry in her eyes told Alex that at least Mae had known what he'd lost that day. The back of Alex's throat tightened. What a terrible thing to relive every time these guys wanted to dig up war stories. She knew Winn would despise her pity, but for the moment he could have it anyway. She could relate to that kind of isolated and secretive pain, so maybe it wasn't pity but honest empathy.

Chapter 14

The next day, Alex took the truck and a small flatbed into town to pick up the supplies for the fence repair. Surprisingly, no one had even asked her if she knew how to drive a truck with a trailer. She figured she'd work it out and was thankful for the showing of trust. Alex had called ahead to the local hardware store and was confident that the pleasant man who took her order would be able to help her out if she managed to get stuck in their parking lot.

The forty-five-minute ride into town was uneventful and she allowed herself a moment to breathe with the windows down and the music up. Every time she allowed her mind to wander, it ended up on Winn. She would shake her head, try to steer her wayward thoughts elsewhere, but she always came back to him and what she'd learned about him the last few days.

Maybe he was right, working at the ranch seemed to suit him, but what if? What if he could have been more, done more? Was it a survival thing to tell yourself where you are is where you belong? That's something I can relate to, but like Winn, am I lying to myself? Am I reaching for a connection with him?

Alex arrived at the store and managed to park the truck and trailer, only taking up three times more room than she figured was normal. As she walked through the door, her heart hit the back of her rib cage.

Blake Martin stood at the counter. He was leaning over deep in conversation with the man standing there. Alex's feet briefly froze, but after a fraction, she regained her composure and replaced her face with a stony nonchalance. Both men stopped and turned at the bell marking her entry. Blake's face instantly fell into a sneer before he threw a mask on it. His lower lip was purple and a small split in his lip still evident.

"Can I help you, miss?" the man behind the counter asked.

Never breaking eye contact with Blake, she replied while slowly walking to the counter.

"Yes, I'm Alexandra, I called ahead with an order for Crooked Brook?"

"Ahh, sure, I've got it here. Let me go tell the yard to load you up. Parked out front?"

"Orange truck." Alex nodded, knowing she was about to be left alone with the man she'd recently publicly humiliated. As the older gentleman left the storeroom, Blake slithered right up next to her.

"Why, hello there, Alex. No warm welcome for me? You'd think I'm owed at least a cordial hello since you cracked me one for no reason."

"No reason? I believe the slap on the ass counts as cause, Blake."

He nodded. "I suppose I was out of line…" He watched her with a cold, unnerving stare, no apology in his eyes. "Interesting question now though."

"What's that?"

"How tough you may be without an entire ranching crew behind you."

She squirmed under his scrutiny. Appearing to notice her discomfort, Blake stepped into her personal space. Alex stepped back against the counter, cursing her kneejerk reaction to back down. Blake took advantage of her prone position and placed a flat hand on the counter on either side of her, boxing her in.

"Do I need to be tough to be alone with you, Blake? Is that the kind of man you are?" She challenged him with her upturned chin, not feeling an ounce of the bravado she tried to force into her tone.

He leaned in so close she could feel his breath on her face. "You have no idea what kind of man I am, Alexandra. What I'm capable of." His tone was low and promised darkness. She willed herself not to look away.

"That may be but understand this: you also don't know me or what I'm capable of when I'm backed into a corner."

"That so? I'd like to find out exactly what kind of woman you are." He leaned in closer, and her stomach flipped over. She swallowed the panic.

"I don't think you would. I'm about to neuter you with my knee if you don't step away."

He raised an eyebrow at her suggestively. "And what if I like it rough?"

The storekeeper cleared his throat from the back door. Alex let out a long-held breath in relief, thanking God she didn't need to find out if she could hold up her end of the threat. Blake immediately took a step back, swiping the back of his hand across his mouth.

"Everything okay in here?" the old man asked.

"Sure thing, Charlie, I was just getting out of your hair," Blake chirped.

Charlie raised his eyes to Alex, looking for confirmation. She only managed to nod. Blake slid away from the counter and left the store. Alex and the older man watched his back until the bell sounded with the door closing. Charlie moved his questioning gaze to Alex. "You all right young lady? That one can be…a handful."

"I'm fine, thank you, Mr. Singer. He's nothing I can't handle." She hoped the lie didn't sound a false as it had tasted.

"All right, you're ready to go and this has been put on Mae's tab. Try to have a good day now."

"Thanks, you too," she managed through the dryness in her throat.

Alex climbed into the cab of the truck and rested her forehead on the steering wheel, taking a moment to regain her composure. She tried to convince herself that she'd been up against worse at drunken frat parties. She stuck the key in the ignition, her only regret being that she hadn't belted a knee straight to his groin. He was owed that and plenty more for what he'd done to Winn.

Alex pulled back into the ranch less than an hour later and found that Mae was waiting for her on the front step. Surprisingly, both Matt and Winn were by her side, hands shoved into their pockets, eyes down in matching poses. When she climbed out of the truck she put her hands up, looking for some sort of direction.

"I'm confused about the welcoming committee here…did you guys think I was going to total the truck or something?"

"Charlie called, said you had an interesting time down at the store," Mae answered.

Alex looked to Winn and then Matt, both of which still wore downturned, unreadable expressions.

"Oh, for God's sake. This small-town gossip hotline is hard to wrap your head around. Yes, I ran into Blake at the store. It was uncomfortable but uneventful. That's the end of it."

Matt finally looked up and let out an exasperated breath. "Charlie said he'd pushed you up against the counter, Alex, inappropriate-like."

Winn pulled his hands from his pockets and balled his fists at his sides but remained silent, first looking up and beyond her and then back at the porch floorboards.

"Blake is a bully, Matt. He tried to bully me. It didn't work. It's over. Can we all get on with our lives, please? I don't understand what you want me to say."

Alex tried to keep her tone light to not let on how much he'd gotten to her. Despite her best efforts, frustration crept into her tone and the tension from the day's events was starting to take its toll on her resolve. Her choices were to break and give in to the strange urge to cry or get defensive. Alex picked defensive.

Mae responded, "Look, kiddo, really we're checking to make sure you're all right. That's all. Charlie said you were shaken up and we wanted to check in. No need to get upset with us. We care about you and want to know you're all right."

"Well I'm fine, I appreciate the concern. I think maybe your friend got a little excited with the drama. Blew it all up out of proportion."

They all stood there unsure for a few seconds.

Finally, Matt nodded and came to her rescue, hopping down off the steps to take the keys from Alex. "I'll have the guys unload. Thanks for running for supplies, Alex. Tomorrow we'll head up and start on repairs."

Winn finally met Alex's gaze, but his expression gave nothing away aside from a small twitch at his jaw. After a moment he turned and stormed off the porch. They watched his back for a moment and then Alex turned to Matt, not knowing what to do next. She said, "Thanks, I'm in for tomorrow."

As she walked past Mae to go into the house, she tried to hold eye contact as long as she could to try to prove her point. As soon as the door shut, she visibly dropped her shoulders. Running into Blake had been unnerving, yes, but coming home to the strange support group had been even more unsettling.

As she made it back to her room, her phone buzzed. Looking down she saw a text alert from Emily. She was afraid to open but strangely excited and relieved.

Hey

                                                                        Hey

How are you doing?

                                                                  I'm doing ok

I'm glad. Can we make up now?

                                                                   Yes please

Thank Christ. So spill, what's it like?

    It's pretty awful, some of the people are ok, but some of them are total assholes and this place is seriously in the middle of nowhere. I miss you.

We miss you too. Tommy and I were talking about maybe taking a road trip, maybe in a week or two to do some in person checking on you.

    That would be amazing....wait... You AND Tommy?

Don't judge me. We've been keeping each other's genitals company. In your absence we've both had some time on our hands...shut up we're dating, kind of....

                                                                     OMG...

.....

                                                                   OMFG

... ...

                                                                SQUEEE...

Leave off it all right?

Ok, ok…but yay..

Ok, enough. See you in like 2 weeks?

Yes, you and your bf.

Shut up

Thanks Em

I love you hun

Love you too

Chapter 15

The next morning Alex was dressed and ready to head out to the pasture to help with fence repair. She felt lighter now that she and Emily were back on speaking terms. It was a fragile truce, but it was a truce nonetheless. When she couldn't find Matt in the house, she headed to the barn. The sound of raised voices poured out of the aisle and surprisingly, one of the louder voices belonged to Matt.

"You need to take a moment to get ahold of yourself, Winn. These are Frank's horses. You don't get a say in this," Matt was saying.

"I'll trailer them back to his place myself then." Winn's voice was tense.

"Trailer for free? Take the morning off from your own work? What for? To make a point? Think Frank'll appreciate being wrapped up in this?" Matt prodded.

"What in the hell is Frank thinking in the first place?"

"I can't tell you that, all he said was he got held up in Cheyenne and that he hired Martin to pick up those horses."

"Hired Martin? Why would he hire Blake Martin to ship horses earlier than we agreed? Since when does Frank not have someone capable of coming to get them? This is bullshit, Matt. You know this is Blake trying to strong-arm his way further into my training business." Winn sounded like he was getting more worked up now.

"I don't know what Frank's up to, but word is making nice with the Martins is important to Frank these days. It's his business. If you want, I'll get Trix. He can handle loading the horses. You go take a walk and calm yourself. There's no reason you have to be here."

"The hell I will. I'm not going to hide, and I'm sure as shit not letting Blake handle a horse while he's at my ranch."

"Well, then fine, don't—" A door slammed, cutting off Matt's reply, and a moment later he came walking out into the sun, his expression grim. He saw Alex and his facial expression deepened.

"Not sure this is the best time for you to be around, Alex. Afraid we're going to get a little later start on the fencing than I thought."

"What's going on, Mattie?"

"Ah, nothing really, I need to be here a little later than I thought. Maybe you could go visit with Tommy and come back in an hour?"

"Matt, it's more than that," Alex pressed.

"No, no, nothing Alex, told Winn I would help put the finishing touches on the paint before he was picked up." His lie fell between them like a stone. She watched him squirm under the weight of his fib and felt like giving him a break.

"All right, I guess I do miss my little man. I'll see you in a bit," she agreed, and Matt's shoulders sagged in noticeable relief. He nodded and turned back through the doorway.

Alex waited a beat until she was sure he was well into the aisle before she followed and bounded up the ladder to her normal spying location in the hayloft.

From her spot in the loft, she could hear murmurings of the conversation continuing between Winn and Matt below her in the aisle, but she couldn't make out what they were saying. A few minutes later, she looked out into the yard and watched a truck and trailer pull into the space in front of the barn. Blake hopped out of the driver's seat and surveyed the property like a chief executive. His ability to show up and look like he owned the place irked Alex. The entitlement in his carriage was one more thing about him that read all kinds of wrong.

Matt and Winn came out of the aisle leading Frank's horses.

"Morning, boys." Blake wore a cocky grin to match his condescending tone.

"Morning," Matt said. "Why don't you open up that trailer and we'll load up here. Won't take but a minute."

"Sure, Mattie, why don't we do that?" Blake said, then swinging his stare over to Winn. "What's wrong, Winn? I don't get a friendly greeting?"

When he only got a hard look in response, Blake worked his way to the back of the trailer and undid the pin to let the ramp down then swung the doors open.

"You know, I've been thinking about you some lately," Blake said as he reached out to take the lead line from Winn.

Winn shifted his body between Blake's outstretched hand and the horse. "You can drive them out of here, but there's no way in hell you're touching a horse while you're on this property."

The corner of Blake's mouth popped up in a half grin. "That's a bit childish, don't you think now, Kid?"

Winn ignored him and walked the paint up into the trailer, climbing back out and clipping the bar in place behind the horse. Matt started up the ramp with the bay.

"So where's your little red head?" Blake started. "Ran into her in town yesterday."

Winn took a step toward Blake, but Matt stepped down out of the trailer between them.

Winn nodded toward Blake's face. "Well you don't look worse for the wear, looks like she let you off easier this time."

Alex smiled, despite the tension in her gut.

"Yeah that little kitten has proven she's got claws, that's for sure." Blake mindlessly ran a hand over his mouth. "But I like 'em to have a little spirit, gives you something to break."

Winn narrowed his eyes, the muscles in his jaw popping.

Matt broke in, his voice cool. "Alexandra can take care of herself and knows what you're about."

"Don't be so sure. This one seems smart enough to bet on a winner too. Guess time will tell eh, Winn?" Blake sneered.

"You and I know this is about getting in a jab at me. I hate to tell you, roughing up some city girl that I don't know from Adam isn't going to do it. You're the only horse in that race."

Winn's words cut Alex closer than she wanted to admit, her ego taking the brunt of that one. Blake stepped even closer to Winn, but Matt shifted his weight and put a hand on Winn's chest, keeping him where he stood.

"Your business is concluded here, Blake. I suggest you get on your way," Matt said firmly.

Blake and Winn held eye contact for an uncomfortable moment before Blake nodded and headed to the driver's side of the truck. Once in, he leaned an elbow out the window.

"Winn, pleasure doing business with you…again." His words were dripping with sarcasm and some underlying meaning Alex couldn't nail down. Matt and Winn stood and watched the back of the trailer until it was out of sight.

"Guy's an ass, Kid, don't even know why you let him bait you like that."

"What, Mattie? You think he should get to run his mouth off whenever he wants? Without any consequence, even when he's talking about your precious pet project?"

Alex reeled from the heat in his voice when he used her to provoke Matt. She was strangely surprised that he could talk about her that way. Were they friends? No, of course not, but seriously, a strange girl he could care less about handing over to Blake? That had a sting to it.

"Now who's running his mouth for the sake of being mean, Winn? I don't buy this jerk thing you've been up to lately. Whatever is going on with you, you need to work it out. It's not Blake Martin, and we both know it has nothing to do with some harmless girl who showed up as you're gearing up for some fits," Matt said, speaking more aggressively to Winn than Alex had ever heard.

Winn spit whatever he was going to say onto the ground and took off toward the woods.

"Get your head out of your ass, Kid!" Matt yelled at his back, and Winn threw both hands in the air and continued without turning around.

Matt watched him for a moment and then headed toward the house. Alex sat frozen in her spot, unsure of what to do next, still feeling uncomfortable and voyeuristic from watching the interaction below.

"Sneaky girl."

Alex whirled around and saw Trix standing at the ladder to the loft.

"Crap, Trix. What in the hell?"

"I was about to ask you the same thing? You doing some spying, Red?"

She opened her mouth to lie and then decided against it. "Yes, I'm spying because no one will ever tell me what the hell is going on around here."

"About what? Blake? You know why Blake and Winn don't really buddy up. The whole high school rivalry thing? Stories like that are common around here. You know, Hatfield and McCoy type stuff."

"It doesn't feel like the whole story, Trix."

"Well, if you're looking for a rundown on the whole history, Red, you're looking at a long list. I can tell you that Blake is a capital 'A' Ass-hat. The Kid and Martin have had troubles for a long time, and they don't seem like they're going away any time soon, and that was before he slapped your backside and you spanked his ego."

"What happened?" Alex pushed, hoping that Trix's love of speaking would work in her favor.

Trix suddenly looked exceptionally uncomfortable. "Um…most recently you mean?"

Finally, he broke under her relentless stare. "Well, most recently, Blake seems to be weaseling into The Kid's training business, no one seems to understand it. Everyone around here knows Winn's the best horseman within five hundred miles, but they're moving their business anyway. Doesn't make sense." He paused, looked at his hand and then looked like he decided to keep talking, so Alex kept her mouth shut.

"Then insult to injury, not even a month ago we were at an auction, and Winn put eyes on Blake doing what Blake always does, manhandling and downright abusing a young horse."

Alex sucked in air and furrowed her brow.

Trix continued, "There's not anything the Kid can do about it though, you know? The Martin family wields a lot of clout around here, and authorities aren't going to step in, so he tries to buy the horse from Blake. Course, the horse isn't worth a dime, and Blake sets some ridiculous price, something like five grand. The Kid doesn't have that kind of scratch, and he's got no leverage, so what's he gonna do? He's got to leave knowing this poor horse is going home with Martin. He was in a piss-poor mood for a week after that." Ho looked up at the ceiling. "Come to think of it that was the weekend before you got here, maybe that's why he was still in such a funk when you showed up."

"Blake beats his horses?" Alex asked through gritted teeth.

"I imagine Blake beats on everyone, but yeah, his horses too. He's one of the truly rotten ones, Red."

"What did this horse look like?"

"Aww, well, little thing, bay. Didn't get a real good look at it. He was filthy and you could tell he was emotionally cracked, you know? I was floored when Winn even made an offer on it. It's never going to do any work again. He's a very expensive pet to keep around to look at, even if it'd been free." Trix finished, looking proud of his gossip rundown.

After hearing Trix's description, Alex was convinced Tommy was Blake's horse.

Had Winn stolen him? Or is that what Blake had meant earlier about doing business with Winn again? Did he somehow manage to buy Tommy?

Alex's anger at Winn's careless words about her started to fizzle, despite how much they had cut her, and she knew exactly where she could find Winn. Matt was going to have to wait on her.

Chapter 16

Alex had to pump herself up for the interaction as she walked to the little barn.

This is about Tommy. This isn't about you. Go for Tommy. Go play nice.

She came around the bend to find Tommy and Winn staring at one another. Winn stood with his foot propped on the outside of the fence, and Tommy stood at the opening to the stall. As far as Alex could tell, this was the extent of Winn's progress with the gelding. Both turned to her when they heard her approach. Tommy picked his head up and his ears shot forward. Winn swore at the ground and then again turned his back to her.

"It's not a good time," Winn said to the air in front of him.

"I know, but I don't care."

Winn shook his head. "What in the hell is wrong with you? Didn't I tell you to leave this horse alone?"

"You did, and I ignored you. I like him and he likes me. The more I learn, the more I know I haven't done anything to compromise your work with this horse." There was no doubt in Alex's voice. "But you coming here frothing at the mouth like this...that's not helpful."

Winn whipped around at her words. "What? Oh, of course...I'm sure you got a whole soap opera update from Matt by now. It was a rough morning, Alexandra, and don't insult me by insinuating that I would ever take it out on this horse. Last time that conversation went badly...for both of us."

She nodded her agreement to that statement and switched tactics. "Why didn't you tell me that this horse belongs to Blake?"

Winn's jaw dropped. "Where did you get that idea?"

"Is it true?" she pressed.

"He's my horse, Princess, that's all you need to know."

"Bullshit, there's more to it. I know Blake beat this horse and made him the way he is."

"Jesus, I'm going to kill Mattie. You don't know the first thing about what you're—" He stopped when Alex boldly started to climb through the fence rails.

Winn reached out to stop her but froze when she shot him a steely glare, almost daring him to touch her. He withdrew his hand and she continued into the paddock.

"Don't blame Matt, he didn't connect these dots for me," Alex said over her shoulder. She kept her eyes on Tommy who watched her from the stall entrance, with his eyes constantly bouncing back to Winn.

"You make him nervous," she ventured.

"I know, but it makes sense," he conceded.

"Can they tell the difference between men and women?"

"Sure." Winn nodded.

"So that's it? You're bigger, too much like his abuser?" Then with sarcasm added, "Whoever that may have been."

"Yes." Winn refused to be baited.

"So what's your plan?" She turned and held his gaze.

Winn eyed her, obviously weighing his options. She planted her feet to make it even more apparent that she wasn't going anywhere and wasn't letting this go.

"You're looking at it. Obviously, it's slow going, but I've got time."

Alex continued to watch him, trying to read his expression. It was guarded but softer than she'd expected. She decided to press her luck. "Can I show you something?"

He nodded, surprising her with an uncharacteristic show of patience—or maybe it was resignation.

"When I first came out here, I was terrified about what he may do. Then I saw all of the marks on his neck and it broke my heart." Alex swallowed and again looked at Winn.

He continued to watch her, but she saw the anger creeping into his eyes. She couldn't tell if he was angry at Blake or at her retelling how she'd blatantly stepped in where she didn't belong.

"So I sat down, right here." She pointed to the spot and then she sat down cross-legged in the dirt. "And then I cried. I mean I cried my freaking eyes out. I was alone, and so was this poor thing, this thing that was so big but so defenseless—I don't know, it hit me all at once and I cried." She turned back to him, expecting to be mocked for her admission. Instead, he watched her. "That's when he came out the first time, came right up and blew nasty horse breath right on to the back of my head."

"He walked out to you?"

"Yes, and you know that he does. The day you caught me, he was all the way out here. Even let me clean off his neck."

"I know," Winn admitted.

"So maybe I can help? Maybe he'll come out, even with you, if you sit." She patted the ground next to her.

Winn eyed her warily then brought his eyes to the horse. "People don't sit on the ground near horses, Alexandra. It's a terrible and dangerous idea."

"Well, it's my method." Alex grinned at him, and he seemed to return the smile before catching himself. Winn put his hands in his pockets and watched the sky for a moment. She couldn't tell if he was contemplating her murder or praying for patience.

"All right." He climbed through the railing, and when he did so, Tommy shot back into the stall and out of sight. Winn shot her a disapproving look, but she shrugged, not deterred by the setback.

He sat down next to her. "So what, I need to start sobbing?" His tone was mocking but not mean.

"If you feel the urge."

"I don't."

"Shocking, you seem to have such a healthy grip on your emotions."

"You do realize you're pushing it right now?" Winn asked, one eyebrow hitched.

"In terms of?"

"My patience with this game of yours."

Alex took a deep breath, reminding herself that she was trying for the sake of their united cause—this horse. "Contrary to your unfounded low opinion of me, Winn, I know this isn't a game. Tommy is important to me. I can't even begin to tell you how important."

"Who?"

"I named him Tommy," Alex confessed while waving her hand toward the still empty door.

Winn started to roll his eyes and she cut off whatever rude thing he was about to say. "Shut up, you certainly weren't going to tell me his name, and it was my first time naming a horse, and Tommy is as good a name as any."

"Fine." Winn capitulated quicker than Alex had expected.

"Tommy is a friend of mine back home, and it's a long story, but Tommy is a survivor in his own way, so I thought it was fitting."

Alex stared at him, daring him to push it, but Winn seemed to let it drop.

"Stay here, and don't move. I'm going to go get him." Alex said, making a little stay gesture at him.

Winn opened his mouth, but she gave him a harsh look, "We're doing this my way, for now at least. Okay?"

Winn's eyes narrowed but he nodded. Alex walked to the stall entrance, murmuring something below her breath, and the gelding stuck his head out quickly. She walked right up to him and planted her hand on the center of his head. The horse, Alex, and Winn simultaneously let out a long breath.

"Thank you for not making a fool out of me," she whispered, then a little louder she added, "All right, come on now, Tommy, time to be brave." She turned, watching Winn, daring him to mock her. He simply watched.

She knew that when Winn thought no one was watching, he always had full-on conversations with the horses. She ran her hand up and down the horse's head then slowly backed away from him. He took a tentative step to follow her. Tommy's worried eyes moved to Winn, but he took another step. After a few tense moments, Tommy had taken several steps and was now only about five feet from Winn, who sat motionless, maybe trying to ensure he didn't spook the little gelding. The progress seemed like a real positive step in the right direction, but there was no point in pushing it.

***

Alex ran her fingers through the horse's mane. She said, "Not sure if you've noticed, but he's looking a little svelte."

Winn opened his mouth and thought better of letting his pride speak for him. Plus, she looked so happy and pleased with herself, he realized he didn't want to damage that.

"I easily run out of things to say to him, but I think he likes being spoken to, so I keep babbling. I'm sure I sound like a freakin' idiot, but you know it's worth it. To have, well, you know...?" Alex trailed off.

"Trust," Winn finished.

Her eyes found his and she slowly smiled. "Yes." The smile spilled into her eyes. "He trusts me."

There was something about her look, the unabashed but surprised pride. Even when he tried to seek it out, he couldn't find an ounce of the frustration and anger that had been coursing through his veins only minutes ago.

She broke through his thoughts. "Confession time?"

"Seriously? What more could there possibly be?"

She shot him a sheepish look. "I'm going to ride him some day."

His face dropped. "Alexandra, please, you're going to ruin my mood. Promise me you won't get on this horse, because I promise that I will throttle what is left of your lifeless body when you get thrown and trampled to death."

"Well, lord knows your mood is my primary concern," Alex said. But as she watched him, she must have sensed his genuine fear. The sarcasm dropped from her tone when she added, "But, for now, I promise to defer to your judgment if you promise to stop stonewalling me when it comes to Tommy."

"So now this is blackmail. We work together on this horse or you kill yourself with it?"

"I suppose that's what's happening if your interpretation has a flare for the dramatic." Alex teased.

He raised an eyebrow at her, weighing his options. "All right, fine. I counter that *if* you learn to ride on a different horse and *if* this one gets better, then we can *talk* about it. Also, you do not ever, I mean ever, get on this horse, or any horse for that matter, without me there."

"Or Matt," Alex quickly added.

He nodded and added, "Or Matt."

He mentally noted that he needed to have a talk with Matt about this ASAP. She squinted at him, walked toward him, and bent down, offering him her hand to shake. He eyed her and realized she was dead serious and then reached up take it.

"Deal," she said and curtly shook his hand.

"Settled," he replied, more than a little amused despite himself.

Alex then turned and walked back to the barn, Tommy following in stride. Once the little horse was back in his safe zone, Winn stood and brushed the dirt from his jeans.

"Guess I owe Matt a few hours of labor on the fences seeing as how my morning derailed his."

"Whatever your issue was, it did seem to ruin his morning also." At his sour look, she added, "Your propensity for drama strikes again." She smiled at him, her eyes holding a little gleam of mischief.

"As usual, Princess, your concept of reality is ill-informed, and because of that, you again have no idea what you're talking about." Winn's words were harsh, but the delivery was almost playful.

Alex laughed the confident laugh of someone who knows more than they let on. "Oh, hillbilly, you don't have a clue what I know."

There was a tease in her tone, but underneath Winn couldn't shake the feeling that she was probably right. They walked to the fence and without thinking, he offered his hand to help her step through. Stranger yet, she accepted it.

As they made their way down the path, Alex started, "So for my first riding lesson…"

She watched him out of the side of her eye and smirked when he winced.

"You're getting ahead of yourself," he said, deadpan.

"A deal's a deal, Winn."

He laughed, shaking his head. "No special treatment, Princess. You learn to contribute at the stables, and you get to learn to ride."

"I can help."

"We'll see." Winn couldn't help but grin. She may be play pouting, but he could tell she wasn't going to let it go.

"You're banking on the fact that I'm going to flake out, and I can tell you, that's a bad bet," Alex said.

"We'll see," he repeated. "But you're right, I'm betting you don't have what it takes. Let's see how you behave the first time you get thrown and you get dirty."

In response to her incredulous look, Winn reached out and rubbed a dirty smear from his dusty hands onto the arm of her shirt.

"I think I've already proven I'm made of more grit than you give me credit for." Alex bent and took a little handful of dirt and smeared it on the side of his face.

"A few moments of temporary insanity do not mean you're in for the long haul." He bent down and swiped his finger through the dirt and then stood to wipe a large swatch down the center of her nose.

"I'm pretty tough," Alex announced right before she gave him a quick light jab in the gut and took off running, shocking Winn with the playful move.

"See," she called over her shoulder. "Tough!"

"Of course you fight dirty," he yelled and chased after her. "Now your true colors are showing, Princess, but I can fight dirty too."

He caught up to her and, with no effort and without breaking his stride, snagged her off her feet and threw her over his shoulder like a sack of grain. She let out a sound of distress and snagged a small branch off a tree as they passed by and began beating his back with it.

"Now, you're in trouble," he said and chuckled at her squirming.

"I've got you exactly where I want you," she countered.

Alex laughed at the growl he let out after particularly brutal swat. The pair of them came crashing into the main barn area as a swarming tangle of dirty limbs, leaves, and battle sounds.

Winn stopped dead in his tracks and Alex grunted as his shoulder dug into her stomach.

"What in the—?" she started as he quickly dropped her back on her feet.

Bishop, Matt, and Trix stood at a fence a few yards away. Mouths agape, Trix even had a hammer raised and stopped mid-swing. All three stared without attempting to cover their shock.

There were a few moments of strange silence, with no one sure what to say. Winn couldn't quite explain the bloom of embarrassment he felt in his gut. It wouldn't be a stretch for the guys to razz him over this, but he usually worked pretty hard not to give them such easy ammo.

Finally, Alex stepped forward and still a little out of breath, said, "Hey, guys." She reached up to comb her fingers through her hair, which prompted him to remember to wipe the dirt off the side of his face.

Bishop was the first to recover. "What's up?" After a pause for effect he added quite formally, "Are you all having a nice morning?"

Next to Bishop, Trix finally lowered the hammer and failed at suppressing a snicker.

Winn's eyes narrowed. "I thought you were fixing the fencing in the north pasture today," he said more gruffly than he'd intended.

"Was waitin' on you," Matt finally said, surprise still evident on his face.

Winn collected himself and decided that if he refused to talk to anyone, he wouldn't have to explain the one-eighty in his mood since he last saw Matt.

You'd have to admit Alex made you feel better.

Winn shook his head at the thought.

"All right let's go then," he said and walked toward the truck without a backwards glance.

※ ※ ※

Alex and Matt stood next to one another watching as Winn walked away, which seemed like it was becoming a habit. Matt looked down and caught her eye, smiling at her. She decided it was still going to be a good afternoon even if Winn had spent all of his available good humor for the day. Alex couldn't pretend to understand the abrupt shift in Winn's mood, but she decided it was silly to act embarrassed. There was nothing to be embarrassed about.

People roughhouse all the time—hell I've seen these guys in more than a normal number of headlocks. Why should I be any different?

As the group made their way toward the truck, Matt leaned in close to her, quietly saying, "Surprised the hell out of me. I thought his mood was a lost cause. Not sure what you did but I'm much obliged."

Alex shrugged. "He got a pretty good look at Tommy today, which I think made him feel better…and I may have promised to not kill myself via horseback, which also seemed to lighten his mood."

Matt made an interesting face but then seemed to make the decision not to question her meaning. Ahead of them, Winn had hopped in the passenger's side of the truck as Trix and Bishop climbed into the bed. She moved to the back and they bent down, each grabbing an arm, and pulled her up while she stepped on the rear tire. Matt climbed in the driver's side, and they were off bouncing toward the far north corner of the pasture.

Alex felt light and happy. When she looked over, she saw that both Trix and Bishop were still smirking at her.

She leaned forward and said, "I've still got some fight left. Who's next?"

The three of them laughed, any trace of tension gone.

They all hopped out when the truck came to a stop. Trix dropped the tailgate and pulled out four of the heavy posts.

"You sure you know where these go?" he asked, and Alex ignored his little dig and consulted her list, pointing at the fence post nearest them first.

"This is first, post thirty-one." Then with a sweeping motion she added, "Then thirty-two, forty-two, and forty-five."

Trix grunted as he put the first post down and then got to the next one. As he was setting it down, she couldn't resist taking some revenge. "No, wait, sorry, thirty-four and forty-two. Sorry."

Trix nodded, bent down, picked up the post and walked it over to drop it at the correct spot. His arms began to show strain with the other two posts.

"Oh wait, yes, thirty-two was right. Sorry." Alex tried to hide her grin.

He started to bend down again, a bit of his smile coming off his face. He looked up at her, and she couldn't conceal her guilt for screwing with him.

Understanding began to dawn on his expression. "You little…"

Trix dropped the armful of posts and took off toward her. Alex threw her head back and laughed, taking off around the truck, aiming to put the bed between the two of them.

"We're not out here ten minutes, and you've already got me sweating like a pig," he yelled.

"Hey, Trix, you've got to cut me some slack. I'm new to this whole complicated counting concept," she hollered, mocking him. As he gained on her, Alex squealed and tried to round the front of the truck.

"All I'm saying, Red, is that fair is fair, and it is not fair that I stink…and you don't."

Alex's eyes widened as she caught his meaning and tried to pick up the speed. He caught her in the middle of the next lap and tucked her head under his arm, pinning her in a headlock. Lord he was right, he did smell like a pig.

She mumbled something unintelligible into his forearm and Trix laughed. "How's that sweet-smelling shampoo of yours holding up against *eau de* field hand?"

Alex was snaking her foot around the back of his knees, when out of nowhere, Bishop let out a war whoop and hopped on Trix's back. For a second, Alex thought they were all going down, and she had a moment of legit panic. But in an instant, Winn was behind her, picking her up and out of Trix's grasp by the hips. When he set her down, she was ready to be annoyed with his interference, but she caught the laughing spark in his eye. He cocked his head and touched the brim of his hat in a mock moment of chivalry.

"Ma'am," he said with a sideways grin. Tossing the hat aside, he comically jumped on the pile of wrestling, squirming men. They became a writhing ball of grunting male, each one trying to get a slap or a playful punch in where they could.

Alex stood back and laughed at the sight while Matt stepped up next to her.

"Overgrown children," he said with faux disapproval.

Chapter 17

A few days passed in a similar fashion, and Alex's closeness with the crew continued to grow. Alex and Winn had seemed to work out a civil understanding. They never got back to the level of playfulness from that day in the north pasture, but they were no longer at each other's throats at every opportunity. Things were uncomfortable at times, but everyone, including Alex, seemed to have settled into an easier routine.

It was a little after lunch and Alex was gearing up for her second riding lesson with Matt. She was excited as she went into the barn to tack up her horse, Winston. She led him out and met Matt, who gave her equipment a quick check to make sure everything was in order.

"All right, you get on yourself this time," he prompted.

After a moment's hesitation, Alex nodded, and with less grace than she'd hoped clawed her way up into the saddle.

"Well, no points for technique, but you're up there now." Matt grinned, and Alex couldn't help but return the smile.

She started Winston off walking along the fence, practicing her balance like Matt had shown her. Winn came around the side of the barn and she felt a little sense of pride perk up. Alex was excited to show him that she was capable of riding. Matt had told her last time that she was a quick learner. He'd even let her trot. Alex opened her mouth to say so to Winn when his expression darkened, as he looked from her to Matt to his watch.

"Matt, what the hell?" Winn called out angrily.

"What?" Matt replied, looking startled.

"You know it's past two o'clock. Did you go into town today?"

"Umm…"

"Matt, I even set the goddamn alarm on your phone." At Matt's blank expression, Winn asked, "Damn it, where's your phone?"

Understanding flashed on Matt's face, but before he could get out the apology, Winn jumped on his case. "Jesus Christ, Matt. Do I have to do everything for you? From now on I'll come and find you, hold your hand, walk you to the truck, and buckle you in myself. Like I've got time to do that. Okay? From now on, that's how we'll do this."

Alex's jaw dropped. She'd not once seen him be hostile to Matt. Matt was always the one who Winn protected and sheltered, he was never in the crosshairs when Winn really got going.

Winn ran an agitated hand through his hair while Matt continued to stare at the ground, obviously gutted from Winn's malicious words.

Winn's face softened as he took a long deep breath, and in an instant, he looked exhausted. "I can't, okay, Matt? I…I can't…" As he trailed off, he turned to leave.

Alex hopped off the horse and went to Matt first. His expression was guilty and distressed.

"What was that?" she asked, even as she knew he wasn't going to be able to answer past the tears brimming in his eyes. Alex wrapped Matt in a hug and watched Winn's back walking toward the fields.

"It's okay, I'm sure whatever it is, it's okay," she soothed.

He nodded into her shoulder and released her.

"I'll be right back, okay, Matt? Can you take Winston?"

Matt silently watched her and then nodded again. She handed him the reins and took off after Winn.

Alex was fuming.

There is absolutely no way I'm letting him get away with such a hurtful outburst. Everyone else may be willing to let Winn get away with this shit, but not me.

"What in the hell was that all about?" Alex yelled at Winn's back while running after him.

He spun around, his eyes seething. "Seriously, you have no idea what a time-wasting distraction you are, do you?"

"Excuse me? You agreed to this, remember? I work, and I get to learn to ride. Now you're mad that Mattic at least has the decency to hold up your end of the bargain?"

"Matt has better things to do than play horsey with you."

"Christ, Winn, I expected more from you." Alex shook her head.

"What in the hell does that mean?"

"Matt's an adult, an adult that understands he has a job to do. He's fully capable of being in charge of his own freaking schedule. You're treating him like a moron that needs to be babysat."

"You're unbelievable. You don't know the first thing about what Matt needs or doesn't need," Winn shot back.

"No, Winn, you better take a good look at yourself and see the way you treated him. You reprimanded him like he was the village idiot, and do you know what's worse? Because he loves you so much, he would never tell you what you did cut him to the core. You think whatever errand he blew off trumps what you did to him? If I'm such a waste of space, how is it I care more about his feelings than his own shitty brother?"

Winn sucked in air at her accusation. His eyes narrowed, and his jaw popped as he gritted his teeth. He slowly raised a hand and pointed at her. "That's enough."

"Oh, I don't think it is. You have no right to speak to him that way. Ever."

Winn held up his palm to silence her. "Not another word," he growled through his clenched jaw. "Not another goddamn word."

Alex flinched at the venom in his voice. He'd been angry at her before, but she'd never seen him like this. Something was wrong. Taking a deep breath, Alex forced herself to take a step back from her rage.

"Winn, what's going on?"

He stared at her for a long time, so long that she thought he may confide in her, tell her what was behind his abhorrent behavior. After a moment, his jaw ticked, and she knew he was done. He wasn't about to explain himself to her.

"You're so concerned for Matt?" he said with a scoffing disdain. "Why don't you go ask him what your little riding lesson took the place of today?"

Winn put his back to her, officially ending the conversation, and took off this time toward the house, leaving her stunned and confused. Alex couldn't even begin to come up with an explanation for his renewed animosity toward her. And his treatment of Matt? There was not a scenario in which he could defend his words. By the time she returned to the paddock, Matt was already gone.

***

Winn struggled to keep his temper in check as he wandered the yard. He needed to be more balanced before he tried to go in the house. The day was an all-over disaster. That afternoon he'd spoken with Frank, who had confessed that he was officially going to use Blake as his horse supplier and trainer from now on. He tried to get more information from the old man, but Frank was tight-lipped. Something was going down, and it involved his business falling to shambles around his feet. Winn knew that Blake somehow was steering the disaster. That's when Winn had noticed the time. His guilt overshadowed all other things.

It was almost two. He'd trusted Matt to go to the doctor alone. It had been years since Winn hadn't been able to find time to accompany his brother to the now regular checkups. The last time they went, the physician had very strongly warned them about keeping Matt's diabetes better managed. He'd again lectured that the degeneration in Matt's vision was because of the poor maintenance, and Winn had felt that the doctor blamed him solely for Matt's lack of care.

The doctor was right. Maybe Winn had been sloppy. He could have, should have done better. He needed to be better, more on top of it, on top of the readings, on top of the diet, on top of everything. He had tried and look what had happened. Not good enough. Always not good enough. For the next follow-up visit, Winn had convinced Matt to go on his own.

When he'd found Matt, not at the doctor, but with the Princess, Winn had wanted to wring her neck but had instead set his sights on Matt.

I'm letting everyone down and then screaming at them for it. What is wrong with me?

Of course, Alex had followed him, and had called him on it. Of course she'd defended Matt. He yanked off his hat and ran an exasperated hand through his hair. She was right, he knew it. But there was no room in that moment for her to be right. There was no room. There was only anger and frustration.

Winn had been right about Alex though. She was a distraction. Matt would have remembered the appointment if he hadn't agreed to teach her today. Winn's eyes rose to the sky, and he took a few deep breaths as he forced his anger at himself and Alex back down below the surface.

Winn finally wandered into the house and entered his shared room in search of Matt. The sight of his brother, sitting so dejected, shoulders slumped, eyes trained on the floor, destroyed him.

Alex was right. I did this. I'm worse than Blake. Blake does this to animals, Blake breaks animals. But no, not me. For the animals, I have patience eternal. I did this to a human being. To the most important human being in my life. I did this. I broke Matt.

"Mattie," Winn said softly.

Matt turned, and Winn could see that he'd been fumbling with his blood glucose monitor.

"I'm sorry, Winn," Matt quietly said to the floor.

Winn's gut wrenched. "No, Mattie, don't. I'm sorry, this was my fault and there is no excuse. I didn't mean those things I said. Can you forgive me?"

Matt stared at the test strip in his hand. He took a long time to speak and Winn waited. "I'm going to be better at this, Winn, I promise I am."

The question dodge was Matt's way of telling Winn it wasn't yet time to ask for forgiveness. Matt was too tender, wounded so easily and things like this landed deep and stuck. It would be a long time before he would truly be able to forgive Winn, and he wouldn't say it until he meant it.

"I'm going to be better too, Mattie. I'm going to figure out how to be better." Winn pleaded.

"Okay," Matt said simply.

"I need your help, though, Mattie. I feel, I feel like I'm…I don't know, man, I need your help."

"Okay," Matt said again, essentially closing the door on any more discussion. He was still too upset.

Winn recognized this plan. The plan to put the conversation on hold, wait for another day, a day when it would be easier to talk about, another day he knew would never come. They would stay this way, careful and barely interacting until Matt forgave him and then everything would go back exactly as it was before. They would be normal and happy together and Winn would be back to feeling like he was drowning. Alone. He pinched the bridge of his nose.

"Okay," Winn finally echoed.

Sitting down next to his brother, he tilted the glucose monitor Matt held to read the display. He then pulled out the insulin, carefully drew the right dose into a syringe, opened an alcohol pad, swabbed the section of stomach that Matt had exposed and pushed in the medication. Like he had every day in recent memory.

"I love you, Winn."

"I love you too, Mattie."

***

Alex stood at the door to Matt and Winn's room. She wasn't sure what she was going to find. Low voices rumbled inside the room, but she couldn't make out any of the words. Unsure of what she hoped to accomplish, she raised her hand to knock and stopped at a noise behind her. Turning, she saw Mae standing in the hallway, a dripping bowl and dish towel in her hand.

"Not a great time for a visit," Mae said simply.

"I know, but I think this may be my fault," Alex responded carefully, trying to keep her voice from projecting beyond the closed door.

"Maybe. But you being there isn't going to help right now. Come and dry dishes." In typical Mae fashion, it wasn't a question.

Alex took a moment to weigh her options, and at the end of it she knew she didn't have it in her to handle whatever would be on the other side of that door.

Turning, Alex followed Mae up the stairs and into the dimly lit kitchen. Silently, she snagged a dish towel and pulled a dish from the rack. Mae had already returned to the sink, not a doubt in her mind that Alex would obey and come with. A long few moments passed wordlessly.

"Want to tell me what happened?" Mae finally asked.

"I'm sure you already know."

"Of course," she nodded. "But I didn't ask what happened. I asked if you wanted to tell me."

"Then no."

"All right."

A few more quiet moments passed, the only sounds the gentle bump of dishes floating in a ceramic sink and a trickle of rinse water from the faucet. Alex surprised herself by suddenly feeling the need to swallow tears. Mae seemed to sense the weakness.

"Being between two brothers who are struggling is not a peaceful place, Alex."

Alex gasped. Of all of things that she expected Mae to say, this wasn't even close. The surprise jolted her from her teary moment, and she could feel her own embarrassment fanning her seemingly ever-present anger.

"Good God, Mae. Don't be ridiculous you know damn well that there isn't anything romantic going on between me and either of them."

"Now who's being ridiculous? Did I say anything about a love triangle? I said between brothers who are struggling. And frankly, if you want to talk about insulting, what's offensive is you thinking you're the cause."

Of course, that little hand slap immediately put Alex in her place, the place where she felt foolish and narcissistic. This admonishment, because there were no accidents when it came to Mae, was completely intentional.

Alex had to bite her tongue to keep from lashing out. Being reactionary around Mae was fruitless and exhausting. These little back-and-forths required well-thought-out arguments or she would hang you with your own casual words.

"You're right," Alex finally said. "The problem is, I don't have a clue about what's happened, and I feel stuck in the middle without all the facts."

Mae nodded agreement as a small knowing twitch found the corner of her mouth, but she remained silent.

"I want to help," Alex added.

"Why?" Mae asked, turning to face her.

"Because I feel responsible."

"So it's still about you then?"

"No. Damn it. I don't know."

"Do not confuse being a target with being an enemy, Alexandra."

There was a long pause as Alex tried to wrap her head around the simplicity of the statement and the convoluted way to apply it to her own situation.

"You don't blame me for this then?" Alex finally asked.

Mae let out a disappointed sigh. "No, I do not blame you."

"Well what then? What do you expect from me?" Alex asked, allowing her irritation through.

Mae answered Alex's frustrated question with a hard stare and more silence.

After several quiet moments, Mae swiftly turned off the faucet and said harshly, "I expect you to comprehend your own distance from this. Comprehend that other people have bigger things going on than what they may or may not think about *you*. So, if you truly wish to understand how today, specifically today, was bigger than you, I expect you to ask better questions."

Alex felt pushed back on her heels. Mae's words were not wrong, but they were sharp and hard to hear. Finally, quietly, with eyes directed into the dishwater, Alex asked, "Do you want to tell me what happened today?"

She looked up at Mae expectantly, feeling like she was testing out the answer to a riddle. Mae's smile was small but approving. She tucked Alex in under her arm, and with a squeeze, kissed the top of her head. Chuckling lightly, Mae finally said, "No."

Alex let out an exasperated breath then Mae added, "But what a great question that was."

Then Mae walked out of the room, leaving Alex alone in the noiseless kitchen.

Alex decided tomorrow she would put the grizzled wisdom Mae shoved down her throat to good use. Tomorrow she would ask better questions.

Chapter 18

Early the next morning Winn was throwing hay and watering the horses when Alex came in. He glanced up, not surprised to see her.

"Can I help?" she asked. "With the chores," she added briskly.

Now Winn was surprised. He searched her face for an ulterior motive and couldn't nail anything down.

"Okay," he said tentatively. "Can you finish hay and water so I can start meds?"

"Yup."

"Thanks." Winn handed Alex the hose and warily watched her over his shoulder as he made his way toward the tack room, returning a few moments later with his arms full of wraps, cotton and bottles.

Winn watched as she reached into the half-empty water buckets to pull hay and debris off the top before wiping her hand on her jeans and setting the hose in the bucket to fill. Next Alex went to the wheelbarrow and pulled down an arm full of flakes to throw into the stall before pulling the hose and moving on to the next stall. Her rhythm and comfort with the chore told him that Matt must have taught her how to do the afternoon feedings. Winn pulled the buckskin gelding out of his stall and pulled the existing wraps off its legs before leading it to a wash stall. He lost himself in his task for a few moments as he cleaned off the stubborn clay poultice the horse's legs were covered in from the night before.

As he scrubbed, Alex appeared next to him. "Ok to feed grain now?" she asked.

"You know how?" Winn asked.

"Yes."

After eyeing her for a second, he nodded. "Okay, yes, thanks."

Winn finished cleaning the gelding's legs and began to dry them. He listened as she made quick time of feeding. There was an efficient rhythm of the sound of the scoop in the feed, the percussion of grain bouncing off the bucket and the squeak of the cart's wheel as she moved further down the aisle. By his count, she was already almost to the end.

What game is this? Is it remorse for yesterday? Did she learn about Matt's appointment?

Winn wasn't surprised to see her this morning, but he was legitimately shocked when the reason for the visit wasn't purely to rip him a new one. He couldn't place a motive for what appeared to be an agreeable and helpful Alexandra. His desire to repent for his sins toward Matt told him he needed to allow this new development to play out more.

"Umm, Winn?" came a questioning call from Alex.

He fought off his knee-jerk cynicism about what her issue may be. She was trying, to what end he wasn't sure, but he was going to try to not blow it up, at least not yet, for Matt's sake.

"Yeah?" he called back.

"Winston doesn't seem interested in his grain, and he hasn't tried eating any of the hay I threw."

Winn started down the aisle, frowning at the alarm in her tone. He joined her at looking in at the gelding. Winston did look listless. Not good.

"This may sound dumb, but he looks…sad?" Alex said it with a little wince, no doubt expecting him to scoff.

"Yes, he does," Winn agreed, which caused a beat of surprise to flash across Alex's face.

Winn continued, "We need to get the grain and hay out of his stall. Do you happen to remember how much water was gone from his buckets before you refilled?"

"No," Alex said worriedly. "Not really, I'm sorry."

"It's all right. Can you grab me a lead rope?" he asked.

Alex nodded and took off down the row as Winn walked in and stooped to grab Winston's hay, tossing the flakes into the aisle. When Alex returned, she handed him the line. Winn fastened the halter and led Winston out of the stall, Alex watching him intently.

"It's colic?" she asked, returning to the horse's head and petting him.

"Maybe," Winn replied, a little surprised that she knew the term and warning signs. "Do you know what we should check next?"

Alex looked up at the ceiling, apparently trying to recall what she knew about this. "Look for manure and check for dehydration?"

Pleased, he nodded and showed her how to check. The results were not reassuring.

"Next step, gut sounds." Winn leaned over and pressed his ear to the horse's stomach and moved it around to several places before switching sides and doing the same. Alex copied his movements but came back around to face him looking discouraged.

"Well?" Winn asked.

"I think I did it wrong, I didn't hear anything." Alex admitted.

"That's the problem. I didn't hear anything either. A happy gut should make some noise, not a ton, but some. I think you identified a colic, Princess." His use of his nickname for her was not meant to sound mocking, but when he looked at her, Alex looked ready to cry.

"Hey, I'm sorry, I didn't mean to make you upset, I didn't mean it to be mean, was that mean?" he rambled, not wanting her to think he was picking a fight.

"Is he going to die?" Alex asked, a tear slipping down.

Understanding washed over Winn. "What? No. I mean I don't think so, no." His voice softened. "You caught it early, you did good, we can help him." Winn was still confused by the motive bringing her to the barn this early, but her fear for Winston was real. She looked up, eyes still wet but determination all over her face.

She took a bracing breath. "Okay, what do we do?"

"Take him out and see if he wants to graze. I'm going to pull an injection that should make him feel better."

Alex followed his instructions and she walked Winston out to the grass. Within minutes, Winn joined them carrying a large syringe and was encouraged to see that the horse had been interested in eating some grass.

"Pick his head up. This is going to help with his pain and once he gets this, he should start looking better in a few minutes," Winn directed.

Alex lifted up on the rope to bring the horse's head up. Winn pinched lightly on the bottom of Winston's neck. A rope-like vein bounced up, and he quickly inserted the needle, pulled back, got a flash of blood and injected the clear medication into the vein. After he pulled the needle, he applied pressure on the injection site for a moment.

"Okay, so now what?" Alex asked.

"Now we walk." Winn pointed toward the path and the three of them started down it. "We'll pit stop over at the pasture and see if we can get him to drink from the trough a bit."

They walked in silence. When they got there, the horse dropped his head and began to take a few large gulps, which was a relief. When Winston seemed to be done drinking, Alex looked to Winn.

"Now we walk more," he said and gestured up the fence line.

"Thank you for letting me help this morning and thank you for teaching me about how to do all this." She waved her hand toward Winston.

"I can tell Matt's been teaching you a lot."

Alex nodded, but the mention of Matt's name had brought some tension to the air.

"Do you want to tell me what happened yesterday?" she asked.

Winn sucked on his cheek. He wasn't sure how much he was willing to get into.

He turned to look at her for a hard second, "I know I do owe you some explanation for yesterday, but I'm not sure how much of an apology I owe you."

His double-sided answer appeared to stoke a quick flash of anger in her, but instead of jumping all over him for it she seemed to force herself to take a breath before gritting out, "That may be fair."

Wary of her capitulation, Winn went on, "Matt's got some health issues, mainly diabetes."

If this was news to Alex, she didn't let the surprise show on her face.

Winn continued, "I usually take him to his doctor's appointments, but yesterday he and I agreed that he could go on his own. Or technically, I guess I decided he could go on his own and he didn't argue. He missed the appointment because he was teaching you. I was pissed off, I let it get to me, and I said things to Matt I should never say. That's the bottom line. I did owe him an apology, and before you ask, yes, he got it."

Alex nodded along as she listened, and it became more apparent that she already knew Matt had diabetes. Winn wasn't surprised. It wasn't a secret or anything, and she spent a lot of time with him.

He watched her and was a bit caught off guard at the careful way she chose her next question without flying off the handle at him.

"Was there a reason this doctor's appointment was important enough that it justified you being that pissed at him?" Alex asked.

"I said I was pissed, not that I was pissed at him." He sighed and decided if they had come this far, he may as well get on with it. "I was pissed at myself. The doctor is getting more and more worried about Matt." That comment seemed to spark some surprise and concern in her expression. He continued, "I feel responsible about the fact that his diabetes doesn't seem to be as under control any more. The doctor being worried scares the shit out of me, and even though I knew I should go with him, I felt buried with work, felt like I couldn't find the time. I wanted to think it was fine, but deep down, I knew it wouldn't work for him to go without me. I tried to pass off this huge thing that I have no business passing off. It was a dick move to begin with and then when I saw him goofing around with you, not a care in the world, I was mad. I guess mad at him that he didn't care as much as me, that he's not afraid like me, that he's not drowning like me."

Winn scrubbed a hand over his face. Then he looked at the ground and braced his hands on his hips, embarrassed by how much had spilled out when the floodgate opened. It hadn't been his intention to spit out so much of his baggage. Winn wanted Alex to understand better, not to invite investigation of his own massive character flaws. He finally looked up at her face, expecting anger—or worse, pity. Instead, he saw understanding.

"That must have felt terrible coming together all at once. I've only known Matt for three weeks, and it kills me to think of him getting sicker or having complications. I can't even imagine how hard that would be for you, loving him as you do," Alex softly said.

Winn searched her face trying to sort out precisely what angle she may be working here. What else could explain a different version of Alex? He felt underqualified to interact with her on this level and fought against a pretty strong desire to bolt from the conversation. He forced his feet to stay planted.

Alex didn't seem to mind his lack of response, as she continued, "I don't agree with how yesterday went down. Seeing Matt hurt by you was seriously awful, but now I understand more about where you were coming from. So, thank you, I guess, for telling me." She paused. "Can I help?" she asked.

He tilted his head, trying to authenticate the sincerity she seemed desperate to impart.

"Help?" Winn finally asked. "Like with my asshole nature toward my brother?"

Now it was her turn for a head tilt. "Do you seriously think that yesterday boils down to your general asshole nature?"

"You don't?" Winn asked, surprised.

"Actually, no, I don't. I know that you're the first to tell me that I don't have a clue about your life and you're right, but it sounds full, overwhelming maybe. Can I help? With, I don't know, stuff, stuff on your plate. I can't train horses, but I can feed and clean stalls. I've been learning some medical stuff. Those wraps you pulled off Bucky this morning? I put those on. I could drive Matt to the doctor, or I could do paperwork or something so you can drive him. You know, help?"

Winn was confused by the sincerity in her tone. This much of a personality swap felt like a trap. He looked from her to Winston and ran his hand over his chin. He pictured Matt's face and felt as though he owed it to him to try harder to get along with Alexandra.

"Morning chores. If you helped with morning chores that would free up the early part of my day," Winn finally said.

She smiled at his obvious discomfort and decided to press her luck. "And Tommy?" she added, grinning.

"And Tommy," he conceded. "But we do that together. I can't give up on him, and if I let you do that without me, I worry he'll think I gave up on him."

"Ok then." Alex smiled then they both looked at Winston, who seemed to raise his tail and poop on cue.

"That's good, right?" she asked.

Winn nodded. "That's good. Let's bring him back, and I'll show you what the protocol for his care will include for the next few days."

As they made their way back to the barn, Winn watched the side of her face when he thought he could get away with it. He knew his initial judgment of her had been overly harsh, but this version of her was different than the annoyed girl who showed up that first day too. Noticing that about her made him feel uncomfortable, so he tried to push it from his mind.

Chapter 19

A week had passed since Winston's colic and Alex's Mae-inspired conversation with Winn. As he'd promised, he'd allowed her to do morning chores. It was a strange feeling that he would *let* her do his work, and somehow, it seemed like a favor to her. Regardless, Alex was truly enjoying the work and the time with the horses that didn't require her to sneak around behind Winn's back.

It was finally time for Emily and Tommy's visit to the ranch and Alex was excited to share this part of her current lifestyle with them. Alex heard the car and ran down the stairs with all the unabashed enthusiasm of a ten-year-old. She tore out of the front door as Emily was climbing out of the passenger side. They made eye contact, squealed loudly and met halfway in a huge hug.

"Oh…my… my crazed little dumpling," Emily said. "Look at this place. You didn't tell me you were living like Hemingway."

Alex laughed into her ear, feeling weightlessness she couldn't explain. Finally releasing Emily, Alex ran to Tommy, who wrenched her off her feet and swung her around.

"I'm so glad you guys are here," Alex breathed into his neck.

Alex didn't know if it said more about Emily and Tommy or the crew, but everyone welcomed them with open arms. The group had decided over lunch that a bonfire was necessary to kick off their official welcome. People gathered at the fire pit where beers were opened, music flowed, and the mood was high. Emily, true to form, plunked herself down next to Winn and tackled him with all of her bear-poking glory. Alex chuckled to herself. Her friend was going to provoke him to come to blows or they'd end up best friends. There was no middle ground with Emily, and the more Alex thought about it, there was a similar lack of middle ground with Winn. The potential for it to blow sky high made Alex reach for another beer.

Emily quickly began chatting Winn up, talking about her life in London and what she thought about Chicago. Eventually, Emily stopped tiptoeing around with safe issues, appearing ready to look around for a raw nerve. It was a common tactic Emily employed when she was trying to test the metal in someone.

"So, you a baseball fan, Winn?" Emily asked.

His eyes narrowed almost imperceptibly. "I am."

"Silly game," Emily said dismissively with a wave of her hand.

Alex bit her lip, furious at the gall Emily had to stir up something based on what Alex had told her in their conversations leading up to her visit.

"Some say that," Winn responded with a little tension in his tone. Alex could recognize his attempt to keep from being baited. "Others call it America's pastime," he added.

"Right, leave it to Americans to idolize a game like that. You all take a game with no strategy or technique, make it boring as hell then put it on a pedestal with apple pies and balding eagles."

"Bald eagles," he corrected. "And you're wrong about the lack of strategy. It *is* a thinking game." Winn's tone was still even, but Alex could tell his patience was running thin. Lord knows she'd been on the receiving end of his short fuse enough to recognize the warning signs.

"Ha!" Emily laughed dryly in his face. "Bullshite. People go to Wrigley all the time, they pay ten dollars for a beer and get sloshed, but you know what they don't do? They don't watch the Cubs. People love them because it's trendy to love the Cubs, not because the game is anything short of awful."

"Watching the Cubs may bore the hell out of you, but most people would kill for a chance to watch a game at Wrigley Field. Maybe you're not informed enough to watch for the nuance." Winn rocked forward slightly.

Emily got closer still. "Not informed? What nuance? You run from one square to the next? Sure, tough thing to wrap your head around."

Conversations around them that had started to die out had been entirely snuffed as Emily's voice rose.

"So, what do you propose we replace it with? Cricket or something?" Winn prodded.

"Real football is a better game than your silly baseball."

"Soccer?" he asked incredulously.

"You've got a problem with soccer?" Emily practically shouted as she leaned right up into his personal space.

"I guess I do now," Winn said through a clenched jaw.

There was silence from the group, as everyone held their breath. Emily stayed there, inches from his face and then, after a dramatic pause, she leaned in and planted a little kiss at the top of Winn's nose. She then proceeded to laugh her ass off. After taking a second to process, Winn surprised the hell out of everyone by bursting out laughing too.

"You scare me, little one," Winn chuckled.

"I'd be hurt if you weren't terrified right to the tip of those natural sun-kissed highlights of yours," Emily replied.

"She'd be afraid she was losing her touch as a Bond villain," Tommy chimed in while Winn stood, still chuckling.

"I've got to do the last night check. Excuse me." Winn partially nodded, touching the brim of his baseball hat. It irked Alex how polite and well behaved he was being. They all watched his back as he walked away.

Emily scooted over to Alex. "Riiiiigggght...so he's an ex-baseball star turned horse trainer, who looks like he's stepped off the cover of Cowboy GQ...and we hate it?"

"Wait. He'll drop this polite-for-company thing he's doing and then you'll see. He's judgmental and unyielding. He's rude and condescending and..." Alex stammered.

"Oh now I get it," Emily teased. "We *wished* we hated it. What's next? You tell me he's actually a rock star, that in his spare time, when he's not rescuing orphaned puppies from burning buildings, he's training with NASA to be shot into space to save the world?"

Matt leaned over and broke in. "He isn't an astronaut, but The Kid plays the hell out of a guitar."

Matt laughed when Alex rolled her eyes.

Emily's grin reached fiendish levels. "Of course he does," she said, sending a pointed look Alex's way. After keeping eye contact long enough to make her point, Emily ventured, "Do you play, Mattie?"

"I've been known to strum a chord or two," Matt replied sheepishly.

Alex noted that Winn wasn't the only one pouring on the country-bumpkin charm for Emily's sake.

Emily clapped, a gesture that completed the character that only Alex and Tommy could tell she was playing. "Oh then boy," she drawled in her best American accent, "won't you play us a little ditty?"

Matt's face lit up as he was already rising to fetch the instruments from the house. He came back holding a guitar in each hand. The other guys around the fire took notice and started moving closer.

"Sing-along!" Bishop hollered toward Winn who was coming back around the side of the barn. A brief look of confusion passed his face until he saw Mattie holding the guitars.

"Sing-along it is," Winn nodded with an almost imperceptible glance at Alex.

Winn took one of the guitars from Matt and sat down next to him, plucking a few strings and twisting to tune them.

"Ah, right then. What are we looking for?" Winn asked the group.

The group called out requests, and the mood was high as Winn and Matt played several songs that invited raucous choruses and arm-linked swaying verses. They had gone through everything from "American Pie," for which everyone tried desperately to remember all the words, to a surprisingly entertaining acoustic rendition of an Usher song.

The camaraderie seemed easy and comfortable. Alex should have known better than to think it would last. It was then that Junior's girlfriend, Maddie, rounded the corner. Alex hadn't even noticed when Maddie had left, but it appeared that she'd returned with another woman, someone Alex didn't recognize.

Junior looked up when he saw Maddie and the huge grin on his face dropped immediately when he saw the other person in tow. The new arrival was tall with golden-tan skin and extremely long, shiny brown hair that was curled and placed perfectly. Her eyes were heavily outlined with liner and smoky shadow. She looked primped enough to be walking into a club in downtown Chicago, and even though it was out of place at a middle-of-nowhere bonfire, it was seriously working for her. She was stunning. Alex hated her.

Emily leaned over to whisper in Alex's ear, "Okay, *that* one you can hate."

Alex had to grin slightly at Emily's equally snap judgment and nodded.

"Who is that?" Emily pressed.

"No idea," Alex murmured.

Judging by Junior's fallen face and the quick way he darted to Maddie's side, they were going to find out that her presence wasn't a good idea.

Junior turned and watched Winn, who was deep in conversation with Bishop and Tommy. Alex also watched Winn, who finally glanced up and did a double-take. His lips pressed together into a stern line and then his eyes quickly passed over to Alex, who couldn't help immediately looking away.

Alex was unsure of the circumstances, but she sensed the unease building in the group as more people took notice of the visitor. Everyone that noticed her immediately looked at Winn. There was no doubt everyone expected a reaction from him, which meant they were connected.

Junior leaned in toward Maddie, saying something under his breath. She shot him a pleading look and Alex could tell her response included an "I know, I'm sorry," followed by more than Alex could make out.

Next to Alex, Emily shot up and wiped dirt from her backside. Alex caught her breath, knowing Emily had picked up on the same vibe. Emily walked up to the new arrival and shoved her hand out. "Hello, I'm Emily, a visitor from out of town. And you are?"

The woman seemed a bit taken aback by Emily's tone, which told Alex that, contrary to the cool reception, she felt as though she had a right to be here. Her eyes narrowed slightly but she took Emily's hand.

"I'm Katherine, I'm a"—her eyes ventured over to Winn—"friend of the family."

"Ah," Emily responded, her eyes traveling to Winn. "Glad you could make it, even if, as it appears, your invitation was…unintended." Emily smiled sweetly despite the pointed words.

Alex stood and looked around. Everyone seemed a little dumbfounded and she felt the need to diffuse whatever Emily was trying to kick off.

"Hi, I'm Alex. I'm also visiting from out of town. It's nice to meet you. Can I get you something to drink?"

Katherine made a point to keep her eyes trained on Winn for a few more lingering seconds and then turned to Alex, making no attempt to hide her obvious scrutiny of her. "Yes, the girl from Chicago. I've heard about you," Katherine said with more than a hint of a sneer. She shook Alex's outstretched hand in a dainty, yet obnoxious way.

Alex raised her eyebrows. "I guess I'm at a disadvantage because I've never heard of you."

"I find that hard to believe."

"I imagine you do," Alex replied, refusing to break eye contact.

Katherine let a small chip fall off her façade before recovering.

"I'll take that drink now," Katherine said.

After a long pause, Alex weighed her options and decided that she needed to keep her irritation in check, but her initial intent to be hospitable was gone. She pointed at the cooler several feet away.

"Beer's in the cooler. Help yourself," Alex directed.

For an awkward moment, no one moved or said anything. Maddie stepped in and led Katherine over to the cooler then to some seats on the other side of the fire. Katherine nodded and said hello to several people on her way. Her greetings were met with a few subdued "Heys" and "How's it going?"

Alex watched her go and couldn't resist the urge to look over at Winn, who also watched Katherine warily. The fact that he watched Katherine annoyed Alex, but she tried to dismiss the uncomfortable feeling. Her eyes traveled to Matt. Alex gave him a questioning look that he answered with a slight shrug and a pinched smile.

Slowly conversations began to resume at a dampened level. Tommy, who had been chatting with Bishop, stood and came over to where Alex and Emily were still standing.

"Ok then girlies, good times." Tommy smiled at Alex and watched Emily for signs of aggression.

"I dislike that," Emily said through gritted teeth.

"Looks like you're not the only one," he answered and gestured to their seats. "I'm proud of you for not escalating that, babe," he said to Emily as they sat.

She made an angry, unintelligible noise in response. Tommy watched Alex and added, "We've been working on her anger management issues."

Alex couldn't help but laugh despite the twist in her belly. "And how's that going?"

"It's literally hit or miss." Tommy smiled and gave Emily a hug that she brushed off violently, which set off a sparkle in Tommy's eye. A bit of tension started working itself out of Alex's shoulders as she watched her friends.

"Who is that bitch?" Emily finally got out.

"According to Bishop, we're looking at an ex-girlfriend." Tommy slid a sideways look at Alex. "Winn's ex-girlfriend."

Both Tommy and Emily watched her for a reaction, so Alex simply said, "Well, obviously."

"How much do you want to know?" Tommy ventured.

Alex watched him and tried to look as impassive as possible. "Why would it matter to me?" she asked, keeping her tone light.

Emily rolled her eyes. "Right, doesn't matter to you. So, Tommy, what's the down-low? I'm always up for dirt on little snatches."

"You sure?" Tommy asked Alex, and she made an annoyed gesture with her hand in response. "Okay," he went on. "Bishop says that's Maddie's cousin. Winn and her were high-school sweethearts."

Emily gagged and Tommy spoke over her.

"Sounds like they were pretty serious, like potential wedding bells serious, up to around graduation, but then something happened that made them fight a lot. I guess they tried to gut it out for a few more years, but about a year ago Winn found out that Miss Perfect was a little less than. Rumor was, she cheated on him with some guy named Martin. It's all speculation, but people think she's still kind of dating that guy and people talk 'round these parts." Tommy looked proud of himself for throwing in Bishop's vernacular.

Alex let the air out of her lungs with a low and slow, "Ooohhh."

"What?" Emily ventured. "A guy named Martin? Seriously? Doesn't really sound like a guy who could give Cowboy Hottie McLevi a run for his money."

"His name is Blake, Blake Martin, and he's not a good guy. Guess this is another piece in the why-Winn-hates-Blake puzzle. Actually, maybe it's *the* piece in the puzzle."

Alex's eyes wandered over to Katherine. *What a bitch,* she thought.

Katherine had sat where she was sure to be in Winn's eye line, playing with her hair as she laughed and joked with those around her who had thawed enough to interact. Katherine was truly gorgeous and she made sure everyone knew it.

"What a bitch," Emily said.

Alex smiled at her friend for repeating what was in her head.

"Makes you want to guess at why she's here," Alex wondered aloud.

"Bishop thinks she wants to get back with Winn." Tommy and Emily again watched her for a reaction she refused to give.

The night carried on despite the mood-dampening arrival. Emily and Tommy made blatant attempts to pull Alex from her own headspace with animated stories and banter about how they had finally connected. Eventually, Alex began to relax.

For at least half an hour she refused to give in to the desire to throw periodic glances over her shoulder toward Winn and Katherine. When she finally peeked, they were both gone. Her stomach flipped before she could convince it not to.

"I've got to pee," she told Tommy and Emily as she stood despite not having a plan.

Are you sure you want to find them? she asked herself.

Even though her mind was doubtful, Alex's feet brought her toward the horse barn. When she heard voices, she knew she'd guessed right and had to admit to herself that she was not too big of a person to avoid eavesdropping. Alex slowly walked until she could see them through a stall window giving a silent prayer that the horse inside wouldn't give her away.

"I'm having a hard time understanding what you're doing here, Katherine." Winn's voice was calm and soft, which irrationally upset Alex, who had secretly hoped they would be engaged in a screaming match.

"Winn, it's been over a year now. I'm finished with feeling so excluded," Katherine replied.

"This is my family, Katherine, it's my life. You're not excluded. You're not a part of it any longer."

"These are my friends too, Winn, my family."

Winn jaw ticked. "No," he said simply.

Katherine watched him through her lashes.

"No," Winn repeated. "You didn't want this life, this family, these friends. You made that pretty clear. It's unfair for you to come back and think that people are going to forget that you discarded them."

"People? Or you?" Katherine asked softly.

"Both."

"Well, I miss *people*. Do *people* miss me?" Her voice was so low and quiet, almost a purr. They stared at each other for a long moment. Katherine took a deep breath when it became apparent he wasn't going to answer, her voice shifting from sultry to easygoing in a blink.

"You know, I have to admit, Winn, you're pretty calm. I was expecting you to go a little atomic."

"Yeah, me too a little. I guess you don't have the same effect on me that we both thought."

Katherine's spine stiffened at that. "I guess we'll see. I know Mae will be a tough one to crack, but Mattie? How hard could it be to bring him over to my cause?" There was stone in Katherine's easy words.

"Leave Matt out of this," Winn answered coolly.

"You know I think he always had a little thing for me anyway."

"Now you're being ridiculous."

"I'm serious, and lord knows I've always had a soft spot in my heart for that soft head of his," Katherine said flippantly.

"You're out of line." There was ice in Winn's voice.

"Oh trust me. I know the simpleton is off limits."

Winn flinched at her words and took a second to seemingly rein in his temper. Alex did the same, finding her fists in balls.

"One more word about Matt and you may get the reaction you're fishing for." His jaw was set, and the anger in his tone backed up his words.

Katherine eyed him, and she appeared to believe him. "And what about that Chicago girl? Is she one of your off-limit topics, Winn?"

"This isn't about her."

"I'm surprised. Cute as a button, little red head, may be a fun change for you. Out with the old, in with the adorably ginger new."

"It's none of your business."

Katherine leaned into him, circling her arms around his neck as he stood stiffly with his hands on his hips.

"But Winn, it is my business." She pressed her body to his. "If you've decided you want a fling with some innocent out-of-towner then maybe it is time for an intervention." Katherine brought her lips to the base of his jaw.

Winn closed his eyes, letting out a long breath while he brought his hands to her hips. Alex bit her lip, shocked at her guttural reaction to seeing them together in this way.

After what seemed like an eternity, Winn's hands pushed Katherine away. Holding her at arm's length, he stared into her eyes for a long moment.

"I don't need something else to know I don't want this." His hands dropped, and he turned to leave.

"It's just as well," Katherine said to his back. "Looks like your little redhead has caught Blake's attention anyway. I'm wondering if that makes your score zero and his two."

Winn turned slowly, his eyes glinting with anger. When he spoke, it was with that low, slow tone Alex had come to recognize as something to be feared. "Alexandra is not like you, Katherine. She's part of this family...*people* aren't going to tolerate Blake messing with her. You can run to him and tell him I've said that. If he wants to discuss it further, he knows where to find me. Now it's time for you to go. That paint you've caked all over your face is starting to crack."

Katherine's jaw dropped as his insult sunk in. She grabbed a brush from the bin on the wall and threw it at him. Winn didn't even flinch as it bounced harmlessly off the wall a few feet from him. Without acknowledging her tantrum, Winn turned and walked out the door.

"Bastard!" Katherine yelled at his back, before she headed down the opposite side of the aisle.

Alex also made a quick exit, running back to the house to use the bathroom before she returned to the campfire. On her way back, she met Tommy and Emily on the path. They looked cozy and on a mission.

"To bed, guys?" Alex asked in a light tone, not wanting to disrupt their evening with her own reaction to the drama she'd spied on.

"Indeed," Tommy said with a grin that earned him a lighthearted punch from Emily.

"Night," Alex called.

"Night," they echoed in unison.

Alex rounded the corner of the barn. Things were winding down, and the few remaining people were talking quietly while the fire was beginning to dwindle. She saw Winn sitting alone a few feet from everyone else. Feeling brave, she approached and sat down next to him. He didn't look up but continued to pluck out a quiet song. Alex turned her ear to Winn. Something was familiar about the flowing and sad melody he was mindlessly picking out.

"I think I know this song," she said.

He looked up at her, tilting his head. "I wouldn't think so, it's kind of...obscure, I guess." He looked back down at his picking hand and continued.

"No, I'm certain actually. It's missing the heartbreaking violin part. I love this song."

Winn's brows crimped, but he kept playing. "Yeah?"

"Yes. There's something about it, something that gets to me. I don't know why. It's... what?" she asked herself. After a pause she continued, "Haunting, I guess. Every time I hear it I feel like I want to cry, and I think that's my favorite thing about it."

Winn watched her for a long time then finally nodded. "It makes me feel...small," he said, all the while his hands moving effortlessly over the guitar.

The notes were crisp and solitary in the quiet night, sounding lonely as one at a time they were dragged away on the breeze. Alex smiled sadly to herself. She knew exactly what he meant. They both listened to the emotional melody for a little longer and Alex tentatively set in to sing with his playing. Winn joined in softly for parts of the chorus. It was a song about loss and feeling the absence of another, the touching tale made impactful by the desolateness of a single guitar.

They both stopped and the guitar carried on alone through the rest of the song. When it ended, Alex stared at her feet.

"I guess it's supposed to be haunting." She tried to fight the tightness in her throat. Alex looked up to meet Winn's gaze.

"Been a long time since I heard that song in a women's voice. Kind of drives home the delicateness of it, makes it feel more—fragile," Winn said. After shifting uncomfortably, he added, "You sing pretty well."

Taken aback by the compliment, Alex bit her lower lip. "Thanks. I had no idea you were such an accomplished player. I guess I'll chalk that up as one more surprising thing about you."

"You do seem genuinely surprised when I can do anything," he said.

Alex looked up, expecting to see a hint of teasing in his eyes, but his face was sober, and he looked tired. She tried to remember when she may have given him that impression.

"I'm sorry if I do. It's not my intent to hurt your feelings."

"Let's not take it that far. I'm making an observation."

Alex opened her mouth and then when she didn't have a clue what should come out of it, she shut it again. Thankfully, as the silence was starting to goad her into reaching for empty words, Bishop walked over and pulled up a stump to sit down by them.

"You all sing a pretty nice duet," Bishop said.

Both Alex and Winn made the requisite dismissive noises one makes when receiving unexpected praise.

"Really sounded good together." Bishop was piling it on now.

Alex watched Winn eye Bishop.

"All right, I'll bite," Winn said. "Why do I feel like you're trying to break the ice on something here?"

"Well, Kid, you've got me...I've, well I've got a bit of a secret." Bishop leaned conspiratorially forward and motioned for both them to do the same.

Winn glanced around at the handful of remaining stragglers laying around the fire, none of whom were conscious enough to eavesdrop. He cocked an eyebrow at Bishop.

"Humor me, Kid, it's a huge secret."

"Oh, a huge secret? Well hell, should we work out a code?" Winn teased.

Alex couldn't help one side of her mouth from pulling up.

"Actually, smart ass, now that you mention it, let's go to the barn." Bishop stood and turned to throw an expectant glance at Alex and Winn. Both had their curiosity piqued enough to follow.

Once inside the barn, Bishop whipped around with a big grin on his face and in a stage whisper announced, "I'm going to ask Belle to marry me."

Alex's jaw dropped, and after blinking twice she managed to get out, "Oh my god. Bishop, that's so exciting."

Winn walked over and shook his hand in a polite manly sort of way then picked him up off the ground in a big bear hug. "Man, that's great news."

When his feet were back on the ground, he turned to Alex who wrapped him up in a hug. "Congratulations."

"Well no congratulations yet, she's still gotta say yes, and that's where you two come in."

"I'm not going to bully a chick into marrying you, Bishop," Winn said with a laugh.

"Ha-ha," Bishop answered dryly. "Here's my problem, see I've been wracking my brain on a super romantic way to ask her. You know, to get to a real fancy restaurant you've gotta drive all the way to Great Falls." For Alex's benefit he added, "That's about a three-hour round trip."

"So if you pack her along for a road trip like that, she'll know something is up," Winn noted.

Bishop nodded. "Yeah, she'll be on to me hours before we even get to sit down to a meal. Plus, the suspense might kill me. I'd end up asking on the side of the interstate, and she'd probably never forgive me. So, I'm thinking about setting up a little romantic dinner here, candles and shit, you know? Then you two can serenade us right before I pop the question...like mood music." His face was expectant and thrilled. There would be no telling him no.

"I'm in," Alex said and then they both looked to Winn cautiously.

"What am I? The damn anti-Cupid? Of course, I'm in," Winn announced.

Alex couldn't help herself, and she let out a little giggle. "I want in on helping plan everything."

"Oh, thank god." Bishop breathed. "Honestly, after the candles part, I was out of ideas."

"Trust me, 'candles and shit' are a start, but this one, this one we can do up even better than that." Alex gave him a reassuring smile.

"You have a song in mind?" Winn asked.

Bishop watched his foot as he dragged a toe across the ground. "It's a bit on the sappy side, but our first date we slow danced to that Randy Travis song 'Forever and Ever.'" He looked up at Winn, with a look like he expected to be mocked.

"Great song, and I know it," Winn said lightly, maybe trying to combat the worry in Bishop's face.

"When?" Alex asked excitedly.

"Soon. It's gotta be soon. The ring is burning a hole in my brain. It's all I can think about. Get it over with quick, like pulling off a Band-Aid," Bishop said.

"Nice, but let's leave that analogy out of your speech." Alex laughed.

"Speech?" Bishop's face fell.

"Well yeah, Bishop, you've gotta say something nice to her before you ask. Even I know that." Winn put a hand on Bishop's shoulder.

"I'm already hatching a plan," Alex said and rubbed her palms together to illustrate.

"Great, you make a plan and fill me in on what the hell I'm supposed to do." Bishop laughed joyfully.

Chapter 20

The next day Alex found Winn in the horse barn where they completed a handful of late-morning chores quickly and efficiently. It seemed to be getting easier for them to share space and duties.

"Where are your friends?" Winn asked.

"Oh we spent the morning playing on the equipment with Trix, and now they're tired, so they were going to take a walk and a nap. Pretty sure it's code for something I don't want to think about my two best friends engaging in. I thought we could go pay horse-Tommy a visit while Emily and person-Tommy are otherwise occupied. Maybe we can talk about the Bishop plan."

"Yeah, now works I guess." Winn put his hands in his pockets and started toward the woods. Alex followed, unconsciously matching her strides to his.

"Does it bother you?" Winn ventured.

"What?"

"English and Tattoos being a couple."

"Tattoos? Is that what we're calling him?" Alex laughed.

"Oh because 'person-Tommy' is so much better?"

"Point taken," she conceded.

"Are you avoiding the question?" he pressed.

"No, and no it doesn't bother me, you know, aside from a little bit of the ick factor."

"Ick factor, huh? Not because you and Tommy…?"

She watched the side of his face as he seemed to be refusing to look at her, his eyes glued to the path ahead. "God, no. Tommy's amazing, but it's not like that with us, and honestly, I don't have any right to call it ick. Tommy has been in love with Emily for years, and she could use a really nice guy. Tommy's a nice guy."

"He seems all right, I suppose. Not really what a typical nice guy looks like though," Winn said.

"Oh?" She bristled on Tommy's behalf. "What does a 'nice guy' look like?"

"Calm down, Princess, no one's insulting your hipster." Winn finally looked to her and put his palms up.

"Okay, one, don't let him hear you call him a hipster, and two, seriously what does a nice guy look like?" Alex motioned toward him with a questioning glance, pointing up and down his body. "Like this?"

"What, me? Absolutely not. No. No, I think nice guy, I think glasses, sweaters over polo shirts, I don't know…khakis?"

Alex snorted. "Perfectly parted hair."

Winn grinned. "Drives a Volvo."

"Has a cat named Mr. Darcy."

"Spends entire weekends at IKEA."

"Makes a hell of a banana daiquiri."

"Plays in a cutthroat game of bridge every Thursday."

"Knits sweaters for homeless cats."

Winn seemed to be at a loss. Alex felt like she'd won their little game then he said, "Avid scrapbooker."

Alex laughed and so did he when she put her hands up in surrender. "I guess you know more about nice guys than me."

He made a little bow of thanks and they continued down the path.

"Our nice guy doesn't sound like much fun," Alex said.

"Glad I'm not a nice guy."

"Me too," she replied without thinking.

Her statement seemed to hang in the air between them, neither willing to acknowledge it. They got to the little barn and climbed into the paddock.

Winn started to sit, and Alex stopped him. "I think you should stand today and let's see what happens."

He shrugged his shoulders. Both of them seemed surprised at how willing he was to give her the reins. Alex walked to the opening of the stall and started talking to Tommy. His head appeared, and he immediately fixed his gaze on Winn.

"All right now, Tommy, lord knows if you were human, you would never be a nice guy, you adorable bad boy, you. Come say hello to Winn so we can all relax, yeah?" She turned and walked away from him. Tommy followed very cautiously.

To keep the constant stream of words that the horse found comforting going, Alex finally decided it was time to put one of her nagging questions to bed. "Are you ready to tell me the story of how you ended up with this bad boy?"

Alex turned to watch Winn's expression and was surprised to receive almost no reaction.

"It's not that juicy of a story, Alex," Winn admitted.

She sighed at his deadpan face. "Humor me."

Winn let out a long sigh but relented, "I was at an auction. I saw Bake getting aggressive with this one, most likely because Blake's training technique doesn't work too well with horses like Tommy. Well, I guess horses in general, but it for sure doesn't work on the timid ones. I got upset, told Blake I'd be willing to take this one off his hands. He set a ridiculous price to spite me, knowing damn well that I didn't have four thousand dollars to give him." He paused when Alex's face got hard, but she waved him on. "So I traded the only thing I had of any real value—my bike. Probably wasn't worth more than two or three grand anyways."

"You traded a bike for Tommy?"

"A motorcycle," Winn clarified.

Alex nodded and bit her tongue a little to avoid letting it show on her face how endearing she found it, knowing he wouldn't appreciate her feeling sentimental about his actions.

"That was *nice* of you." She chuckled when he rolled his eyes. "Can I ask a follow-up?"

"Taking advantage of my immobility here, Alexandra," he said, gesturing to the slowly shortening gap between himself and her and Tommy.

Alex shrugged unapologetically. "I'll take what I can get."

"Fine, fire away," Winn said.

"What's Blake's beef with you?" At his narrowed eyes, she felt the need to explain further. "I get why *you* hate him, he's an awful human being, but it feels like he singles you out for his wrath. Why?"

"A handful of reasons I'm sure." Winn watched her, maybe wondering how much he could get away with not saying. Alex put on a firm face, hoping it would convey she would not tolerate glossed-over details.

Winn appeared to relent. "I'm guessing you've gotten our whole family history from Matt? The stuff about our dad, Matt's mom, my mom?"

Alex nodded, feeling guilty like she'd plucked it unwillingly from Matt, even though that hadn't been the case.

"So, when my mom bounced out of here, she made a pit stop over at the Martins', may have stirred up some trouble in that marriage before leaving town for good," Winn said with a strange matter-of-fact tone.

"So it's your fault your mother left when you were an infant and broke up someone else's marriage?" Alex asked, her face scrunching up.

"When you put it like that, it sounds too simple, but I guess yeah, that's the gist of it. Blake's folks are still together, not happily I would assume, but they're still together. When we were younger, Blake used to lash out at classmates, me, the world, whatever. He was an angry kid and I was one of the few who never backed down when he got like that. I guess he didn't appreciate it."

"I would suspect not. Seems ridiculous to start a feud over something you had no control over. Blake's father is the scumbag who cheated on his mom when she had a newborn," Alex said.

"Maybe scumbag is learnt behavior," Winn replied. There was a finality to the way he spoke that sounded like he was unwilling to delve any further into his history with Blake. Katherine's face flashed in Alex's mind. It wasn't that tough to understand why Winn wouldn't venture down that path with Alex. She decided to leave well enough alone.

"Yeah, probably." Reaching for something else to say for Tommy's sake, Alex tossed out a lifeline in the form of an abrupt change of subject. "So, Bishop and Belle, huh?"

Winn kept his voice quiet, his eyes trained beyond the cautious horse edging closer. "Yeah, she's a great girl. I'm honestly happy for them. You have any idea yet on how you're going to set up the proposal?"

"I think that we'll put out a table off the back porch, some white Christmas lights in the trees, candles, roses, nice wine, nice meal."

"Sounds like what he's picturing. How can I help?"

She turned, raising her eyebrows at him. "You want to help?"

"I may not be a 'nice guy,' Alexandra, doesn't mean I'm a bastard who's unwilling to help one of my best friends land the woman of his dreams."

"Understood. Okay, yes, you can help. I'm working out now how to get Belle dressed up without tipping her off. But for you, you can work on getting Bishop into a tux."

"Why would he need a tux?" Winn said louder than he intended, and Tommy stopped in his tracks. Alex shot him a nasty look.

"Yes, a tux, and watch your freaking mouth here," Alex said in a syrupy-sweet tone that placated Tommy.

"I'm having a hard time understanding what the point of that would be," Winn replied, matching the sugary level of her tone through gnashed teeth.

"Well, think about how floored you are by the idea of Bishop in a tux. Now imagine how surprised Belle would be. We're going for wow factor here, aren't we?"

"Well, that'll certainly floor everyone," Winn conceded.

"That's the plan." Alex smiled. Tommy was now only a foot away from a standing Winn.

"Okay, I'll give you that it will have wow factor, but I'm not sure I can pull it off. What else?"

"I'm working on the details, but I will let you know when it's time to call in for reinforcements. A few more of the guys are going to have to help on the day."

"That won't be a problem."

"We should practice the song," Alex ventured.

"Yeah, I have it somewhere. Maybe even on a CD I can give you so you can learn it."

"I know it already. I may even have it on my phone," she replied.

Winn cocked his head at her. "You know that song?"

"I know it doesn't fit your image of me, but I know a lot of country songs…mostly because of my dad." Alex mindlessly ran her fingers through Tommy's mane. He dropped his head and pressed it gently into her chest, a simple gesture of support.

"Oh," Winn said dumbly and then took a small step toward her and the horse.

"Of course, I don't know most of the new stuff, the stuff that's on every radio on the property. I kind of fell out of the country music scene for a few years." Alex watched Winn get closer, and Tommy tensed but stood his ground, leaning his head more into her chest, almost unwilling to walk away from her.

"You don't like newer music? The contemporary stuff is good too, a little more rock and fewer spoons and jug blowing," Winn said, now standing right next to her and Tommy.

"I guess I listened to it because my dad listened to it and it was something we had, for us. We used to go driving whenever he was having a particularly brutal fight with my mother. He'd say there was a country song for everything. You could laugh along when you were feeling high, scream when you were pissed, and cry along when you needed. It was country or…" Alex swallowed and then added wistfully, "or Springsteen. That was all that was allowed."

"There's truth to that," Winn said, his eyes soft but trained on her face. When she didn't respond, he asked, "Did you do that a lot? Go driving to laugh, scream, and cry with your father?"

"Yeah." Alex couldn't prevent some of her sadness from showing on her face. Tommy pressed harder into her, and she swayed before catching herself. "Yeah, I suppose we did. Before he died, our family was kind of like two teams, you know? It was my brother and mother on one, me and my father on the other. Things usually broke along party lines with us. When things got really bad, he would take me with him when he stormed out. Looking back on it, we did that more than should have been necessary in a happy, well-adjusted family."

If Winn was surprised to learn that her father had passed away, he didn't let it show. "Happy and well-adjusted are myths," he murmured.

"Maybe," Alex said and then after a few moments of silence, "I used to think that way, but recently I'm wondering if maybe happy is possible."

"What changed your mind?"

"Here," she said simply without thinking.

It was then that her eyes met his. Alex sensed his unease and felt foolish for her detour into personal drama. Getting into the inner workings of her family was unnerving regardless of who it was with, but it felt rawer getting into it with Winn. Unsure why she'd even shared what she had, Alex needed to change up the conversation. She needed to distance herself from the memories kicking their way to the surface. She reached her hand out and held it in the space between them.

"Give me your hand," she told Winn.

Even though he looked surprised by her request, he complied. Alex took Winn's hand in hers and brought it up to Tommy's neck, pressing her hand over the top of his. The horse flinched briefly but didn't move. Alex looked up to find Winn watching her instead of the horse.

Without breaking eye contact with Winn, Alex said, "Tommy, this is Winn. He's going to fix you."

"Thank you for the introduction," Winn said quietly, keeping his intense eyes locked on her.

Alex smiled shyly, suddenly very aware of his nearness and the warmth of his hand under hers. Embarrassed by her reaction, she looked down and pulled her hand from his. Leaving one hand on Tommy, Winn reached out with the other hand and cupped her chin to bring her gaze back to his own.

"Seriously, Alexandra. Thank you."

In the shade, Winn's eyes were almost the color of dark copper, and in them was an emotion Alex struggled to identify. The callouses on his hand felt rough on her face but were strangely comforting, and she had to resist the urge to turn her cheek into his palm.

"You're welcome," Alex murmured, closing her eyes for a long second. There was an uncomfortable twist in her gut and in an instant, her mind began to race.

You need to get out of here.

Alex opened her eyes and plastered on a cracked, shallow smile before pulling away from his touch. Winn's hand dropped to his side.

"Now that you guys have met I think I'll leave you to get acquainted. It's rude to leave Emily and Tommy up to their own devices for too long—and probably a little dangerous," Alex stammered.

"Right," Winn said simply, confusion in his expression.

"Right," Alex repeated. She slowly backed away from them, gauging Tommy's reaction to her retreat. He was wary but seemed prepared to stay where he stood. Winn appeared the same.

"Okay," Winn said, brows still crimped.

"See you later, we'll run through the song," Alex said, trying to interject an airy, carefree note.

"Okay," Winn said again.

Alex reached the fence and climbed through, willing herself not to run once her back was to them.

Chapter 21

Alex needed to catch her breath. Opening up about her family and her father was a rare occurrence for her and doing it in front of Winn made it feel even more exposed. That part of her family life was something she fiercely guarded, not something she put on display in front of someone who already made her feel off balance.

Alex needed space, desperately wanting to distance herself from the memories that were bubbling up to the surface. Regardless of where she tried to force her thoughts, there was an unrelenting pull to revisit old pain. Even as she fought against it, her mind began to replay the last time she'd seen her father. Two months before his death, Alex had visited the shabby studio apartment where her father had secluded himself from the world after her mother had kicked him out of their family home because he was unable to control his addiction.

***

He looked old. God, he looked so much older than he should, than he was. Alex would never forgive him for what he'd done to himself. The previous two years had aged his face ten. His dull, vacant eyes broadcasted his sleepless lifestyle and the self-hatred that drove it. She despised him for taking those years away from her. She could vaguely remember the man she'd idolized, but this man had stolen him from her. She wasn't looking at her father. She was looking at his killer.

He sat across from her, his lit cigarette sending a listless curl of smoke climbing into the unmoving air. She watched its lazy path curl to the ceiling, which now permanently bore the yellowed scar. Clearly, he sat here often, and she wondered how many hours a night he hunched over this table lighting one after another.

The lines in his face were deep, cracking the corners of his eyes, drawing harsh creases down toward his mouth. The broken capillaries on and around his nose were the only color keeping his face from being entirely washed out, and the pallor of his skin was so corpse-like it made her stomach turn.

The heft of his brow cast a shadow halfway down his face, which he peered out from while he slumped forward. As he leaned, the bones of his shoulders pushed awkwardly against the seams of his graying t-shirt, making him appear even more frail and underweight.

He looked sick, chemo sick. He *was* sick, she reminded herself, except he wasn't plagued by cancer or a virus: he was plagued by having to live inside his own mind and the war he waged against it. His only weapons were booze, smokes, and pills.

Alex had been a casualty in that war. Her life was different now. Changed, not snatched away quickly, but slowly tugged and destroyed one agonizing inch at a time. She'd fought at the last minute, screaming and clawing, trying to keep her hold on the future he'd promised, but she couldn't do it alone, and by then he was already gone.

Her father blinked hard, pupils dilating and constricting too slowly. Strangely this was what brought her back to this garage-sale table in this pathetic kitchen of his rented studio apartment.

The need to act was so overwhelming that remaining seated at the table became excruciating. She stood, waiting for him to speak, needing him to say something, the right thing, the wrong thing, anything. Her chest felt so full she needed to scream, to empty every last molecule of air from her body. She clenched her jaw, feeling her teeth pop against one another, as if sheer willpower could keep the force of her rage buried and silent. Slowly she clenched and unclenched her fists, feeling her nails bite into her palms and then retreat. She focused on the minute pain each finger caused.

Finally, her father spoke, low and slow. "You and me, we were the pretenders." Quoting Springsteen like she was ten again.

All the air involuntarily gushed from her lungs, not a scream, but a burst of silent stunned breath. Not knowing what to do, what to say, Alex betrayed her feelings by crying. Her father remained silent, eyes never really focusing. Pulling her gaze from him, she turned her back, staring hard at the door through her tears.

Leave, leave, don't look back, today is the day. The last day. This apartment, this table, this stained ceiling, erase it from your mind, walk away and keep walking until the smell of stale, desperate air is out of your lungs and off of your clothes. Walk until it doesn't feel like mourning, until the grief softens and lets you breathe, until the wasted years feel less expensive.

Finally, before hitting the door, Alex replied, "No, Daddy. It was me. *I* was the pretender."

At the time, she felt like that was all that was left to say. She was wrong. She'd had plenty to say to the lid of his closed casket. So many things that she should have said sooner.

***

Alex bounced back to her current reality. Remembering that day was like remembering a hole in your chest, deep and festering, even though you managed to deny its existence. The memory made her feel bare and uncovered. She needed to get a handle on it before she saw anyone, or this crack in her façade would be exposed.

Alex retreated to the house, praying she could make it to her room unseen. As she made it to the top floor and staggered into her room, she exhaled, feeling like she was nearer to getting her emotions back in check.

There was a soft knock, and she spun around to see Winn leaning against the open doorframe. He looked confused and uncomfortable, but something in the way she must have looked had his expression shifting to concern.

He furrowed his eyebrows. "Hey, I, uh, was coming to see if you wanted to run through the song tonight after dinner. You kind of made a quick exit back there and…"

"Oh, yeah, sorry, I, um, needed to…" Alex trailed off and waved her hand at her phone on the desk, hoping the vague gesture made some sort of sense.

"You're all right then?" he asked.

"Oh yeah, yeah, of course." She swallowed the strange guilt she felt for lying.

"You sure? You seem a little, I don't know—"

"I said I'm fine." She cut him off more tersely than she'd intended.

Winn watched her for a second through narrowed eyes and sucked the inside of his cheek. Finally, he put his hands up in surrender and shook his head. "Fine," he said and then turned and walked away.

At dinner, Winn seemed to be making a point to ignore her. They both spoke to the people around them, and when she allowed her gaze to travel over to his side of the table, he never once looked her way. The rebuke felt personal and left her feeling even more confused.

Is he punishing me for being short with him this afternoon? Is this how things are going to be between us, a slight thaw and then another cold front?

Alex decided she needed to come to terms with the fact that she was being affected by Winn and it wasn't the same for him. Her cheeks flushed at the embarrassment of what was beginning to feel like a one-sided school-girl crush. At best, he was starting to tolerate her. She was the one touched, and then flustered, by their interaction earlier at Tommy's pen. She was the one that had verbally puked up a bunch of unsolicited information about her family, and then she'd been the one to overreact to his brief and innocent moment of sincerity.

Alex reminded herself that not even two weeks ago he'd written her off when talking to Blake. Alex was the one that he'd chosen to throw his wrath at when his mercurial moods swung the other way. Her resentment toward him began to grow, fueled by her shame for allowing herself to feel something for him, something he didn't feel in return.

Bishop cornered her and then to her dismay motioned for Winn to join them.

"So?" Bishop asked, brows raised, pointing from Alex to Winn and back.

"What?" Winn asked defensively.

"What, he says. The song, you dipshit. How's the song?" Bishop made an annoyed hand gesture.

"Oh." Alex recovered first, and seeing Bishop's strained look, she opted to lie. "It's coming along, honey, and we've got to put the finishing touches on it."

"Yup, it's gonna be fine, Bish, no worries," Winn chimed in, giving Alex an extended hard look.

Bishop narrowed his eyes. "What's going on with you two? You've got my back on this one or not?"

"No nothing, of course we've got it. We're going to go over it tonight right after dinner. Like I said, no worries." Winn comforted him.

"Fine, well it's after dinner now, isn't it?" Bishop asked and continued to watch them.

Alex pinched her lips together. Despite her darkening mood, his worried mother-hen routine was amusing. "Yes, it is. You're right. We're going right now. You can relax, things are going to work out beautifully."

Bishop nodded curtly and stormed off.

Winn faced her and with a slightly aggressive tone said, "I'll meet you in the barn in twenty minutes." It wasn't a question, and he walked away without waiting for her confirmation.

Alex found herself staring daggers at his back. Between thinking herself into a froth over dinner and his current behavior, her anger and frustration were back to a boil.

Emily appeared in her line of sight, breaking up the hate-fest she was throwing in Winn's direction.

"Can I talk to you for a second?" Emily asked, no humor in her tone.

Alex resisted the urge to roll her eyes. She wasn't in the mood but nodded toward the corner of the dining room.

"What's up? I've got to run really quick and work through something, should only take a few minutes." She tried for easygoing, but Emily was smarter.

"Okay, so I leave in like twelve hours, so I need to get this off my chest before I go." Emily looked for a reaction from Alex but continued when she didn't get one. "I know I don't know everything about what's going on here, but I would be remiss as a best friend if I didn't tell you it may be time for you to pull your head out of your ass."

Alex let the shock show on her face. "Well you're right about one thing, Em. You don't know what's going on here."

Emily's expression was grim but determined. "Here? This place? It is a good thing. You refusing to see that is bad for you. Like whatever was going on in that dining room tonight? I have no idea what's about but picking a fight with Winn every few minutes has got to be getting old. He's a decent bloke, and you need to either get on it or back off. Throwing dirt like a kid with a crush on the playground is beneath you."

"Okay. You've proven your point, Emily."

"I don't think I have. What I'm trying to say is, I know you're planning on coming home in a month or so, and maybe…maybe you should stay longer." Emily dropped her eyes as Alex let her hurt out on a whoosh of stunned air.

"You…what? Don't you miss me?" Alex said, not hiding the pain in her voice.

"Of course I miss you. I miss you terribly every day. But honestly, I missed you before you left the city. This version of you is, I don't know, calm. Settled. It fits. This place fits."

"Not everyone is how you're seeing them, Emily. You can't even give me the benefit of the doubt on that?"

"Right, you have trouble with one pouty guy who's in the middle of having a freak-out about his life. How in the hell could you possibly be expected to relate to that?"

"Your logic is that he's wounded and I'm broken, so we should get along swimmingly?"

"God, you're so dramatic when you're self-pitying. I'm saying, I haven't seen you give a shit about anything in a long time and there are things here you genuinely care about. Horse-Tommy, Matt, Mae." She brought her eyes to Winn and Alex followed her stare. "Maybe that's worth some more time to explore."

"Well to that I'd say if you've had these deep concerns about my life for so long maybe you should have piped up sooner."

"Agreed," Emily said sadly. When Alex didn't say anything else, Emily turned to walk away, leaving Alex to watch her back and wonder how in the hell she'd ended up in the same place with Emily all over again.

Still reeling from their talk, Alex made her way to the barn where Winn's guitar and sour face were waiting for her.

What in the hell does everyone want from me and why the hell does he get to look at me like that? I'm the one who rode the emotional rollercoaster of past family bullshit today and all I did was refuse to let him pity me in the process.

"Okay, look," Alex started. "Today I didn't want to fight. I'm not trying to fight. This is for Bishop and so whatever is making you feel like I've pissed in your Cheerios let's table it for a different fight, a different day."

Winn's eyes narrowed in the calculating way she was getting used to. He opened his mouth, closed it, nodded and started playing the song.

"Okay then," he finally said. "How about you sing the song, and I'll join in on the parts where it makes the most sense for there to be a harmony, then we clean it up from there?"

Alex's first instinct was to argue, but even she could recognize the petulance in that, so she nodded and waited for the timing to come around to begin the first verse.

They made it through the song once, and she had to admit that he had a great feel for when the two should sing together. After the first run-through, she made a few points about when she thought his voice alone would be better, the parts that made more sense for a man to be saying them. He agreed, and they started again. After getting through the second time with the changes, it was beginning to feel like a cordial collaboration.

As if he heard her thought, Winn said, "Seems like despite our best efforts at playing enemies, we may make a good team on this."

"Now's not a great time to dissect why we don't get along. I know you're counting down the days until I leave, so can we get through the song please?" Alex said, her face taut.

That seemed to catch him off guard. "Where did that come from?" he asked stiffly.

"I heard you talking to Blake about me. You told that asshole he could have me and it wouldn't make a difference to you one way or the other."

"What in the hell? When did this supposedly happen?" He seemed to be scrambling to keep up with the abrupt turn in the conversation.

"When he picked up Frank's horses."

His face fell. "How in the—?"

"Who cares? Stay on task here, farm boy." Alex squared her shoulders.

"Why is this coming up now?" His eyes searched hers.

She held his gaze for a few seconds before brushing him off. "Forget it. Play the song one more time."

He shook his head and set the guitar down on the hay next to him. "Seriously, I don't get why this is coming up now. I honestly don't, but if you want to throw out another accusation I guess we can do this now. You have no idea how ugly things would be if Blake thought I had something he wanted."

"You make it sound like I'm some new G.I. Joe or something, and worse than that, you make me sound like a liability."

"Well, what else would you call it?"

"Nice, Winn, really nice." Alex let sarcasm mask the hurt his words caused.

"Get this straight, seriously, because at the end of the day if Blake thinks he can get to me by hurting you, that's not good for anyone. It's better for you to be off his radar. He needs to know that you're not some weapon he can use against me."

"Oh, I think we all *know* I couldn't be used as a weapon against you. We all *know* exactly how you feel. We should invite him for dinner—all he'd need is to spend five minutes with us to hear the tone dripping with disdain when you cease ignoring me long enough to talk at me."

"You're way off base here, Princess, and now you're pitching a fit because your ego took a hit." He stood now, his growing agitation showing.

"This isn't about my ego, Winn. This is about me insisting that you treating me this way isn't okay."

"This way? What way? What does that even mean? There's no right answer with you, is there?"

"There is a right answer. Is it so impossible for you to believe we could be friends? I'm such a terrible person that you don't care when that freaking sleazebag corners me in a store and presses his disgusting body against me? The very next day you tell that same man that it's open season on the city girl you don't know from Adam?" Alex's lip quivered, and she forced herself to breathe and get ahold of her emotional freight train.

Winn ran an exasperated hand through his hair. "Christ, Alexandra, what do you want me to say? That when Charlie called, I was livid? That I was so out of my head that I got in a damn truck and had to be talked off a ledge by Matt because beating on Martin would cause irreparable harm to this ranch and my training career? Is that what you want to hear? That it took every fiber of my being not to rip the bastard's arms off when he showed up here the next day? 'Cause that's the truth." He exhaled in resignation. "That's what happened."

Alex was so floored by his admission that she opened her mouth then slammed it shut again. Speechless, she stood there and watched him start to pace.

"Then there's you, you come back from the store, blowing it off, all nonchalant like you could care less that Martin tried to come onto you again." Winn swallowed hard before continuing. "You're calm and collected like you're fine. Then I'm the fool, right? Because I care, and you don't. Then to top it off, you're mad at us for even having the audacity to ask after you."

Trying to keep up with his confession, Alex tried to find words to explain. "It wasn't like that. When he finally walked away I was, I don't know, shaken. When I got home, and you all had already heard about it…I was…embarrassed. I was embarrassed that I let him get to me, that I let him scare me. You guys being there, it was too much."

"That day, and earlier today, it's the same. You don't get to pick and choose when people care about you, Alexandra. You can't push people away and then get pissed off when they follow your lead."

"I felt foolish," she admitted.

"That's not a good enough excuse." Winn shook his head.

"So what now? I reacted badly so we can't be friends? I'm an offering to Martin now because I didn't lean on you after?"

Winn took in a long breath and looked over her head. "You don't listen."

"I'm trying to listen," she insisted.

His gaze came back to her, and he watched her intently for a few tense moments. Alex could sense he was wrestling with something, trying to work out what to say.

Finally, Winn said, "Forget it. I've got to go."

"Seriously?" she asked.

"Seriously. Work on getting this through your head: I do care if Martin takes an interest in you. It would be bad for you, bad for this ranch, and bad for me. So now you know."

Winn turned and left her standing with a gaping mouth staring at the doorway long after he'd left it.

Emily and Tommy left the next morning. The mood between Emily and Alex was tense but strangely didn't feel irreparable. Emily's words echoed in her mind. She'd been right about one thing—Alex was calm here, relaxed. But Alex needed to find a way to make that her state at home, not when she was on vacation from her life. She felt confident that when she returned to Chicago, she would be able to show Emily she'd taken her advice and changed without needing to stay in Montana longer than necessary.

Alex spent the next few days throwing herself into the preparations for Bishop's proposal. She felt as though she owed them, and this place, her best effort on making someone's happily ever after coming true.

Chapter 22

Finally time had come for the big proposal day. Hours of work had gone into Alex's master plan and she'd spent the day cracking the whip over all the guys until everything was set and perfect. She'd rush-ordered five dresses online, four of which she knew wouldn't come close to fitting her. Working with Maddie, they convinced Belle to come over for a girls' night. Alex had made up a grand story about needing to find a dress to wear so she could go out to the debut of Tommy's photo showing in a gallery. It was kind of a true story. No one needed to know that this exhibit had taken place a year ago.

When Belle and Maddie arrived, Alex whisked them up to her room, claiming to be desperate for help in this crisis moment. It felt funny to play the part of a high-maintenance city girl, and she wondered momentarily if this is what they had all expected from her since the beginning.

"Okay, girls...here are my options." She laid all of the dresses on the bed. Belle seemed immediately drawn to a silky midnight blue slip-like dress. The woman ran her hands lovingly across the soft and alluring fabric.

Internally Alex squealed. She'd bought it in Belle's size and had been picturing her in it all week.

"I love that one," Alex cried, and then she pouted. "But I'm too short for it and I don't have the boobs to make it work."

"Oh, but it's incredible," Belle replied.

"Try it on," Alex prodded.

"What? Why?"

"Have you ever tried returning anything you bought online? It's a nightmare from way out here. If it fits, it's yours."

"Um, that's okay. Thanks, though."

Alex died a little inside and then desperately looked to Maddie for back up.

"Alex, try this one." Maddie handed Alex a black dress off the bed trying to keep things going, reminding Alex why Belle thought they were there.

"Yeah, this one is nice and simple right?" She pulled her sweater over her head and slipped into the slim-fitting black cocktail dress with a simple scoop neck and a dramatically dipping back.

"It suits you." Maddie smiled.

"Yeah, thanks, I like it. Think it'll work at an art exhibit?"

"Oh sure, you know me, I'm very hip to the art scene," Maddie said with more than a touch of sarcasm. Belle laughed.

"Okay, now I feel like a dummy. Please try that on, Belle, so I'm not the only crazy person walking around a ranch dressed to the nines. Maddie, you try this one. We'll have a fashion-forward evening."

Maddie grinned and caught the dress Alex threw at her as she started stripping. Belle watched them both like their heads had fallen off. Alex sent her a pathetic look, so she shrugged.

"So this is what real girls do at sleepovers," Belle mused as she started to pull off her jeans.

"Oh, you've not seen anything yet, my friend," Alex promised.

All three now stood barefoot on the hardwood dressed in formal evening wear, awkwardly picking at the clinging fabric. Alex needed to rally.

"Okay, now what in the hell should I do with my hair?" She made eye contact with Belle in the mirror and was pretty sure Belle's expression matched what she would look like if she came across a talking dog.

"Up?" Belle ventured, barely able to hide how out of place she felt.

Alex smiled to herself.

What a good-hearted woman. She thinks I'm out of my damn mind and she's still playing along. Hang with me a little longer, Belle, I promise the nightmare is almost over.

"Do you mind being my practice doll? I think I know what I want, but it's faster for me to do it on someone else."

Belle's eyebrows practically hit her hairline. "You want to do my hair?"

"Is that okay? And Maddie thinks she's going to show me something about makeup too…although she can't do my makeup while I do your hair."

Belle shot Maddie daggers, but at the end, her kindness won out, and she visibly caved. These women feeling sorry for Alex was working more to her advantage than she'd anticipated. After an uncomfortable few minutes, the final result was that they had found bumbling excuses to throw Belle's hair into a trendy loose up-do, and she was now wearing a perfect amount of natural but breathtaking makeup.

"Okay, so now that you've seen it, can I take this off?" Belle ventured.

Alex and Maddie panicked and threw quick looks at the clock. It was six-fifty p.m. She thought back to the panicked phone call from Winn earlier in the day:

"He won't wear it." Winn hissed.

"What? Why?"

"He says he'll look like a fool walking around in a monkey suit."

"I swear to god I will murder your face if you don't get him in the tux," Alex threatened.

"You're gonna what? I…? What do I do?"

"He won't be alone if you rent one too."

"What in the hell? Why? No way I'm—"

And then Alex had hung up on him. Later she'd received a beleaguered text stating they were on their way home, and about two hours out. Winn promised to have Bishop and himself dressed and waiting at the table by seven. Trix and O'Reilly were on lights, candle, and wine duty. They should be working on their tasks now. She needed to get through ten more minutes without Belle disrobing.

"Ok let's pretend my hair is up like yours." She tugged her hair into a messy bun. "I still can't work out the makeup. Maddie, please help?"

Maddie nodded. "Sure, let's do this again."

Belle threw Maddie an incredulous look, but Maddie shrugged and seemed to try to power past Belle's pleading eyes.

"I'm sorry, girls. I know this is odd, I'm—anxious, you know? Fancy party, and I'm worried and all that." Alex hoped Belle wouldn't disrobe right that instant.

Belle's good nature took over, and she knelt next to Alex, touching her arm. "No, of course. It would be scary for anyone. We'll help you."

Alex exhaled, sending a quick thank-you to the heavens. After a few minutes Maddie had painted Alex's face up, and even though her hair was in a careless knot, she felt as though she could walk into a formal event and kick its ass. The clock said seven. It was go time.

"I know what we need," Alex announced.

"Flannel PJs and cold cream?" Belle ventured.

"No. We need wine," Alex insisted.

"Yes," Maddie agreed.

"What?" Belle asked in confusion.

"Let's go to the kitchen. I could seriously use some wine." Alex refused to take no for an answer, and they all padded barefoot down the stairs.

Once down to the main floor, Alex looked out the back window and saw the lights twinkling in the tree.

"Hey, what's that? What's going on outside?" Alex said in her best stage voice.

"What?" Belle asked for a second time in as many minutes.

"Look, do you see that?" Alex said, trying to keep the glee from her tone.

"Umm..."

"Let's go find out," Alex pushed, and when they came out on the back porch, the entire scene came into view.

Bishop stood uncomfortably in a tux under the tree decorated with hanging little white lights. He held a fist full of roses and was near a table draped in a white table cloth with two candles burning in the center. It was breathtaking. Alex heard the small sound of surprise Belle let out.

"Babe?" Belle asked hesitantly.

"Hi," Bishop answered awkwardly as he glanced over his shoulder toward the tree. "Join me for dinner?" he asked stiffly.

"What on earth? Bishop, what is this?" Belle asked.

"Please?" he pleaded.

Belle sent a quick and mildly accusatory glance toward Alex and Maddie. They both returned her look with wide and exaggerated grins, practically pushing her down the stairs and following close behind her.

Winn appeared from behind the tree.

Alex's feet stopped mid-stride, and her mind went blank. He wore a tux, and he wore the hell out of it. Winn's hair was loose and tussled, falling over the collar. The jacket fit him as if he belonged in a window display, hugging his broad shoulders and tapering to his waist. His smile, as he watched Bishop, was deep and genuine.

Winn's gaze bounced up. His eyes locked on hers and his lips parted slightly on a sharp intake of breath. She was frozen as they stood staring at one another. Out of her periphery, Alex barely noticed Belle approaching the table and that there were muted words exchanged. Alex heard and saw nothing else. The world was replaced with Winn's intense gaze.

She first became aware of her heartbeat as a loud and foreign pounding in her head, and then more aware of Maddie standing at her side with a vise-grip on her elbow. Finally, she broke eye contact with Winn and looked down at Maddie's white-knuckle grasp and then up to her talking face.

"What?" Alex asked dumbly.

"It's tanking. Fix this." Maddie briskly nodded toward Belle and Bishop both standing and fidgeting near the table close enough to touch but not touching, not speaking.

"Oh, yes…right," Alex said, gaining her composure and stepping closer to the table, her eyes briefly passing over Winn who still watched her with intensity.

"Belle, welcome to a very special night that Bishop has planned for you," Alex announced.

Belle kept her eyes on Alex, and Alex glanced at Winn, who was shaking his head at Bishop. She couldn't help but smile when Winn made frantic "pull out her chair" motions to his friend. Understanding splashed across Bishop's face, and he walked over to the chair and pulled it out. Belle watched him curiously.

"Sit," Bishop said.

Winn cleared his throat.

"Won't you please have a seat?" Bishop corrected and then smiled, no doubt delighted with himself when Belle obeyed. He crossed over to his own side then reached across the table and thrust the flowers in front of her.

"These are for you."

"They're lovely, thank you."

"I'm not sure where you should put those though…sorry."

"Baby, this is all a huge surprise, and it's, my god, it's beautiful. I don't understand though." Glancing around self-consciously, Belle leaned in a little closer to Bishop and said, "What's going on?"

"I wanted to do something nice for you, and these guys are helping."

"But we're not staying," Alex interjected quickly, while she filled two wine glasses from the bottle on the table.

Alex watched Maddie retreat back into the house, no doubt on her way to find Junior. She then willed herself to look back at Winn, who also seemed to have snapped out of it, his heated gaze replaced with a more panicked and questioning look. Winn pointed at the guitar and shrugged. Alex nodded, crossed over behind Belle, and mimed dancing at Bishop.

"Would you care to dance?" Bishop asked as Winn started picking out a few notes.

Belle's shoulders relaxed a fraction, and with a happy sigh, she nodded. "Yes, I really would."

Bishop stood, took her hand as she rose, and after walking a few steps, pulled her into his arms. She visibly relaxed further. Alex smiled to herself when Belle closed her eyes and rested her cheek on Bishop's shoulder. Winn started strumming out the song in earnest as Belle's mouth turned up.

"This," Belle said quietly into his lapel.

"This," Bishop answered her.

Winn began to sing as the couple started to sway in time. Alex joined in with a soft harmony. They quietly sang through the song as Belle and Bishop clung to one another, lost in their own world. Winn dropped off and let Alex softly sing the last line.

Alex and Winn stood there next to one another in silence as Belle and Bishop continued to dance in the quiet night. Alex bit her lip and looked up to Winn who looked down at her and offered a small smile.

"Good?" he whispered.

"Good," she replied.

Winn tilted his head toward the barn, and she nodded. As they turned to go, she heard Bishop clear his throat and start to speak. She couldn't help herself. She stopped in the shadow of the yard and turned.

"Belle, I know this is an out-there kind of thing and this outfit is by far the craziest thing I've done yet." Bishop tugged gently at the tie around his neck. "But this is all to show you that I would do *anything* for you. You deserve the world. You deserve candlelight and romantic songs and to be swept off your feet every night. But we both know I'm a more than a little rough around the edges." He waved his hand at the table. "And this? Hell, we both know this ain't really all my doing. The point is I'm a simple man, Belle, a simple man with simple tastes, and simple dreams, but my love for you has pushed me, pushed me to try to be the kind of man you deserve, a better man."

Belle shook her head. "Baby, I love you exactly as you are."

"I know that, and that makes me so damn lucky." Bishop got down on one knee, producing the ring from his pocket. Belle gasped.

Alex held her breath and pressed the tips of her fingers to her lips.

Bishop looked up at Belle from the ground. "I *am* going to love you forever, and if you'd let me, I'd like to spend every day, for the rest of my life, showing you exactly how much love and happiness a simple man with simple dreams can give you. Will you marry me?"

Belle nodded and began to cry as he tried to get the ring on her shaking hand. Alex started to turn around, feeling guilty for spying, but she froze when she felt Winn's breath at the back of her neck. He leaned down and said softly in her ear, "You did a good thing here, Alexandra."

Alex turned around and found his closeness affected her deep in her gut. Her eyes were wet, and she didn't trust her voice. They held eye contact for a long moment before she was able to nod and blink back the start of tears.

"Let's give them some privacy," she managed, and headed toward the horse barn.

Chapter 23

As they walked into the barn, Alex had almost regained control of her emotions. Having Winn so close to her during such a touching moment rocked her more than she'd care to admit.

"I think that went well, right?" he asked, his voice sounding a little rough. Maybe the emotion of what they'd witnessed had gotten to him too.

"God, I hope so. Looks like she said yes, but honestly, how could she not, with a proposal like that?" Alex couldn't help but smile.

"And it only took him two hours in the car to commit that speech to memory." Winn chuckled at her wide-eyed disbelief.

"You *didn't*." She joined him in a light laugh.

"Hey, you said not to bring up the ripping off the Band-Aid thing, so we needed a plan. Lord knows what that boy would have said if left to his own devices, especially with his nerves all frayed like that."

"Then I'm impressed with both of you, because that speech was movie-grade romance." Alex tilted her head at him. "You're a good friend."

He blinked hard, appearing embarrassed by her comment. After a beat, Winn nodded and started down the aisle. She walked with him as he made final night-checks, peeking in on every stall, clucking and cooing softly once in a while, his version of tucking them in.

Winn threw his jacket over a hook and unknotted his tie, which he let hang lopsided on either side of his unbuttoned collar. The combination of the half-worn tux, surrounded by the sounds and smells of the stable, was out of the ordinary, but it seemed to work.

She remembered Emily calling Winn the GQ Cowboy and acknowledged how fitting the label was at the moment. He stopped and looked down at her bare feet with a grin.

"What does it say about me that I find a barefoot woman in a formal dress walking around the barn weirdly sexy?" he said with a little hitch of his lips.

Her eyebrows shot up, not believing that he would so overtly compliment her.

"You said something nice about me, Winn." Alex poked him in the side.

"Yeah, well, I guess there are limits to how stubborn I can be, and I'm not blind. You look nice tonight, like I damn near swallowed my tongue nice," Winn admitted.

"Well, if it's confession time, you in that tux knocked me on my ass. It's a good look on you," Alex said.

He smiled shyly and then brushed some imaginary dirt from his white shoulder. "When I first put it on, I felt like a chump, but I gotta admit, it feels a little James Bond."

"You wear it better than Bond."

"That's what the girl at the shop said." He gave her another sheepish smile, and she could tell that he thought it was more funny than true.

"Oh, I'm sure she did." Alex laughed at his ignorance. She didn't doubt for a second that there was now some poor love-struck shop-girl pining for her tuxedoed cowboy to come back to her.

They both took a moment, each seeming uncomfortable with their admissions. Winn watched her for a long moment, and she couldn't tell where his mind was taking him.

Eventually he asked, "Now that you've orchestrated the happily ever after for Bishop, have you given any thought to what you're going to do next?"

"What do you mean?"

"Well, you must have had a life in Chicago. English and Tattoos were proof of that. What's happening in that life while you're here?"

"Oh well, that ended up getting put on hold a little, I guess. I lost my job, or quit it, rather, so I need to lock down some employment before I can go back and start paying for my apartment again."

"Who's paying for it now?"

"My brother is subletting it. He had an internship downtown this summer." Alex shrugged.

"Any chance his internship will turn into a job?"

"I guess I don't know. I don't even remember where it was. Some pharmaceutical company."

"He's a chemist or something?"

She surprised herself. "I don't know."

"You don't know what he's studying?" Winn turned to face her. Alex felt judgment dripping in his tone and didn't appreciate it.

"No...I guess not." She frowned a little, trying to work out how she couldn't know that. She did not like having to admit her ignorance to Winn.

"I guess I would have thought you guys would be closer after what happened with your dad."

That got her spine up even more. "I didn't say we weren't close," she said, annoyed at how much it tasted like a lie.

"I'm saying after our father left, Matt and I learned to lean on each other more."

"Sounds a little like codependence to me." She knew it was a shitty thing to say, but she was in full-blown defensive mode now.

"I guess you'd see it that way." His tone matched hers.

"What do you mean by that?"

"Only that it seems like being there for people isn't your strong suit."

"Are you serious with this right now?" Alex pinned a hard look on him.

"I'm calling it like I see it," Winn said, his face looking impassive despite the heavy accusation he'd leveled.

"You don't know the first thing about me."

"Whose fault is that?" He returned her hard stare.

"Oh sure, like you're some kind of open book, Winn."

"At least the people I care about know it and know they can count on me."

"Are you sure about that?" Alex challenged.

"It doesn't mean anything when someone like you tries to make me feel bad about my life." Winn's dismissive tone was infuriating.

"Someone like me? I'm a good person!" She surprised herself with the force that she mustered.

"Good people don't ride out on their family when things get hard," he gruffly countered, his anger appearing to come through.

"You're right, good people stay. They stay until they resent their family so much that they can't even speak a civil word to them." Alex knew she was hitting below the belt, but he'd struck a nerve.

Winn nearly snarled. "How dare you come in here thinking you know the first thing about my family and what I feel about them?" The fire in his eyes threw her for a loop, but she wasn't going to back down. This was too important.

"Do you think that this is what Matt needs? For you to hover and babysit and scold him every time you're having a bad day?" Alex snapped back.

At the mention of his brother's name, Winn sucked in a huge breath of air, but Alex wouldn't and couldn't stop. "And Mae, you think Mae needs you around throwing tantrums every time the stress gets away from you? She's got her own crap to worry about—she doesn't need to be placating you and your perceived misery all the time."

That was it. That was the blow she'd wanted desperately to land. The one hand she had left to play. Now that it was down on the table, she felt sick looking at Winn as the pain she'd inflicted washed over his face.

The silence was long and ragged. He drew a deep breath as she drew short, painful ones.

When he spoke next, the tone was quiet and saturated with contempt. "You'd be the expert then. Family is something to take for granted, something to be thrown away after use. You're the poster child for that level of selfishness, to be sure."

Winn's soft words hit her like a thumping fist to the chest. He was right and terrible at the same time. Her breath hitched as they stared at one another. The dense silence between them grew fingers and wrapped around her throat, causing tears to threaten. Alex wouldn't cry, not wanting to give him that. Keeping the unblinking eye contact, she exhaled.

"Such awful things you think about me." Her words were hollow, deflated. Alex wanted to push back, to defend herself, but Winn was right. The unspoken defiant words died in her mouth. She had nothing to rebuke his claim.

His face looked grim and tired as he sighed before running a hand through his hair. "Alexandra, I'm not going to do this with you any longer."

"And what is this? Some exercise in futility?" she asked.

"You're right. All this has done is proven that we can hurt one another." Winn nodded and pulled his eyes to the ground.

"And was that the point?" Alex asked quietly.

"It feels like it, doesn't it? Children lashing out, men pissing off rooftops, two broken people climbing over one another to prove something to themselves, to what end?"

Alex studied him, felt her remaining pride and bravado wane, and suddenly all that remained was weight—pressing, suffocating, unnamed weight.

"I'm tired, Winn," she confessed. "I'm not tired tonight, or tired of fighting with you. I'm tired in my heart. I'm tired and…used up…and…*broken*. You're right. I'm not worth it, not worth the words, the anger, or the energy it takes to fight with me. This idea that I'm okay, that I have an ounce of spirit left in me to keep me moving—it's not real. I have to own that. I have to own the falseness of that, and you've shone a light on it. I want to hate you for it, but I'm not strong enough to get there. I don't have the strength to hate you anymore."

There was nothing to add, nothing to contest. They had thrashed against one another long enough, used one another as tools to inflict their self-punishment. There were no words, only the raw and painful reality between them.

When she finally allowed herself to look up, Alex saw that his expression had softened. There was regret in his eyes, and it was not her own reflecting back. Winn approached her and wrapped his hand around the base of her neck, gently pulling her cheek to his chest. His arms surrounded her.

Alex murmured, "No," but didn't mean it as she leaned into him and rested her head on his shoulder.

This wasn't anger and it wasn't possession.

"I'm sorry," Winn said softly.

Alex closed her eyes and let out the air she held in her lungs. She allowed herself to register the strength in his arms, the heat of his chest, the slow and deep feeling of his heart beating. She turned her face into his chest, pulling in his scent, drawing comfort from the strength, the pure maleness of him.

His hand trembled slightly as he drew it up her back and tangled it into her hair. He pressed his cheek to the top of her head and pulled in a long, deep breath.

Alex's hands flattened against Winn's back, pulling his body to hers, closer, tighter. There was pain in the embrace, tension in the arms, the muscles locked and desperate. Alex found her hands sliding up to his shoulder blades as she lifted her face from his chest to look up at him. They were so close. There was confusion in his eyes, and something else, something more profound than sadness. He was lost, like her.

"Alex, I need..." he trailed off, sounding unsteady.

She closed her eyes and shook her head to silence his words.

When she opened them, she watched him for a reaction as she slowly brought her face closer to his. Winn closed his eyes as her mouth found his. The touch of their lips was light and tentative. There was a feeling of sadness in the low simmer but a softness, a rightness that was delicate and frail.

As the soft, slow kiss continued, the sadness began to boil, allowing pent-up desperation to break free. Winn leaned into her and grasped both sides of her face tenderly. She retreated a step, her back pressing against the wall as he followed. The kiss gained strength.

Alex sighed and poured herself into their connection. Winn responded, taking from her frantically. She couldn't feel enough, taste enough of him.

Winn withdrew slightly and spoke, his voice hot against her lips. "Alex, you have to stop me."

"I won't," she breathed, dragging him back to her.

His hands slid down her body, down the outside of her thighs and back up, bringing her dress with them. His mouth trailed down her jawline to find her neck.

"Alex, damn it. Stop me," he growled into her ear.

"I can't," she rasped, as her hands, eager to find him, roughly untucked his shirt and slid up his abdomen.

He hissed, "Alex. Tell me to stop."

"No."

His stomach muscles clenched at the contact with her desperate hands. He groaned against her neck, and his wide hands gripped the back of her thighs as he wrenched her off her feet, pinning her against the wall. She wrapped her legs around his hips as the rough, unfinished wood dug into her back.

As suddenly as things had picked up, Winn pulled away.

"Not like this," he mumbled into her neck.

"What?" Alex's confusion gave way to an unbearable realization about what he was saying. "Winn, no," she stammered as he started to pull away further. "Please don't leave me here with this, stay here." Her emotions were raw and open as her eyes pleaded. "Stay with me, Winn."

"Not like this," he repeated, but he didn't release her.

Her chest constricted when Winn turned his head to look away from her, her panic palpable.

What to say? How to explain? Make him see.

"Winn, I—I need you. You need something too."

His eyes snapped back to hers. "I don't need something…"

Alex's breath hitched, and she reeled as if he'd struck her.

Without releasing her, Winn pulled them away from the wall, and in two long strides, carried her to a horse blanket strewn across a bed of stacked hay. Laying her down, he hovered over her.

"I don't need *something,* Alex." Winn paused. "I need *you.*"

His fingers toyed with the ends of her hair that splayed out along the bales behind her. "But I need you like this."

His eyes soft, he studied her face. His fingers trailed down her neck and ever so delicately followed a path across her collar bone. "And like this." His eyes followed the trail of his fingers.

Alex shuddered as his calloused hands traced slow lines down her body. Down the long line of her leg and back up past the inside of her knee. He brought himself down to kiss her. The kiss was strong and deep, but patient, lacking the desperation from before.

Her hands wrapped around his torso then up his back, feeling the shift of muscle as he positioned himself over her. He reared up, and she helped tug his shirt up over his head, allowing herself to admire the hard planes of his chest, the ridges in his abdomen, the sculpted arms that trembled now as they caged her in. The strength they held was intoxicating.

As he came back to kissing her, Alex laid her hands everywhere she could reach, moving down to tug at his pants. Winn briefly leaned back and pulled her hitched-up dress over her head. He paused a moment, dress in hand, to look down at her. She had to fight the urge to cover herself, but the hunger in his eyes made her brave.

Winn took a few steadying breaths, working to rein himself back in. Slowly he lowered himself over her, and his mouth found hers.

She lost herself in him, in the feeling of the length of his body pinning her. Lost herself in the feel of his heated skin against hers, the feel of his mouth dragging her under with him. She was captive to her own body's response to his firmness now pressing at her core.

He reached a hand up to hold her face. He drew away from the kiss, and they locked eyes, his expression questioning. She had no words. She answered him by leaning up and retaking his mouth softly as she wrapped her ankles around his legs. As he began to enter her slowly, she bit his lower lip, causing his barely leashed control to snap, and he moved swiftly to fill her.

On a quick intake of breath, she arched up to meet him. He banded an arm under her waist, pulling her up and to him, pulling himself deeper. He dropped his forehead to her shoulder. "Jesus," he groaned into her neck.

Alex tried to catch her balance, overwhelmed by the rightness of being with him, being lost with him.

***

They lay quietly wrapped in the horse blanket, surrounded by the soft sounds of the horses shuffling and eating. Alex couldn't decide if she was feeling timid or brave, but as her heart rate dropped back to normal, there was a solid sense deep down, and she knew that she wasn't sorry. She didn't regret making love to Winn.

Making love? Was that what that was?

The fight before had been brutal and cutting. The kiss at the wall was harsh, demanding, abrasive even, but after moving them to the hay, Winn had been gentle, attentive…amazing. She looked up from her head's resting place on his chest and to evaluate his face. The soft satisfied grin he gave her made her think maybe he was also not sorry.

"Hey," he said softly.

"Hey," she repeated.

"This changes everything, doesn't it?" Winn asked.

"God, I hope so."

He chuckled. "Me too."

"You're not sorry?" she ventured, allowing a touch of insecurity to creep into her mind.

"Not even a little. You?" She could hear the tint of worry in his tone.

"Not even a little," she echoed, dropping her head back to his chest.

A comfortable silence fell between them. Alex tried to force her mind to stay still so she could take in the feeling of calm they both seemed immersed in. He slowly trailed his fingertips up and down her arm and exhaled deeply. After several moments, his fingers stilled, and she could tell he was about to speak again.

"Alex, I don't know what this means."

"Me neither."

"But," he continued. "There is something here. I mean, we're tough on each other, I'm not convinced we're good for each other, but there's something here. Right?"

"Yes," she admitted.

"Maybe our reaction to one another is strong for a reason, maybe not, but the spark is undeniable, even to me." She looked up to see him popping that sexy half grin. "Now, that spark may lead to a full-on dumpster fire," he added, and she laughed with him.

"Very true, but a fire nonetheless, and I could use a little warmth."

"Me too. There's something about you that kicks off a reaction in me, a visceral, sometimes ugly reaction, but I'm done telling myself that gut response isn't there, or that it doesn't mean anything. I'm not going to say it's there for a mentally healthy reason, 'cause I don't know what it is, but I'm willing to let it ride. Does that feel wrong?" he asked.

"No. Maybe it should, but it doesn't. You get to me, that's undeniable, but I don't know why you affect me like you do. I've never been so easily riled up. I know you won't believe it, but I never have screaming matches with anyone. Never."

"I can't say the same." Winn smiled at his self-deprecation.

She laughed softly. "I can see that, but I'm willing to let it ride too. I think it may be worth whatever fallout may come."

A moment of content silence followed before Alex confessed, "You know, half of the terrible things you say about me piss me off so much because I know they're true."

"I know," he responded, but before she could react to his words, he continued, "I know because they're true about me too."

She calmed herself and quietly said, "I'm pretty broken. I wasn't lying before."

"That also appears to be true for me."

"I know," Alex said as he tightened his arms around her.

He sighed. "I think I hated that you made me feel broken, but I was broken before you got here. Hard to admit to myself, but you being here held up a mirror that was already cracked." After a pause, he added, "I don't expect you to fix me, Alex, but maybe you give me a reason to fix myself."

It was her turn for a deep exhale, his sincerity hitting close to home.

She decided that he deserved her honesty. "I seem to sabotage anything good that I come into contact with, and I'm not sure that part of me is fixable."

"Or maybe you need something you can't break."

Winn's gentle words brought tears to her eyes, and she couldn't respond. He seemed to understand and resumed his silent stroking of her arm.

Eventually, a chill began creeping into the aisle, and they began to rise and dress. Pulling his shirt over his head, he asked, "Do you think we should keep this to ourselves?"

Alex bristled a little at the idea he may want to hide whatever this was from his family, but she tried to keep her knee-jerk insecurities at bay. "Why? Do you?"

"No. I thought you might feel—I don't know, embarrassed, seeing as how you've tried pretty hard to make everyone think you hate me."

"They're smarter than that. Plus, I've only been trying to convince myself that I hate you."

"Well, all right, then," he said. "Tomorrow is a big workday. We need to round up the herds to bring them for vaccines and a headcount before the auction. I think you're ready to join us on Winston if you're interested."

"You happily allowing me to play ranch hand will clue them in." Alex laughed, pleased that he would consider allowing her to participate.

"For sure it will," Winn said with a chuckle as they got ready to go back to the house.

Can you trust this change? Alex wondered before she could force the anxiety from her mind.

As they walked through the door into the kitchen, it felt like an end to a timeout, as if returning to the house could break the spell. But as she'd let the idea take hold, Winn turned to her and brushed a soft, chaste kiss to her lips. "Night," he said softly before heading down to his room. She smiled at how perfect and reassuring the gesture was.

Chapter 24

The next morning, Alex had butterflies in her stomach about how they would break the news to everyone and how it would land. She came around the bottom of the stairs, and, as usual, the dining room was already full of life and chatter. Winn was facing the stairs waiting for her, and when she came into the room he stood, took three long steps, and without speaking pulled her to him and drew her into a slow, soft kiss. In the room behind them, a few utensils hit plates before it went silent.

Winn pulled away from her face and pressed his forehead to hers. "Morning."

"Morning," she replied breathlessly as he turned back to the room.

There was a brief moment of stunned silence that made Alex's stomach drop before Trix yelled, "Well, it's about goddamn time."

The guys all laughed, but Alex searched out and made eye contact with the one face she was most worried about. Mae's expression was unreadable for a tense few seconds before a tiny smile broke through, and she gave a slight nod. "Breakfast is getting cold," she said.

Alex let out the air that she didn't realize she'd been holding and followed Winn to the table. Griz, who had been sitting next to Winn, stood and moved to the other side of the table, leaving her room to sit. It was a small gesture, but it seemed to prove that the group approved of her place being next to Winn.

After breakfast, she went to the barn with Winn, Matt, and Trix to tack up all the horses. The round-up today was going to be almost all hands on deck. They fell into an easy rhythm of pulling out horses, grooming, and tacking. Idle chatter partially filled the barn. She took a moment to realize what she was feeling. It was happiness, but something more. Purpose? Alex couldn't nail it down, but it was pleasant, and her strong desire to not let it go was a bit of a surprise for her.

In all, they tacked twelve horses. They would ride out in two groups of six and each team would round up and drive as many cattle back toward the barn that they could. There they would drive them into chutes, so the remaining crew members could snag them, evaluate their health and administer vaccines before they were confined to a close, smaller pasture. When they were almost ready to go, Junior, Bishop, Griz, and Tiny appeared and helped put bridles on the horses. They were all mounted and heading toward the field in a matter of minutes.

Her group reached a sprawling herd of cattle and Alex watched as the men, horses, and dogs all took part in a choreographed dance. Alex laughed as she watched Holden, not so much chase cattle, but chase the dogs that were chasing the cattle. She tried her best to follow their lead and for the most part had to focus on not falling off while Winston performed the job he understood better than she.

The sun was getting higher in the sky, and they had managed to round up about a hundred head of cattle into a tight herd that they started moving toward the barns. Alex looked over the ridge and noticed a horse and rider coming over the hill. She narrowed her eyes when she realized who it was.

"Hey," she called to Winn, who looked up at her questioningly. She nodded toward the horizon, and his gaze followed hers.

"What in the hell is he doing here?" Winn said gruffly while he brought his horse right alongside Alex and Winston.

Winn whistled to get the attention of the others, and when they looked to him, he nodded toward the rider. The men tensed but stayed in their places to keep the cattle together. They all waited as Blake approached them on a little palomino that was snorting and prancing, seemingly uncomfortable with being ridden.

Under her breath, Alex mumbled, "...and I looked, and behold a pale horse: and his name that sat on him was Death..."

Without taking his eye from Blake, Winn humorlessly finished, "...and Hell followed with him."

"Morning, Crooked Crew," Blake announced as though it wasn't out of the ordinary for him to be riding around on land that didn't belong to him.

"You lost?" Winn asked.

"Appreciate your concern, Kid, but no, I know exactly where I'm at. Actually, I was taking a quick little ride to survey the lay of the land."

"I'm not playing games with you today. What are you doing here, Blake? We've got work to do, and you're trespassing."

Blake maintained steady eye contact with Winn for a few long seconds before turning to Alex, as he pretended not even to hear Winn's question. "Morning, city girl. You taking to your ranching job? Looks like you're already pretty accomplished in the saddle. Came with some mounting experience, did you?" His tone dripped with arrogance.

Winn visibly tensed, and Alex reached over and put her hand on his thigh to keep him from getting off his horse.

The move caught Blake's attention. "Ah," he chuckled. "This is a thing now, huh? Was wondering if you'd be able to pick any low-hanging fruit."

Winn's gloves creaked as his fist tightened on the reins. "Blake, watch your mouth. You're outnumbered here. I'm going to ask you one more time, what are you doing here?"

"There's talk this land is going to be for sale in the near future. Thought I'd come to take a look to see if any of this shithole is salvageable." Blake brought his eyes up to scan the acreage around them.

"You've been misinformed, and by my count, you're more than an hour's ride from any land you own, so you better get on your way," Winn said icily.

"Misinformed, huh? So you think Mae will ride this all the way to the poor house before she realizes the mistake she's made? Not sure what you think you're going to do with all these cattle, but I have it on good authority folks won't be buying a lot of Crooked stock this year."

"Come on, asshole, move along," Trix volunteered from the back of the pack.

"All right now," Blake said, tipping his chin to the guys behind Winn. "You boys think about if you still want a job after C.B.R. closes its doors." Then turning his eyes back to Alex and Winn, he said, "Guess I'll be seeing you both at the auction tomorrow. Frank says he's planning on picking up a few horses to put in my program.

He's even got eyes on the River Rock mare. Figure that'll be enough high-end babies to keep me in business for years to come."

"You wouldn't even know where to start with stock of that quality, you hack," Trix yelled.

Winn put up his hand. "Leave it alone, Trix, he's leaving."

"Guess I am." Blake grinned then looked to Alex and added, "See ya…Red."

"Eat shit," she told him, her voice level.

He chuckled. "I like 'em to have spirit."

With that, Blake spun his nervous mount and took off back over the hill.

Alex let out a long breath and watched Winn warily to see how the unwelcome guest had impacted his mood. His expression was stony as he watched Blake's back until he was out of sight and then looked down as he forced his fist to unclench.

After a brief moment, Winn called out over his shoulder, "Trix, ride up to the top of the hill and watch to make sure that jackass doesn't make any detours. Everyone else, back to work."

Winn's eyes found hers, and he gave her a reassuring smile, which she returned.

Trix, as usual, broke through the tension, saying, "Sometimes I hate Rule Ten."

She cocked a questioning eyebrow at Winn.

"Don't throw the first punch, throw the last one," he recited, and Alex chuckled toward Trix's back as he rode away from them.

"Guess I'm not going to get to see an auction after all?" Alex asked, trying to keep her voice light.

Winn surprised her by saying, "Blake and his bullshit shouldn't keep you from going if you want. But I am going to bust out my condescending false sense of chivalry and ask that you don't wander off alone since we know there'll be a snake in the grass."

She smiled as he threw her own previous words back at her. "No promises, but I'll try."

Winn laughed and nodded.

"What's he talking about when he says the River Rock mare?" Alex asked.

"River Rock is a bloodline, ranching horse royalty. Horses out of that line are worth quite a lot of money and for a good reason. They're smart and athletic and do well in the rodeo and show circuits. Rumor has it that an infamous mare from that bloodline is going to be at the auction. She's five years old, and she's supposed to be un-rideable, unbreakable, and all-around impossible to handle. If Frank wants her, it'll be to breed her with his stud and throw babies he can sell for top dollar."

"So she'll live on the ranch having babies the rest of her life?" Alex asked sadly.

"If what people say about her is true, then that may be the only thing she can do, assuming they can get her gentled enough to be bred."

"What's her name?"

"River Rock's Red Flag."

Alex laughed, "Sounds like my kind of girl."

"Mine too," Winn said with an irresistible grin.

Chapter 25

The next day they all rose extra early to herd the auction-ready cattle into the back of three huge semi-trucks that arrived before dawn. Alex was excited to see the other side of the business, and for the rodeo and dancing she was told would follow the auction. The crew loaded into several pick-ups and headed out for the two-hour drive to Billings.

The ride was a little sullen. Alex could tell Winn was mulling over the words Blake had thrown at him the day before. She'd no idea what would happen if Blake's prediction was right and none of the cattle sold.

As they pulled into the fairgrounds, Alex took in the ordered chaos. There were large rigs parked everywhere and huge pens filling with livestock. Hopping from the truck, Alex followed Winn and Mae through the crowd as they made preparations for where their cattle would go and received details about when to expect their stock to be herded into the sales pens.

Alex was pleased to find out that they would be going through the process early in the day. Everyone seemed to know both Mae and Winn. Their interactions, while professional, were filled with warmth and an ease Alex admired. Again, she followed them back to the livestock trailers, where they directed the drivers to their assigned pens. Once finished, it seemed they only had about an hour to wait before the bidding would begin.

"Well, now what do we do?" she asked Winn as he scanned the area, no doubt trying to put eyes on Blake.

"Let's go grab some coffee and a place to sit," he said without looking at her.

"Okay, when do we get to see that mare?" Alex asked gingerly.

He finally stopped his incessant crowd-skimming to look down at her.

"Never one to back down, huh?"

Alex could sense that he was sad and imagined that a few weeks ago, the prospect of Frank buying that mare to put into Winn's program would have been career-changing. A little pang of guilt came when she implied they should still look at the horse, but she knew, despite his disappointment, Winn probably really did want to see the mare for himself.

"Not a fan of backing down," she quipped.

"The horse auction will start on the other side of the grounds in about three hours. I'm sure they'll put her out before that," Winn explained.

When he didn't offer to go and look then and there, she didn't push. Alex hoped the auction would go well, despite the threats from the Martins, and that after, she would have a less stressed version of Winn for the rest of the day. They stopped off to grab a coffee and then climbed into the bleachers next to Trix and Mae, who had already staked out a row of seats. They made idle small talk, but everyone seemed tense.

She watched as large groups of cattle were herded into the sale pen, coupled with quick announcements about details such as average weights, ages, breeding info. Then the auctioneer was off. The words seemed like gibberish and Alex decided that instead of trying to glean meaning, she would allow the words to bounce off her ears, rather enjoying their rhythmic beat.

Winn nodded every once in a while, with Mae chiming in occasionally with comments like, "Not bad for that stock." Alex watched them both for any signs of increasing or decreasing worry but found them both too hard to read.

Finally, the announcer said, "Lots 96 through 104, stock of the Crooked Brook Ranch."

Everyone in their group sat up straighter, and Alex forced herself to try to understand what he was saying as the bidding started for their first group. It was over so fast that Alex had to lean over to ask Trix what had happened.

He whispered back, "Sold for 142 bucks a head. That's not terrible, but it's not good."

"What should it be?"

"Well, 150 was the average last time. And 155 would have been great."

Alex stared at the sky and tried to do the math on the money. Mae stood up and dusted off the backside of her jeans. She didn't look upset, but she looked like she was on a mission. Mae made her way over to where a bunch of bidders were sitting. Alex watched and caught sight of Blake seated with an older version of himself, who she assumed to be his father. Blake sensed her stare and looked over at her. He leaned over to say something to his father, who also looked up and gave her a matching sneer. Alex felt dirty holding eye contact with them, so she looked away, noticing that Mae was already on her way back over.

"Spineless sheep, the lot of 'em," Mae said in exasperation. As she sat down, the bidding started on their second lot.

Their remaining lots sold for $147 per head.

"What's really going on here?" Alex asked.

Mae was the one who responded, "Ted Martin is a rich asshole who inherited a lot of land and a ton of money from his father. He's been buying up more land and more property in town. The more he buys, the more power he has over the market, and it gives him leverage over some of the other folks around here. Or at least he makes them think he has leverage. They're afraid of him and what he could do to them if they pushed back. He's a bully, and they're chickenshits. I'm tired of it." Mae narrowed her eyes as she scanned the bleachers.

"At least people still bought them, right?" Alex asked, referencing Blake's threat from the day before.

"I suppose. They seem to think underpaying me for my stock will placate Martin but not burn the bridge with me. I think it's time I make them pick a side," Mae said and then rose again to no doubt go draw her line in the sand.

Now that the cattle had sold Alex knew it was time to turn up the pressure on Winn about going to see the mare.

She turned to him and opened her mouth, but he spoke before she could.

"All right, I know. Let's go," he said

Alex smiled to herself. *Well, that was easy.*

The area for the horse auction was set up similarly to the cattle area on a smaller scale. As they made their way through the pens, Winn perked up. There was a trailer backing up to a round pen numbered 24. Alex wasn't sure how he knew it, but Winn's body language told her that the notorious mare must be inside.

A man jumped out of the passenger side of the truck and opened the gate to the round pen. The trailer continued backing until half of it was inside. The guy came around and undid the latch at the back, letting the ramp slam down to the ground as he ran back around the trailer and out past the fence.

"What the hell?" Alex asked.

"Guess that guy doesn't want to be around when she gets off," Winn answered, smiling a little.

They watched the back of the trailer and nothing happened. Finally, the driver got out and stood on the wheel of the trailer, making a shooing noise through the window. The response he got was a loud bang that resulted in a pushed-out bubble of metal right next to him.

Winn laughed dryly. The driver banged on the side and made more noises. Finally, the mare appeared at the back of the trailer. She jumped down and started trotting an agitated lap around the round pen. She was beautiful, a shiny deep-red chestnut, with a mane and tail a few shades lighter. Her body was solidly built, and her muscles flexed as she seemed to float around the pen. The driver climbed back into the truck and started slowly pulling out, dragging the still open ramp on the ground.

"Good lord," Winn sighed. "It's like a scene from Jurassic Park."

The passenger seemed to have drawn the short straw as he stood nervously next to the gate, getting ready to close it as soon as the back of the trailer cleared the opening. The mare eyed him balefully. As soon as the trailer was clear, she ran at him while he frantically tried to slam the gate. She arrived in a flash of dust with her ears pinned and her gaping mouth aiming for his face. He shoved the gate the rest of the way closed and fell back over his feet, while the mare bumped the railing with her chest, still desperate to get ahold of him.

"Well, I guess the rumors are true," Winn said, gaze fixed on the mare.

"I've never seen a horse act like that," Alex said with a gasp. "She wanted to hurt him."

"She wanted to *kill* him," Winn corrected.

"Unreal. What could make her like that?"

Winn shrugged, absently replying, "A lot of things. Sometimes they're kind of naturally a bully, and if you don't handle those ones the right way in the beginning, they can grow into monsters."

Alex watched his face, seeing thoughts brewing that he didn't seem ready to articulate. She could tell that Winn was going to stand here for a while, so she decided to let him be. Her eyes wandered to the stands where Frank Powers sat with Blake's father. Her face wrinkled with disdain and she thought about Mae's words earlier. Alex too was convinced that Ted Martin was the reason Winn's training business was slowly diminishing.

An idea struck her, and she started hatching a plan. She would need to get away from Winn, but as it was, he was so deep in thought, he didn't even notice as she started walking away. She looked back and knew his laser focus was unlikely to move from the mare.

Time to stir up some shit.

Alex approached Frank and Ted in the stands, sitting down behind them.

"Excuse me, sir, are you Frank Powers?" Alex asked.

He started slightly and then turned to face her. "Yes?"

"My name is Alex. I'm Mae Becker's great-niece. I wanted to introduce myself. I've heard nice things about you."

"Oh, yes. Nice to meet you. I heard that they had an out-of-state visitor up there. That must be you."

"It is." She smiled sweetly, letting her eyes bounce to Ted Martin, who was watching her with narrowed eyes. Alex continued, "I heard you're planning on buying this mare?" She tipped her head toward the round pen.

Frank seemed slightly surprised, but he nodded.

"She's beautiful," Alex said.

"That she is." Frank nodded. "I'm counting on being able to get a few better-mannered foals out of her."

"I'm pretty new to this, but I was wondering, wouldn't her babies be worth way more money if she didn't have this reputation for being so scary?"

Frank furrowed his brow. "Yes, of course, but I think everyone knows that about her already. Best to hope for is that the babies come out more even-tempered and still fetch a good price."

"Ah, yes, that makes sense." Alex nodded. "But, boy, what a shame, huh?"

"Indeed," Frank agreed.

"I bet Winn could fix that mare," she said wistfully, trying to make it sound like an external musing, not a challenge.

Ted Martin's alarmed eyes bore holes through her as he finally cut in. "If that mare is breakable, Frank, and that's a big if, you know my boy is the one who could do it."

Frank looked slightly uncomfortable.

Stay with me here, Frankie.

"Oh, I'm sure your son is a great horseman, Mr. Martin, but I've seen Winn work wonders," Alex added pleasantly.

"Blake is the man for this job, sweetheart," Ted responded with a little edge.

"Maybe," Alex mused. "I know I'm a city girl, but seems to me, the only way to know would be to have them both give it a try." She left the challenge sitting between them and hoped that Ted would take the bait.

"Frank, if you're going to try to have that mare broken, you know it should come home with my boy."

Frank narrowed his eyes, seeming to be weighing his options. Alex had to assume that he didn't like being strong-armed into moving his business to Blake. Perhaps she was opening a door for him that he wanted opened.

"I suppose we could take a look at how well each of them gets along with her so that we pick a good fit, training-wise," Frank murmured.

Ted's eyes iced over, but it looked like he wasn't going to back down. "I'm telling you that Blake could break that mare here and now if you wanted him to."

Greedy, power-hungry men. You're so predictable. I've got you now, asshole.

Alex schooled her expression. "So could Winn," she countered.

"Okay, okay, let's let both of those boys take a crack at her. I'll make a decision then," Frank said, which Alex took as her cue to bow out before he changed his mind.

She stood. "It was nice meeting you," she said to Frank while refusing to look at Ted Martin's angry face. She started down the bleacher steps and only then noticed that Matt was walking down right behind her.

Where in the hell had he come from?

At the bottom, Matt gave her arm a little poke and pointed in the direction he wanted her to go. It was evident that he'd caught most, if not all, of Alex's exchange with Frank and Ted.

"Alex, this is none of your business, and it's a dangerous game you're playing," Matt said, his face stern.

It was the closest Matt had ever come to being upset with her, and it was pretty hard to take. Of course, defending Winn was the only thing that could drive him to such measures. But Alex wasn't deterred. She was confident this would work.

"Matt, I know this sounds crazy, but please hear me out. Doesn't it hurt you to see Winn losing his business through no fault of his own?" Alex pleaded.

"Of course, Alex, but—"

"Well, it hurts me too. I know how talented he is. He deserves to be successful, and right now Ted Martin forcing the hand of people around here is what's getting in the way of that. Imagine though, Blake failing and Winn succeeding in this public place, with this spectacular horse that *everyone* has heard about. No one will be able to make the case that Blake should have Winn's clients. Ted won't have a leg to stand on when peddling his bullshit."

Matt didn't say anything, but she could tell that he was softening, perhaps deciding not to get in the way. Alex decided to push her luck. "Why don't you go break the news to Winn? I think you can make him understand better than I can."

Matt watched her for a long minute then nodded before heading over to where Winn stood, his foot on the rail of the pen. The mare had quieted and now stood directly across from him as they watched each other.

That's a familiar sight.

Alex smiled to herself before sending a silent plea to the sky that she was in fact right.

Moments later, Winn came marching up to her with balled fists and raging eyes. "Are you trying to get me killed, Alexandra? What in the hell were you thinking?" he demanded.

She squared her feet up to him. "You can do this, Winn. Do you want your training business back? Rule Eight. Right here, right now.

Put on your big-boy panties and show these idiots why you're ten times the horseman Blake is." Alex grabbed the sides of his face and forced his gaze to hers. "You want this? You've got to fight for it."

He stared into her eyes for a long minute, and then his gaze hardened. With a sense of triumph, Alex knew he'd resolved to do it.

Chapter 26

Less than an hour after Alex had engineered the horse-breaking contest, Frank officially bought the mare. When Blake heard what happened, he'd insisted he should get first crack at the mare. Winn didn't object.

Blake boldly stepped into the pen while Alex and Winn stood outside watching next to Frank and Ted Martin. Blake had a whip in one hand and a lasso over his shoulder. The mare paced as far away from him as she could get. Her expression appeared tense, and her eyes never left him. Blake dropped the whip at his feet, unwound and rewound the lasso, watching her.

"All right, you little bitch. Time to learn," he said louder than necessary, playing to his audience.

Blake started a slow, sweeping circle over his head with the lasso, and the mare bolted into action, running the perimeter around him. He threw the line expertly, and it looped over her head and down to her shoulders. The moment the rope touched her skin, she became a flurry of movement, running, bucking, stopping to rear and turn around. Blake left some slack in the line as he bent down to pick up the whip. The mare took advantage and charged at him, ears pinned, teeth bared. Blake righted himself quickly and ran back to avoid the bite. Reaching out with the whip hand, he cracked her hard on the side of the face.

Alex bit her tongue to keep from crying out, realizing at that moment exactly what she'd done.

I unleashed this monster on a poor horse for selfish reasons.

Horrified, Alex turned to see Winn watching her.

He nodded at her in sympathy. "Don't blame yourself. This would have happened at Blake's place regardless. He would need to catch her to get her to breed, and he would do exactly this. At least here, Frank has to sit and watch, not bury his head in the sand when it comes to what Blake's really about."

Alex nodded, still wanting to throw up knowing it was going to get worse.

After being struck in the face, the mare turned sharply and again began to run the perimeter of the fence line, trying to get as far from Blake as she could. He drew up slack and forced her into running an increasingly smaller and smaller circle until she was almost on top of him. She took another opportunity to spin and charge him and again he ran backwards while delivering a sharp blow from the whip, this time on the side of her neck.

By now, word of what was going down had spread across the auction. People were beginning to gather around the edges of the round pen. Blake leaned hard against the rope and roughly pulled the mare into a halt. She faced him warily and snorted. The mare danced to the side, and Blank yanked the rope and struck her with the whip again. They repeated this dance for what seemed like an eternity. Whenever she moved her feet, there was a wrench and a whack. The crowd murmured, but no one spoke up.

Under his breath, Winn said in frustration, "That's going to take a month to undo right there. You're asking me to fix that in ten minutes—with an audience."

"It would take a month with Tommy because he's tender, softhearted," Alex muttered. "This one? She's steel, look at her. He can't break her." She tried to soothe Winn's nerves.

They watched the mare as she planted her feet, appearing to have the measure of the brutal arrangement Blake was trying to strike with her. With a sinking heart, Alex realized the horse was backing down and standing still.

Blake turned and flashed a nauseating triumphant smile toward her and Winn. "They all break," he said in triumph.

Blake waved over a guy holding a saddle. The mare watched him but stayed planted in place as he walked over to pull the saddle through the bars of the round pen. Her muscles ticked as he roughly threw the pad and saddle onto her back, but she did not move. Blake approached the mare's head, and when she flinched and stepped away, he hit her with the whip. He approached again, and she stood, watching him as he brought a bridle to her face, forced the bit in her mouth, and then removed the lasso.

Alex began to worry. What if Blake's brutal methods *did* work with this mare? Could she be wrong about all of this? Had she created a platform for Blake to showcase his "talents"?

Alex knew in her heart that his way was wrong, but if Blake broke this mare, then she'd singlehandedly doomed Winn's training business.

Winn had once told her that horses didn't think like people and they weren't capable of human emotions. But at this moment, Alex looked at the horse and thought she saw a calculating intelligence living behind that uneasy eye.

Blake brutally wrenched up on the girth, and the mare danced to the side. She was punished with another sharp crack from the whip and a rough yank on the bit. Alex looked over at Winn's hands on the fencing. He was gripping so hard all of the blood had left his knuckles, and they stood out stark white against the dark red paint. Her gaze traced his arms, where the veins bulged, and then up to his face, where there was tension in his jaw and ice in his eyes.

Alex's eyes landed on Frank and Ted. Frank had a hard line for a mouth, and she could tell that he wasn't thrilled with the display in the pen. Ted, however, almost looked jovial as he slapped a hand on Frank's shoulder and said, "That boy's tough, and he won't back down. You made a good choice. You'll be riding that one after all, Frank."

Alex watched as Blake put a foot in the stirrup, and when the horse moved, he struck her. He put weight on the stirrup, and she danced. When the horse finally stood still, Blake threw his weight over into the saddle, and the whole crowd held its breath. Nothing happened. Blake looked up and around at the people gathered. He held out one arm and called out to the masses, "They all break."

A few people tentatively clapped. Alex felt like throwing up.

"Winn...I—I'm so sorry." She looked up at his face, afraid of his reaction. He never pulled his eyes from the mare and Alex was shocked when a small twitch pulled up the corner of his mouth.

"No...she's got him." Winn let go of the fence and placed a hand against Alex's abdomen, pushing her with him as he took a step away.

Alex trusted Winn and stepped back with him. After a beat of stillness, the mare blew up in a spectacular clamor of movement and dust. She jumped forward, lurching Blake out of his triumphant wave. He gathered the reins and attempted to yank her head up while landing the whip hard on her flank. The horse completely ignored the whip and galloped straight at the fence line. Blake flailed atop her back while the mare charged the gate, bucking hard as she stopped and spun. The resulting force threw Blake into the fence, which he bounced off, landing on the ground in front of them. The mare took off around the pen and began looping back with a vengeance toward Blake's dazed form.

"Aw, hell," Winn muttered as he quickly stepped through the bars and put himself between the charging horse and Blake's prone body.

With hatred in her eyes, the mare buzzed the two men with her ears pinned and teeth bared. Winn kept his feet planted as she came and didn't even flinch when at the last second, the mare diverted and started around the pen again.

Winn looked over his shoulder as Blake came to his senses. "Guess that means it's my turn?"

Blake's eyes filled with rage, but as he watched the mare coming back for a second pass, he chose to step out through the bars. His father and Frank approached.

"You okay, son? That one's a lost cause," Ted said theatrically.

"That bitch won't even breed, Frank, she's Alpo," Blake spewed venomously, still bent over, hands on his knees.

"We'll see," Alex quipped.

"She's going to kill your boyfriend, city girl, and it will be your doing," Blake hissed as he righted himself.

Alex's eyes narrowed, but she gestured toward the side of her head. "You've got sand in your hair."

With that, Alex stepped past Blake and stood at the fence line, training her eyes on Winn and the mare.

Please don't let Blake be right.

Winn made it to the center of the round pen. His eyes were glued on the horse that was still crazed and running circles around him, the reins flailing around her front legs. He bent down and picked up the lasso Blake had discarded, never taking his eyes off the horse. She charged, and Alex held her breath. Winn calmly straightened himself and stood, feet planted. As the mare got closer, he stepped to the side, twisted his body, and slapped the lasso rope on his calf. The horse diverted without striking and continued to run. She tried to come at him three more times, each time with aggression and speed, and each time Winn held his ground until the last moment, then sent her away with a step and a wave of the rope.

He started calmly speaking to her. "Easy…easy, girl. You're all right. You're all right. Easy there, Red."

Alex smiled to herself at the name. The horse's gait became slightly less frantic, and her sides heaved.

"Shh, easy now," Winn cooed.

The horse stopped running and began jogging. Winn stepped to the side and lined himself up with the front of the horse. She stopped on a dime and turned to face him. Winn turned his back to her and took several steps away. Alex's chest hurt from not breathing. She'd seen him do this before but never with a horse hell-bent on maiming a man. The mare watched his back and took a tentative step forward. Winn turned back around to face her again, and they sized one another up for a long moment.

Finally Winn said, "All right, that gear's gotta go. You gonna let me over there?"

He took a step forward, and she stayed still. He dropped the lasso and slowly approached her, his empty hands low at his sides. She eyed him and rocked back on her heels, readying herself to bolt. He shushed softly to her and reached a hand to her neck. She flinched, and he froze, eyes trained on the ground.

A moment passed, and the mare finally let out a breath. Winn mumbled something inaudible and moved his hand down to get a hold of the rein. She shied and danced away from him, and he followed her, keeping slack in the rein so as to not pull on the bit in her mouth. She danced half a lap around the pen before her feet quieted again.

Winn moved to the horse's side and while one hand stayed on her neck, the other pulled off the tack. "We'll need to come back to that saddle…someday," Winn quietly said.

Alex smiled to herself. She knew what he was going to do, and although it called out her bluff to Frank, she knew he was making the right call. The compassionate call.

Blake yelled from the side of the ring, "You're not her stud, man, you don't need to woo her unless you're planning on actually mounting her." He laughed at his own crass joke and looked around at several sullen faces that didn't appear to give him the grins he was hoping for.

Winn twisted his arm around his back and flipped Blake off without taking his eyes off the horse. A few uncomfortable chuckles came from the crowd.

Now that the horse was relieved of all of the tack, Winn returned to the middle of the pen. The mare stayed at the fence and he sent her off trotting before stopping her and turning her around to go the other way. All this was done with only the twist of his body and flick of his wrist. They repeated this several times until the mare was watching and waiting for her cues from Winn.

Finally, he stopped her. She turned to face him. Winn gave her his back and walked away. This time he kept walking, and she followed about fifteen feet behind him. When he stopped, she kept walking until she was right behind him. Winn stayed facing away and began to walk again. The horse followed, her nose right behind the center of his back.

Alex finally allowed herself to breathe easy. Winn had her. He walked to the side of the pen and motioned to Trix, who handed him a halter with a lead rope on it. Winn pulled the halter over her head, uttering more softly mumbled words. He turned, and the mare followed, no tension on the line, heeling like a well-behaved dog. Winn stopped, and she stopped.

"I'm done," Winn said to Frank. He turned to face the people outside of the pen for the first time since he'd stepped through the bars twenty minutes earlier. "She's done."

"So you chicken out even after I get it tired for you, huh, Kid?" Blake sneered. "Guess that proves who's willing to get the job done."

Winn nodded to acknowledge him but then turned to Frank. "This mare has been through enough trauma today. I'm not willing to force her to do more to prove that I can train a horse better than Blake Martin."

The mare nudged him from behind, and he turned to rub the middle of her forehead gently. "Frank, you know me. The horse comes first. She's exquisite, hell, they all are. And for what they do for us, they deserve to be fiercely protected. This one is rideable. I'd stake my career on it, but I'm not going to harass this mare to save my ass. She's done right by me now. She's proven she can listen to reason. That's good enough for today. If you decide to take her home instead of sending her to Martin's, I'll give you some pointers, and help you when I can. I owe her that. Now, where do you want her?"

Frank silently pointed to his trailer and opened the gate to the pen. Winn walked through the crowd that had parted, and the mare followed quietly. They reached the trailer. She stood near him as he dropped the gate, and then she followed him right up the ramp.

Winn stepped down from the trailer and locked in the mare before coming back to the group. There was a silence in the air that was hard to read. Alex looked at Frank, wondering what he would do.

Before he could speak, Blake broke in. "Frank, you know that this guy will take a month to put a saddle on her and even then, he's not capable of breaking her. He can't ride her."

Trix made an annoyed sound, and Alex jumped in. "When that horse got here, it wouldn't let a man within twenty feet of her. She followed him like a puppy through a crowd. That's training."

"He's made her a pet, not a working horse. The only reason that worked is because of the time I put in before he stepped into it," Blake rebutted.

"You beat that thing mercilessly in front of dozens of people, Blake. Everyone here can see that horse is never going to let you on her back again," Alex shot back.

"Oh, she'll let me on her again, city girl, I won't give her a choice. Today proves once and for all, Winn doesn't have what it takes to break and ride a real horse." Blake gloated.

Both Trix and Alex opened their mouths, but Winn finally spoke up. "Enough," he said firmly.

Winn looked over Blake's shoulder at the sign advertising the night's rodeo. "You want to ride something?" he asked pointedly. "Let's ride something."

Chapter 27

Rock music blared as the cowboys entered the arena to be introduced for the bareback bronc event that both Blake and Winn had entered at the last minute. Winn was the only one wearing a baseball cap instead of the classic cowboy hat.

He seemed to move in slow motion as he took long, easy steps through the sand. When he looked at Alex out of the side of his eye, he gave her a sexy smirk and little hike of his chin. Alex's heart hit the back of her chest. It was undeniable—she was in love with Winn, but God, in that moment, who wouldn't be?

After the announcer gave the crowd a quick introduction to the dozen or so participants, the men began to file out. Winn stayed behind and started talking to a pair of men sitting on horses in the ring. After a quick talk, Winn nodded and shook each one's hand, and they all smiled.

Alex turned to Matt. "What was that about?"

"Those are the pickup men. I imagine Winn stopped to check that they were still his friends. Feeling out if Blake had tried to arrange some kind of deal." Matt said.

"What's a pickup man? What kind of deal?" Alex asked.

"They're the men who get him off the bronc when the buzzer sounds. They have his life in their hands. If Blake wanted to get Winn hurt, these guys could see to it."

Alex swallowed hard. She knew this was dangerous, but her faith in Winn's riding had made her confident. It hadn't even dawned on her that Blake could try to cheat.

Matt spoke again, pulling her from her thoughts. "I would think he's having the same conversation with the guys at the chute." He saw her stricken face and added, "Don't you worry none. All these men have known and liked Winn since he was a boy. They'll take good care of him."

Alex nodded, trying to take Matt's words to heart.

The announcer's voice boomed through the loudspeaker. "First to ride, locally grown Winn Taylor, better known to some of you as The Kid, and he's drawn Pick Up Sticks. This big horse is new to the circuit, so let's see what he's made of. You know how this works, ladies and gentlemen. Our cowboys have to try to ride out eight seconds atop these broncs. You think The Kid's got it in him?"

The crowd cheered.

Alex watched Winn climb onto the back of a heavy-bodied dark bay in the chute. The animal jostled some but kept four feet on the ground. There was fussing with things that Alex couldn't make out. There was a beat of stillness when Winn leaned way back, slowly cracked his neck to the left, then the right, coming back to center, then gave a quick nod and the door flew open.

The horse turned out, head low to the ground as it bucked high and hard over and over again. Winn's chin was pinned to his chest as his free hand bounced a rhythm over his head. Alex held her breath and kept darting her eyes to the timer three seconds in.

Good God, how long did eight seconds take?

Winn's feet were up on the shoulder of the horse and swung high and away with the jarring movements. Alex thought he had it, he looked solid, but still, only five seconds in. The horse made a quick shift in direction and Winn went a little to the side but seemed to right himself again before the buzzer sounded. Alex let out the painful air in her chest. The men from earlier ran their horses at the bucking horse, one pulling at a strap near its hind end the other reaching for Winn.

"Uh oh," Matt said beside her.

"What?" Alex asked.

"He's hung up." In response to her blank stare, he continued, "His hand is stuck, he should be off by now."

Alex didn't have an idea for how quickly he should be able to dismount, but Matt would know. She chewed her bottom lip, "Please" she said, under her breath. A few more agonizing seconds passed where Winn was thrown around the top of the horse while trying to free his other hand.

"Come on, Kid," Matt mumbled.

Finally, Winn was loose and able to lean over the back of the pick-up man's horse before sliding down to the ground. With his feet back on terra firma, he looked up at her and Matt in the stands, giving a little bounce with his eyebrows. He mouthed, "Whoops" before breaking eye contact and removing his hat to wave at the cheering crowd. The announcer said his name again and then his score as seventy-four. The crowd booed.

"Is that not good?" Alex asked.

"It wasn't that great of a horse. Winn rode it fine, but without a horse that's trying harder, you can't score much higher than that. High eighties will be the winners."

"The horse is supposed to buck more than that?" Alex couldn't believe it. In her eyes, the entire thing had looked tremendously violent.

"He gave some good bucks, and that little turn helped some, but they want to see them get more airborne. It wasn't a good draw, but maybe a blessing seeing as it's been so long." Matt explained.

"Can we go see him before his next ride?" Alex asked.

Matt shook his head. "We shouldn't. He's going to want to go over that ride in his head a few times before he gets on another. Especially since getting down was dodgy."

The loudspeaker boomed again. "Next up, another guy from down the road, hometown boy Blake Martin, and he's drawn Leather and Lace. That spunky little mare we all remember from last year, don't we, folks?"

The crowd cheered again.

Alex couldn't tell if they cheered for the horses or the cowboys or both. In the chute, Blake lowered himself down onto the back of a little freckled gray horse. He repeated the same fussing that Winn had done, leaned back and dipped his chin hard. The door to the chute burst open, and the mare took off at almost a dead run before stopping and launching her entire body full into the air.

Alex gasped. She now understood what Matt had been talking about. This one didn't buck. It jumped all four feet into the air before kicking out violently with her back feet. Blake was thrown backwards over and over again, bouncing off the horse's haunch. He too had his feet way up by her shoulder blades and appeared to be finding a rhythm in the hard impacts.

Time seemed to move faster than it had during Winn's ride. The buzzer sounded, and Blake didn't wait for the pick-up men. He released his hand and swung a leg over the horse, riding the next buck into the air and landing on his feet. The crowd lost their minds yelling and clapping.

"Well, the little mare doesn't disappoint, does she, my friends?" the announcer yelled.

Blake lifted his hat and waved it in the air.

"That's an eighty-eight, ladies and gentlemen! Eighty-eight for Blake Martin! Going to be tough to beat, tough to beat indeed."

The crowd's fervor was renewed. Blake's eyes bounced around the stands until his icy stare found hers. He placed his hat back on his head without breaking eye contact, and then brushed the rim of his hat while giving her a greasy grin.

The evening progressed through the rest of the first round. Four different cowboys had failed to ride out their eight seconds and had received no score. Of the others that did make the time, only one had scored lower than Winn, and Blake still held the lead. Alex's knee bounced in apprehension. She knew she shouldn't be this upset. After all, this was a sport, a game. This didn't mean anything about horse training, but she was worried nonetheless. Had she helped create a situation where Winn had to put his body on the line to defend himself?

The announcer broke into her thoughts. "Okay, people, we're all set up for our second go-round in the bareback bronc event. These men have come here to prove themselves against time and beast. Who's going to prevail?" The crowd cheered on cue and the announcer continued, "Back in the chute and bringing forward a disappointing first go-round score of seventy-four, this is Winn 'The Kid' Taylor."

Cheering.

"Y'all like this guy, huh? Well, this time he's drawn…Haymaker."

The people in the stands made a collective "Ohhhh" sound that worried Alex, and she looked to Matt for translation. His face was stern, but she couldn't tell if he was also concerned.

"That's a strong horse," Matt said. "It's been around for a while. Has a reputation for quick feet and sharp changes in direction. Tends to throw men early, right out the gate."

Alex looked for Winn to appear near the chutes. When he did, he looked up at her, and she made a questioning face and a little okay-sign with her hands. He nodded and gave her a tight-lipped smile.

The horse in the chute was a sizeable golden palomino. This new horse was way less content to stand still than the last one, and every time Winn went to lower himself onto his back, it would rear. After struggling for several tense moments, Winn was finally on, and the horse was visibly vibrating with anticipation. A long second passed, Winn pulled in a big breath, leaned back and tipped his head. The chute door swung wide, and the horse spun out rapidly, tossing Winn slightly off to the side when the horse's front feet hit the ground.

"You got this, Kid," Matt whispered.

Alex's hands gripped one another so tightly she couldn't feel her fingers. Winn seemed to pull himself to the middle of the horse's back, but the horse launched straight up in the air, throwing Winn's upper body backwards. There was a moment when Alex thought he was losing it. She looked at the clock—two seconds in.

The height the horse reached in the air was spectacular and was followed up with a quick-as-lightning twist when it hit the ground. It was mesmerizing and terrifying, beautiful but disturbing. All of it was happening in slow motion. She looked at the clock: five seconds in.

The roar of the crowd and the announcer's excited words became a low din in the background. All Alex heard was the sound of the horse's feet pounding the sand before it pushed off and catapulted itself and Winn back into the air.

Finally, the buzzer sounded.

The crowd went wild, but Alex waited, learning from the first ride that they weren't in the clear yet. Much to her relief, the pick-up men were there in seconds. Winn smoothly transferred over to the back of their horse and then to the ground. Alex finally allowed herself to breathe in.

Never again. I can never watch him do this again.

"How about that!?" the announcer excitedly yelled. "Our very own hometown hero rides the Haymaker. You can say you were here when. Okay, we're waiting on a score, it's gotta be a good one, don't you think?"

Winn pulled his hat off again and gave it a big wave back and forth as the fans roared. His eyes met hers with a huge smile, which she returned despite the knots in her stomach. He was nothing short of gorgeous.

The announcer's voice cracked as he yelled, "Ninety-one! We've got a ninety-one for that amazing effort. A thing of beauty when a cowboy can ride a horse like that. Ninety-one, hoo boy!"

In the ring, Winn stoically nodded to the crowd again before jogging back to the fencing. Alex ran the math in her head. With a ninety-one that put Winn's final score at 165. Blake would only need a seventy-eight to still come out on top. She looked at Matt, who seemed to be trying to work out the numbers too.

Matt looked up to her finally and said, "Blake only has to ride eight to beat him."

A few other guys rode, some putting up good scores, some getting bucked off. For Alex, the others didn't register or matter—this was a two-man race.

The speakers squawked to life. "Okay, folks, it's looking like a little regional rivalry is rearing its head here today. Next up is Blake Martin. Can he put up a score to surpass our current leader The Kid? He'll try his best to do that atop Bells and Whistles."

Again, the crowd stood to applaud and yell. Alex refused to watch Blake go through the motions of getting prepped and instead searched the areas near the chutes to see where Winn had ended up. She finally spotted him leaning against the railing, eyes trained on the ring, with an easy smile on his face as he chatted with Trix who had somehow secured a spot in the staging area.

As if he felt her looking at him, Winn's eyes bounced to her and held her gaze. She felt stuck in his stare, unable to look away from everything it seemed to convey despite the distance. There was a restless need in his eyes that was so unmistakable, her heart beat faster anticipating being closer to him. Trix slapped Winn on the back, laughing at whatever he'd said and Winn broke their eye contact to turn to him and share in the laugh.

Alex shook off the spell of being held by Winn's gaze in time to watch Blake nod to the chute operators. The door flew open and the horse bolted out, launching a kick that barely landed before it was airborne again. The force tossed Blake back and to the side. He desperately tried to keep himself in the middle while keeping his free hand above his head. A quick check of the clock told Alex he was halfway through. Then another buck with a twist tossed Blake even more off-center. He was half on and half off, clinging to the side of the bucking horse with one arm. When it looked like he was about to fall, he brought his free arm down to the ropes.

"Oh, no. That's a disqualified ride. Blake Martin with the DQ," the announcer yelled as Blake bounced free of the horse, landing on his knees in the sand as the buzzer sounded. He slapped the ground in frustration.

"No score. No score, cowboy. Better luck next time," the announcer shouted.

Alex couldn't help herself—she stood and cheered before she quickly realized that everyone else around her was making sad, disappointed noises instead of clapping. She promptly sat, shoving her hands under her seat.

Winn had beat Blake. Alex giggled to herself and turned to Matt who wore an unabashed grin. Alex gave him a hug that she cut short because her mind focused on one thing.

Winn. Get to Winn.

The need to see him, to be near him, pulled at her insides. Alex stood, made an apology to Matt, who was lagging behind, and tore down the bleachers.

As Alex rounded the corner down at ring level, she saw Winn taking huge strides as he made his way toward the stands. His eyes landed on her, and his face hardened. For a moment she thought he was angry, then she recognized the look for what it was: predatory. She shuddered in anticipation of what he would do when they crossed the hundred feet that separated them.

People clapped Winn on the back as he passed, but he didn't acknowledge them, his eyes pinned on her. Thirty feet. Twenty feet until she was snared. Ten feet.

"Congra—"

Winn cut off her words by grabbing the back of her neck and pulling her to him. His mouth was hot and eager, and she was alone with him in an instant. She wrapped her arms around his waist in an attempt to remove all of the space between them. His fist knotted in her hair as he pulled her deeper to him. The exhilaration of the day, the adrenaline from the fear she felt for him, the heated stare from across the arena—all of these things were kindling that had found a match. Alex caught herself as she started to untuck his shirt, remembering that they were standing in a crowd.

She broke from his lips in time to hear a polite throat-clearing.

"Ahem."

When they pulled away from one another, Alex saw Frank Powers standing off to the side, making a face that was hard to read. Alex felt like she could die from humiliation. Winn smiled down at her and then put on his professional face as he released her.

"Sir," Winn finally said after taking a half second to casually poke part of his shirt back down into his jeans.

"Can you spare a minute, son?" Frank asked.

"Ah, yes sir, but only a minute," Winn said with a little sideways grin at Alex.

"I'll be quick. I want you to know that I admire your work, Winn, and this mess was never about what I think of you as a horseman." Frank paused. Winn nodded but let him continue. "Now, with that show Blake put on with the mare, there's not a person here who could argue that he should train my horses regardless of the hold his daddy has on this county."

"Appreciate you saying that, Frank. I understand that there are forces here that impact your decisions," Winn said graciously.

"Have to admit, the bronc riding didn't make a difference. It was a little foolish, and you didn't need to do that," Frank said with an almost scolding look on his face.

"I know. I did that to shut *his* mouth, not change your mind," Winn admitted.

Frank chuckled. "Right, okay then. That paint horse has been at Martin's for almost three weeks and I need it to go back to work soon. I'll bring it over with the River Rock mare in the morning. Provided I can get her reloaded at my house."

"Yes, sir, thank you."

Frank and Winn shared a firm, brief handshake and a nod before Frank walked away. When Winn turned to Alex, he gave her a relieved smile. The intensity of their moment was washed away by the break but also by Matt and Trix joining them.

"All right, Red, now that your meddling has borne fruit, what do you say we grab a drink and a dance?" Winn asked.

Alex laughed. "So glad you're admitting that was all me, so I don't have to point it out."

He returned the laugh, looping his arm around her waist while they made their way over to the tent where the band was starting up.

They hit the dance floor as a bluesy, sultry song blasted from the stage. Couples buzzed around them, but Winn pulled her close, and they swayed together slowly in their own world. Winn's scent, sweat, leather and a hint of Old Spice, combined with the feel of his body pressed against her was starting to drive her mad. Alex decided to invite him into her torture.

She leaned up to whisper in his ear, "Too bad we're Matt's ride. I need to get you out of here before I do very naughty things to you in front of your adoring fans."

Winn's feet stopped, and she watched his jaw pop out as he clenched his teeth. "He can walk," he replied, without a hint of humor in his tone.

Alex threw her head back and laughed. When she brought her eyes back to Winn, his face was serious.

"God, you're beautiful," he said huskily.

She watched him for a long second. "I'm really lucky you think so," she said, shifting under the weight of his unrelenting gaze.

After a beat of silence hung between them, Winn simply said, "Stay."

"What?"

"I'm not saying don't ever go back to Chicago—honestly, I don't know what I'm saying…"

"Winn—"

"No, at least let me say this. I truly don't know what I'm asking for, but I know I want you to stay—stay longer than you planned. If you were going to stay for three months, stay for five, if you were going to stay four, stay six. I feel like we wasted so much time. I don't feel ready to lose this right as we've found it."

Alex caged her knee-jerk desire to counter his argument, but deep down, she knew that this conversation needed space, time away from the events and emotions of the evening.

"I'm not saying no, but I'm saying I can't make a decision right now. Can we enjoy tonight? Let reality hit tomorrow?" she asked.

Winn watched her and seemed to briefly war with himself before he pasted on a smile that didn't reach his eyes. She sighed, feeling guilty but not wrong. The conversation had put some cold water on their heat, but as promised, Winn let the issue drop and softly pulled her along through another song.

There was a presentation of awards for the night's rodeo. After all was said and done, Winn had ended up in third place for the bareback event, which had earned him a belt buckle. Alex laughed—of course it was a belt buckle.

After a few more dances, the group decided it was time to start the long drive home. Trix had come to them earlier in the night acting dodgy and stating that he'd found his own way home. She assumed he'd found a lady friend and was embarrassed to delve into details with her.

Alex sat in the front seat as Matt slept in the back. As he drove, Winn reached over and lightly held her hand on the center console. His thumb traced light, small circles on the back of her hand. The silence was comfortable, and her feelings of contentment wrapped around her. She decided to log this moment mentally. She wasn't sure how long it would last or if she'd ever have another one quite like it. It needed to be remembered.

When they got home, Winn followed her upstairs in silence, no words needed, and they made love softly and quietly. A tinge of sadness replaced the explosive connection they had earlier.

Chapter 28

In the weeks that followed the auction, Winn and Alex settled into a bit of a routine, neither willing to be the first to rock the boat by mentioning her leaving again. They spent almost all day together, morning chores in the barn, time with Tommy before lunch. As promised, Frank had brought over the paint horse and Red Flag the day after the auction. As a result, much of their afternoon time was spent putting Trix through the wringer as his training education continued to take flight.

With a little patience and another fall for Trix, they had the paint working around the farm equipment and running through the creek without a care in the world. The River Rock mare was learning her interactions with humans didn't need to be combative.

Their nights consisted of exploring one another, sometimes soft and other times playful and full of laughter. Their bubble was made of magic and denial, but it was perfect if you didn't look closely enough to recognize its fragility.

It was afternoon and Alex was sitting on Winn's desk, thumbing through a magazine for cattle farmers.

Who knew that was a thing?

Winn sat in his chair flipping through a pile of unruly mismatched sheets of paper on which he'd taken notes about horses he'd trained so far that summer—hours spent, arrival and departure dates, along those lines.

He sighed. "You ever heard anyone say you shouldn't take something you love and try to make money doing it?"

Alex nodded. "You understand that a little better now?" she chuckled.

"I love the training. I hate the invoicing."

"You know you could show me the billing. I'm pretty Type A when it comes to stuff like that," Alex offered.

There was an uncomfortable beat where they both must have simultaneously thought about how futile that would be. She felt foolish, but Winn seemed annoyed as he let out a ragged breath.

"Well, helping with paperwork for the next seven days doesn't help me much," he said tersely.

Pop.

Alex's eyes darted to the calendar on the wall. It was July 25. Winn was right. She had exactly one week before she was going to leave. Alex realized that they had never spoken of it. Mae must have told him, and he must have been thinking about it often enough to have the countdown so precise. She wasn't surprised that this had been going on under the surface, or that he'd kept it from her. She'd done the same.

"I may be able to help you get caught up, and it would be time together before I have to go."

He let out a dry, cynical laugh. "Have to…"

"Yes, have to," Alex said firmly.

"Well, the more time we spend together before you *have to* go makes the hole you leave that much bigger. Not sure I want to sign myself up for that."

"So how is that different than the last three weeks? What have you been doing during this time?"

"Lying to myself mostly," Winn said bluntly, gaze bouncing to hers. "Same as you."

"So what do you propose we do, stop talking now so that in a week me leaving is easier? Would that make it easier?"

"Of course not," Winn scoffed.

"So if you don't have a better idea, I'm sticking with enjoying the last part of the summer and recognizing it for what it is."

"And what is that?"

"A beautiful few months in a place and with people that changed my life."

"Glad to be of service then," he said rudely.

Alex popped off the desk, frustrated at her lack of ability to explain and his complete lack of willingness to understand.

"Okay, if you're going to be like this, I'm taking a walk. Enjoy your pouting, you dick."

Alex left the stable and headed to see Tommy. She figured he at least may appreciate spending time with her before her departure. As she approached, she whistled, and Tommy responded with a nicker before trotting out of the stall to stand in the paddock.

"Hey, handsome," she said to him as she climbed through the railing, and he leaned into her so she could scratch his head.

"Tell me I'm doing the right thing, Tommy. This was a time out, a time for recalibrating, but now I have to go home and put my life back together. Don't I?"

Her little horse remained frustratingly silent.

"I'm going to miss our little chats, my friend." Alex smiled to herself.

Tommy picked his head up, and she followed his gaze. Winn had come around the path, expression hard to read.

He held up his palms in surrender. "I'm not here to fight or pout."

Alex nodded and watched him climb through the fence.

"Knew I'd find you here," Winn said softly as he got closer.

"Guess my huffs are getting predictable," she said, keeping her tone light and trying to determine if this was a true olive branch.

"I don't know how we're supposed to act with this thing looming over our heads, Alex, so if you want to make this week about enjoying the time we have left, then I'm willing to try."

"Okay," she said cautiously, unsure of what to make of his quick change of heart.

"So, on that note, I have a surprise for you." To her raised eyebrow, Winn added, "Well I guess *we* have a surprise for you."

"Okay," she repeated, curious.

He lightly grabbed her shoulders and marched her over to the fence.

"Sit, please," he told her.

She scaled the fence and sat on the rail while watching him climb out and jog into the barn. When he returned, he had a bridle over his shoulder and a saddle propped up on his hip.

Winn gave her a tentative grin, and Alex gasped, "Oh my God."

"All right, Tommy Boy, you ready to perform for your number-one fan?" Winn asked as he made his way back into the paddock.

Alex's throat got tight as she watched Winn approach her brave little horse. He stood stock-still as Winn placed the tack on him, all the while cooing and whispering calm words in his ear. Once the bridle was on, Winn turned to Alex to watch her face.

"You've been—he's been letting you? How?" she asked, struggling to find words.

"Some bossy little redhead gave me crap about this horse once, decided to prove her wrong," Winn said with a crooked grin.

He walked around Tommy once, giving his body a firm rub down, gauging the horse's reactive responses and level of ease. When he was back on the horse's left side, Winn put a foot up in the stirrup and softly swung himself over.

Alex held her breath.

Tommy and Winn looked to her. She could swear they wore matching expectant expressions waiting for her reaction. Alex couldn't contain herself. She buried her head in her hands to hide her tears.

"Aw, Christ," Winn swore. "You're happy, right? Please tell me that's happy crying."

She wordlessly nodded, trying to get a handle on herself.

"Good, 'cause it gets better, but I can't let you sit on this one if you can't see."

At that, she jerked her head up, no longer caring if he saw her blotchy cry face. "Really?"

"We had a bargain and seeing as how we're coming down to the wire, I figured I needed to make good on my end. You worked, you learned, and he's ready—so do you want to ride him?"

She made a sniffing sound and then nodded. "When did you do this?"

"We've had a few late nights lately, haven't we, friend?" Winn said, rubbing a hand up and down Tommy's neck. He clucked, and Tommy started a slow and wobbly jog around the pen.

"He's still really green, so I think walking may be all you can do," Winn said to her as he tried his best to help the horse find a straight line.

Alex's heart warmed, seeing the two of them trying so hard and she enthusiastically nodded again. "That's all I've ever wanted."

Winn pulled his rein hand up, and Tommy stopped. Alex bit her lip. Their horse was such a good boy. Winn climbed down slowly and offered his hand to Alex as she approached. He helped her foot into the stirrup and gave her backside a little shove to help her get into the saddle smoothly.

She couldn't believe it. She was sitting on her broken little lost cause. She leaned down and ran her hand up his neck, showering him with happy words, unable to shake the wide grin from her face. He stood like a perfect gentleman, and she had to force back another round of grateful tears. Winn walked up past Tommy's head, and Tommy followed him like Alex had seen so many do before.

***

Winn turned to take in the look of pure joy on Alex's face as her hair tumbled around her shoulders and her eyes glimmered with tears. *This* was the image he knew would haunt him after she left. When she'd bolted out of the office, he'd had a momentary flash of panic where he envisioned never getting to see this look on her face again and decided the empty feeling it would leave was worth it. He knew that giving Alex this gift would break him a little more, but he couldn't let her go without sharing it with her.

Winn looked away and took a deep breath to shove all the thoughts and feelings down into his gut and off his face before he brought his eyes back to her. They took a few laps around the paddock in what was essentially the world's greatest pony ride. After a few minutes, Winn turned back to look at her again.

"Good?" he asked.

"Better than, Winn. Thank you. Thank you so much for this."

He held her stare for a long time, batting back words he knew wouldn't change the situation.

"Just holding up my end of the bargain," Winn finally said.

She shook her head as she got down, and keeping a hand on Tommy, she walked up to Winn.

"You've given me the most amazing gift—I don't know how to thank you." She leaned forward and placed a soft kiss on his lips.

"You're welcome," he said quietly, watching her for a few seconds before directing his attention to heaping praise on Tommy.

"I think your boy is ready for his move to the main barn," Winn announced ceremoniously.

"Really?"

"Since he's no longer overwhelmed by every little sight and sound, he should be at ease in the main barn even though it's so busy. Plus, he needs to learn how to make horse friends. Before he was too skittish, and the herd would have eaten him alive, but you've manned up a bit lately, haven't you, friend?" he asked, rubbing Tommy's head.

"My little man's all grown up," Alex said with genuine pride in her voice.

Winn turned to look at her while her attention was directed at Tommy. The sinking feeling in his chest from the words he wouldn't say was almost unbearable.

She's leaving me. I can't do anything to stop it.

He reached out to guide a lock of hair back around her ear. Alex turned to face him, her damp eyes shining. He couldn't make words, so he drew her into a long, slow kiss that had her melting into him.

***

After Winn had kissed her so gently, Alex felt like she was supposed to say something, as if the kiss was almost a challenge she was supposed to address. Instead, when he broke away from her, Winn silently turned away and started to un-tack Tommy.

Winn pulled the saddle off Tommy then produced a mint from his pocket. The two looked solid and at ease. Alex had the strangest sense that this was a sign that they both were going to be okay without her. She smiled sadly to herself. Winn and Tommy weren't fully healed, but they were healing. Could she say the same about herself?

After they ceremoniously moved Tommy over to the main barn, Winn turned to her, unsaid words swirling behind his eyes. He looked uncomfortable, and she knew he was uneasy with the way they had agreed to spend the next week. Trix came waltzing into the aisle.

"I heard this one was moving in today," Trix said. "You guys make one hell of a team." He slapped Winn on the back with a wide grin.

"That we do," Alex agreed, giving Trix and then Winn a reassuring smile.

"I'm going to go close up the office, so I'll see you guys at dinner," Winn muttered, making a quick exit.

Trix and Alex watched his back as he made his way out the door. Alex shifted her gaze back to Trix, expecting to see his usual jovial face, and was surprised to find it more sullen than she'd ever seen.

"So, we going to talk about this?" Trix asked.

"What are you defining as *this*?" Alex asked, nervous about his abnormally somber tone.

"You're leaving? You're actually going to leave?"

"Yes, I need to go home."

"Well, I call bullshit." Trix braced his hands on his hips.

She was surprised at comment, but his tone was soft.

"It's not bullshit. We all knew that I would leave eventually. I have to go back. This place, you guys, Winn, you're all so important to me. I don't think I'm overstating when I say knowing you all has made me a better person. But it's time for me to start planning what I do next."

"Staying here with Winn can't be the plan?"

"Winn is amazing. There's no questioning that, but he and I? It's not a sustainable situation. I can't bear the thought of staying long enough to watch it disintegrate, because it will."

"I get it, Red, honestly, I know what it's like to hate everything about someone. Hate everything they've ever done, everything they've ever said, but still every fiber of your being yearns to be in her orbit, even though it would ruin both of you if you succumbed to her pull."

Alex's jaw dropped. "Pretty sure we're not talking about Winn and me anymore." Trix blinked hard, shaking his head a little. "Trix, I'm sorry I've been so selfish. Obviously, you've got something of your own going on that we should talk about."

Trix blinked again and seemed to snap back from the hundred miles away he'd traveled to. He pasted on a mask and finally looked at her. "What? Nah, I'm good. Right now, this is about if you're going to run away from someone I can honestly call one of the best damn men I've ever known. You know I love you, Red, but if you leaving brings back Winn one-point-oh, I'm never going to forgive you." There was a thin veil of humor over a genuine threat.

"I'm not the creator of Winn two-point-oh, so that's not going to change when I leave," Alex insisted.

"You sure?"

"Positive. He's going to be okay, Trix. I know he will be."

"And you?" Trix asked, his eyes kind but worried.

"Less sure about that." Alex tried to laugh but couldn't muster the energy to sell it.

Chapter 29

The next week passed exactly as Alex had assumed it would. She and Winn played her denial game, but there was always an undercurrent of sadness to everything they did. Rides in the fields, evenings in the office, sitting out by the creek before dinners. It was magical, but it was painful. Both of them swallowed so many words they were full from pretending. It was less severe but the same with all of her friends, many lighthearted moments cut short when the realization that in days they would no longer have one another.

Time flew by, and soon it was the night before she was supposed to leave. She stood in the kitchen, drying dishes with Mae, and there was a quietness between the two of them that Alex knew better than to trust.

As expected, Mae spoke up. "You know, twenty-three years ago I stood at this sink, doing this exact thing with your mother the day before she left."

Alex nodded, feeling uneasy with the correlation.

"When I think about that night, I think about what I wish I had done differently, maybe what more should have been said. At the time, I never would have guessed that she'd never come back, so I can't be too hard on myself. Then there's the fact that all the decisions she made led to you being here right now, so I also can't be too sorry for that."

"You haven't talked about her since I got here."

"You haven't asked."

"I'm asking now."

"What are you asking, Alex?" Mae didn't look up from her washing.

"Do you think it was a mistake for my mother to return to Chicago?"

"When your mom left, I was sure she was making the wrong decision. She had nothing in Chicago and everything here. I couldn't understand why she felt such a strong pull to go back, and I told her so. I tried to force her to see it the way I did. We had pretty harsh words for one another that last night, words I regret, words I'm sure she regrets. I think that fight made it hard for her to see that she truly had options, even after she got back to the city. Right after going back, she met your father. To her, he represented options, and regardless of what I think about your father, I know that he loved Becky with a fierceness that was undeniable, and she returned that love with the same honesty."

The back of Alex's eyes started to sting.

"The way your parents' love burned out was a shame, but because the ending was tragic doesn't mean that it should never have happened. I missed your mom something terrible, but I don't resent her for deciding to go home again. Leaving gave her you and Caleb, a gift I'm sure she'd never wish away."

"What would have happened if she stayed?" Alex asked.

"No way to know."

"Part of me wishes I could talk to her about this," Alex admitted, surprising herself.

"What's stopping you?"

"Pride, I guess."

"Stubborn pride."

Alex chuckled. "You're right about that. Plus, as selfish as this sounds, this is about me and my life. There are obvious parallels, of course, but this is different."

"So earlier you were asking if I think it's a mistake for *you* to go back to Chicago?"

"Maybe. It seems like going back is what I'm supposed to do. You know there are so many things there that I need to fix. Being here seems like I'm avoiding the mess I've made of my life back home. Plus, isn't it crazy to consider moving across the country for a guy that you've known for two months?"

"Let's put the 'Is Winn worth it?' conversation aside for a little bit."

"It's not about if he's worth it, I know he is. He's—he's changing. He's going to be—already is—someone I don't deserve."

Mae considered her words. "Regardless of Winn and that truly misguided interpretation"—she gave Alex a hard stare—"I agree that it's wrong to stay for a man."

"See," Alex said, ignoring Mae's pointed words about her assertion that she didn't deserve Winn.

Mae continued. "I knew the moment I put a foot on this property that I would never leave it. I'm lucky, though. The important decisions in life don't usually come with a big glaring neon sign like that."

"Nothing feels that clear to me, Mae, nothing ever has." Alex admitted.

"If you think going back will help you piece together your life, Alex, then it's what you should do. But if life here is what you want to build, why would you drive across the country to repair something else?"

"Life here is a fantasy."

"So also too good for you?"

Alex paused and looked at the ceiling. "I'd blow it up. I care about you, this place, and everyone here too much to bring it down around us with whatever self-destructive nature drives me to destroy everything."

"Doesn't give us much credit."

"Even if you're all strong enough to endure, how could I ask you to?"

"We love you. You wouldn't have to ask."

"I can't take that risk. If I broke this place, I'd never forgive myself."

Mae tipped her head to the side while watching Alex. "You're so sure that you're still that same person?"

"I don't feel different."

Mae nodded slowly. "Maybe you won't feel different until you get this version of yourself back into your old life. Maybe then you'll see the fit is not the same. If that's the case, you're always welcome to come back."

Alex caught herself fighting back the tears again. Mae wrapped her in a hug. "I guess that's the big thing I needed to get off my chest, kiddo, the thing I didn't flat out say twenty-three years ago. You're always welcome to come back, whether it's two months, two years or two decades from now. You'll always be welcome even if I'm not here to hold open the door for you."

Alex stopped fighting and allowed herself to cry into Mae's shoulder. The older woman held her and rocked slightly.

After a long, cathartic cry in the kitchen with Mae, Alex wandered toward the stairs, and she caught sight of Matt in the front room. Her heart thumped, wondering how many of these she was going to be able to endure.

I should have written everyone a sappy heartfelt letter and left unexpectedly in the middle of the night. It would have been easier than facing these all too real goodbyes.

Matt looked up from a book when she appeared.

"Was hoping to run into you," Matt said with a soft smile.

"Me too," Alex lied.

"I'm not great at goodbyes, Alex."

"Me too," she said truthfully.

"But I've got to say one thing to you before you go."

She popped an eyebrow at that, wondering what version of pressure she would get from him. "What's the one thing?" she asked.

"My heart's going to miss you when you're gone. It's really going to miss you."

Alex let out a puff of air. Way to twist the knife. Of course, there wasn't judgment or coercion from Matt. Of course, all he had was shameless, pure emotion. God, she loved him for that but hated how it made her feel.

"My heart is going to miss you so much, Mattie." Alex sat down and buried her head in his shoulder as he wrapped her in a tight hug. He held her for a few quiet moments before they were interrupted by Winn emerging from the basement steps. She leaned away from Matt and wiped the tears from her eyes.

"I'm going to let you all have the room. See you in the morning," Matt said, rising from the couch and disappearing down the stairs.

"Night, Matt," she called toward the open door but got no response. She turned to Winn and watched as he slowly lowered himself to the chair across from her before he looked up.

"Seems like the clock has run out on us, Alex. No more pretending."

"I know, and I know that you disagree with spending the last week like we did, but I don't know what we could have, or should have, done differently."

"You're right, there wasn't a better choice, but you're leaving, and that doesn't feel like the only option."

"It is for me. I can't begin to tell you how important knowing you and your family has been to me."

"You've had an impact on us all too."

"I know you don't understand what's drawing me back to Chicago, but you have to understand why staying isn't best."

"Do I?" he asked.

"We knew that we were damaged and that we couldn't fix one another. We knew what we've meant to one another was important but not built for the long term." Alex winced saying it, feeling foolish for assuming he was looking for anything long term.

"We knew that?"

"I thought we did."

"I feel less damaged," Winn admitted and then broke eye contact.

"I don't," she said softly, knowing those words would hurt him, but felt like she owed him honesty if nothing else.

"We wasted so much time when you first got here." He sighed, and she nodded her agreement even though he was no longer looking at her.

Winn continued, "My anger and my stubbornness for sure got in the way, but you believe in me, or at least you did, and you pushed me, and I guess for what it's worth I want to thank you for that."

"You make it easy to believe in you, Winn."

He quickly brought his eyes back to her. There was an emotional softness in them she hadn't seen before.

"But I'm not supposed to believe in you?" Winn asked quietly.

"I don't think I've earned that." Alex looked down to avoid the look in his eye.

"I would suspect there's not a damn thing I can say that would change your mind about that."

"You're probably right. Even though I know that I've grown since I've been here, I know that the things about me that are jagged are going to stay sharp until I address what broke them. I have to do that back in Chicago."

"What are you going to do there that you can't do here?" he pushed.

"Honestly? I'm not sure," she confessed.

"If you don't know what it is you should do, why are you so convinced whatever it is needs to be in Chicago?"

"Because it's where I live, it's where my family lives. It's where my life should be. Staying would be ridiculous, it would be like asking you to move to Chicago, it's a non-starter, not plausible."

"For the record, that's not something you've asked me to consider."

"What?" Alex was caught off guard by his words, shocked by them. "Of course not, I'd never ask that of you. Thinking you could leave here is as unrealistic as thinking I could stay."

His teeth clenched as she stared at him unbelievingly. She could sense his horror at the accidental way he'd put that out there. She braced for the embarrassed and angry defensiveness she assumed would follow.

"Then, maybe it was wrong for you to stay past those first few days," he said slowly. It wasn't the flash eruption she expected, but still remarkably hurtful.

"Maybe it was," she shot back.

Too hurt and overwhelmed to stay in the house any longer, Alex stood and made for the front door with frustration and doubt coursing through her veins. She decided that she may as well keep the emotional train wreck rolling and say her final goodbye to Tommy and the other horses. She entered the barn, trying to bring her breathing and frustration levels back down. She stepped into his stall and he nickered at her.

"Oh, my baby boy, I'm so proud of you. You've come such a long way. Listen to Winn, okay? He's going to make you the best cattle horse the world has ever known." She smiled at the thought as he placed his head in her abdomen and pushed a little. She rubbed his ears and traced her hand up and down the part of his neck she could reach. After a few minutes, she heard the door open and knew that Winn had come to find her.

"Alex?" he called.

"In Tommy's stall," she answered. Alex listened to Winn's feet getting nearer and then saw his grim face appear at the stall opening.

"I'm sorry I said that," he said simply.

She nodded, trying to work out what to say that hadn't already been said.

Winn nodded toward Tommy. "He's going to miss you."

"I'm going to miss him too. Will you send me updates on how he's doing?"

Winn looked at the ground. "I'm sure Mae will," he finally said after a long pause, which made Alex's anger flash again.

She left Tommy's stall so that her frustration wouldn't radiate to him.

Latching the stall door, Alex turned on Winn. "So, you won't be bothered?"

Winn sighed again. "I guess not. You're choosing to leave. That means we carry on here without you. It's not fair to ask for updates like we're some sitcom you'll need catching up on."

"That's dramatic and not what I'm asking for, but you're right, Mae will update me. You don't need to waste time on that."

"What did you think, Alex? That you'd leave, and you and I would become pen pals? Maybe I'd see you again in a few years when you come back for a vacation? Maybe you'll bring a boyfriend back with you? A husband? What does that look like in your mind?" His eyes searched hers.

"I honestly don't know, Winn, but I didn't think twelve hours from now we'd have to stop knowing each other."

"I think it does mean that. I think that's how it'll have to be for me."

"Well, that's what you're choosing then."

"Not a ton of great options on the table." He shook his head.

They stared hard at each other for a long moment.

"This wasn't how I wanted our last hours to go," Alex said with frustration.

"What is the right way to spend this time? Should we stick with your drug of choice and go with denial?"

"We could stick with yours and go brooding silence."

He watched her for a long moment, eyes desperate and stewing.

"Damn it," he muttered as he walked up to her and pulled her to him, his mouth overtaking hers in an instant. Her body was on fire immediately, and she responded to the harshness of his kiss with her own brutal attack on his mouth.

Everything she couldn't say, everything she wouldn't let herself feel, she poured into their connection. She held the back of his neck as his hands roughly toured her body. He broke from her mouth to rip the shirt over her head then brought his lips back to her neck. She untucked the front of his shirt and yanked it open, sending buttons spraying to the floor. His muscles constricted as her nails pressed into them and then raked down the ridges, leaving small welts in their wake.

"Goddamn it," he growled, roughly spinning her around so he could explore her front while he wrapped one arm around her collar bone to pin her back against him. She reached an arm up to find his head behind her, filling her hand with his hair she pulled hard, and he responded by sharply biting her neck.

They needed to mark each other, leave the other with evidence that they had existed, even if only for a short time. They tore into one another, aggressive and hard, both trying to communicate their frustration and their angry sorrow.

Afterwards, as their breathing started to come back to normal, he rested his forehead on her shoulder, his breathing quick and shallow.

"God, Alex, I didn't hurt you, did I?"

She knew he was talking about the fierceness with which they had taken one another. She shook her head, staring at the ground, her arm bent over her head, braced on the wall.

"No. That was…amazing…powerful," she said between ragged breaths. She couldn't find the will to lie, even though that may have been more humane.

After a few seconds, she asked, "Did I hurt *you*?"

As she said the words, they felt bigger than this last encounter. She wondered if he heard them that way too.

Winn took a long time to respond, which made her think he too sensed more meaning in the question. "No," he said quietly, and it sounded like a lie.

Chapter 30

Following their intense final night in the barn, Winn had come upstairs with her and he'd held her all night long as they lay in bed, not speaking and not sleeping. Alex had dozed off somewhere in the predawn hours, and when she'd woken, he was gone. She decided to stick with her favorite coping skill, avoidance, and skip breakfast. It felt like her sadness and doubt would be on display, and she couldn't muster the strength to do that in front of an audience. Alex packed her room all the while staving off the tears.

She knew that saying goodbye to Winn was going to be heart-wrenching, but she didn't know what to expect from him. Cool dismissal? Mercurial anger? She loaded her car and did everything she could think of to put it off, but now it was time. She went to the main barn to find him, knowing he wouldn't come to find her. He was standing in the feed room with the inventory clipboard in his hand. Business as usual, she thought sadly, knowing better than to believe he was as unaffected as he looked.

"Whelp," she said as he looked up at her, his face sullen. "I'm, uh, I'm heading out."

He nodded at her. "Are you sure that this is what you want to do?" he asked, holding her gaze.

"I have to go back. I have responsibilities, relationships to repair, a career to establish."

"But what do *you* want?" He held her gaze.

"What I want and what I need have always been too far apart. I can't trust myself."

"This isn't the same," he said, shaking his head.

"Regardless, staying here would be hiding from my real life."

She could tell that her words hurt him. Silently she urged him to argue more, but simultaneously recognized the ridiculousness of the wish.

"Alex, I—" he paused and seemed to gather himself, and his eyes got hard with resignation. "I wish you the best."

She let out a breath and nodded. "I desperately want you to be happy, Winn. I know you will be."

There was a pause where neither knew what should come next. She finally stepped up to him and placed a soft kiss on the side of his jaw before whispering, "Goodbye, Winn."

He sucked in the air but remained silent. She turned and walked down the aisle, refusing to let herself look back.

***

Alex made her way to the main house. Mae and all of the other guys had gathered and were waiting on her return. Alex rushed through the hugs and well wishes. She laughed at the lighthearted jabs and went through the motions of promising visits and letters and offered tours of the city if anyone felt inclined to road trip. It felt wrong, all of it, so she hurried through in a blur, refusing to let any of it truly sink in.

She and Holden hopped into the car, and she waved one last time to a Winn-free crowd before turning down the drive. She made it through the forty-five-minute trip into town in shock, but then the tears started in earnest. With her vision blurred and her mind whirring a mile a minute, Alex pulled into the same country store she'd met Matt in a hundred years ago. She needed to catch her breath.

Before she knew it, an hour had passed, and still, she sat. The tears had stopped, but the weight of the decision she'd made remained. She had to keep going. She needed to start her life.

Like Emily had said, people were growing up, learning to stow their baggage and move on with their life. Alex tried to force herself to imagine a life in Chicago, and struggled to fill in any of the blanks.

Out of nowhere a familiar busted orange farm truck came pealing down the street and blew past the parking lot she was sitting in. A hundred yards down, it screeched to a stop in the middle of the road before it hung a U-turn and came careening into the lot. Pulling in like a bat out of hell, Winn hopped out of the cab and jogged over to her open window.

"You been sitting in this parking lot for over an hour?" he asked, out of breath.

She nodded.

"Yeah, that's about how long I tried to convince myself not to chase you down, plus whatever time it took to give training notes to Trix."

"How long were you planning on being gone?"

"However long it took."

She gave him a skeptical look to which he responded, "Honestly, with that head start, I wasn't sure I'd catch you before Iowa."

"And what if you hadn't?"

Winn shrugged. "I think for all the talking we did in the last few days, I never said what it is I want. If I had to drive to Chicago to tell you that I want you to come home, I would have."

"Chicago is my home," Alex insisted.

"We both know that's not true anymore."

She let out a long breath and got out of the car. "We talked about this."

Winn nodded slowly, eyes downturned, fingers splayed on his hips, one leg cocked out to the side. "We did."

"We talked about appreciating what an amazing end to the summer we had, but that it was time to go back to reality."

"We did."

"You and I both know that we have the things we need to work out. We knew we weren't going to fix one another and that it wouldn't work if we tried."

Again, he nodded. "All of that was said."

"Well, it's time."

"There were things left unsaid too, though. Things that I should have said to you before you drove away."

He looked up at her, liquid entreaty whirling in his eyes. "This isn't about fixing one another. This is about making a choice, and I'm saying, pick us. Pick us because it's right. I think the ranch is the right place for you, and I think you being there makes it that place for me again. I think it's where you belong. I think...I think so many things, but I know..." He broke eye contact briefly before landing a hard gaze on her. "I know I'm in love with you."

Her breath caught. Winn went on. "And I know I needed to say that before I let you leave."

"Winn, I—"

"Please don't. I'm going to get back in my truck, going to go up to that stop sign there and I'm going to turn right. I'm going to foolishly let myself hope that you'll do the same and that you'll finish that sentence at home. But, if you go left, I won't be able to bear the memory of you saying those words to me before walking out of my life."

He placed a palm on both sides of her face, pulling her into a long, slow kiss that had her sinking into him. When they finally broke apart, he looked as if he was going to say something else, and then changed his mind. He gave her a short nod and turned to walk back to his truck. As promised, he pulled out to the stop sign and turned right.

Alex looked down at her shaking hands then up to the stop sign and the empty intersection. The idea of going left genuinely hurt her heart. The thought of leaving Winn and the ranch behind was devastating.

But the idea of going right scared her to the core. How could she pretend she deserved what was at the end of that drive?

She chewed on her lip and felt time slow to a near halt. After a few minutes, which felt like an eternity, she said, "Okay" to the vacant parking lot.

She got back in, started her car, pulled out of the parking lot, hit the stop sign, and turned right.

Next up: *Breaking Wicked*
Trix's story, plus Winn and Alex starting their life at Crooked Brook Ranch

PLAYLIST

Hamilton Leithauser "In a Black Out"
Rag'n'Bone Man "Human"
Kodaline "All I Want"
Travis Tritt "T-R-O-U-B-L-E"
The Allman Brothers Band "Whipping Post"
Travis Tritt "Where Corn Don't Grow"
Cam "Burning House"
Justin Moore "I Could Kick Your Ass"
The Duhks "Annabel"
A Great Big World "Say Something"
Randy Travis "Forever and Ever, Amen"
Birdy "Skinny Love"
Pistol Annies "I Feel a Sin Comin' On"
The Civil Wars "I Had Me a Girl"
Jason Aldean "You Make It Easy"
Imagine Dragons "I'm So Sorry"
Imagine Dragons "I Bet My Life"
Imagine Dragons "Polaroid"

ABOUT THE AUTHOR

E. J. is a wife and mother, a foster parent, a reformed corporate lackey with a degree in something unhelpful, and is a twenty-year veteran of the horse training industry. Currently, she works part time trying to teach adults and children how to not damage themselves on horseback. In her spare time - when she's not ignoring laundry, bathing one of the multiple dogs and/or children, or acting as an unpaid chauffeur - she gives in to her persistent craving to tell a story she hopes you can lose yourself in.

Connect with EJ:
website: ejnickson.com
instagram: author_ej_nickson
twitter: twitter.com/EJNickson1
facebook: facebook.com/EJNicksonWritesSometimes

Boroughs Publishing Group

www.**BOROUGHSPUBLISHINGGROUP**.com

If you enjoyed this book, please write a review. Our authors appreciate the feedback, and it helps future readers find books they love. We welcome your comments and invite you to send them to info@boroughspublishinggroup.com. Follow us on Facebook, Twitter and Instagram, and be sure to sign up for our newsletter for surprises and new releases from your favorite authors.

Are you an aspiring writer? Check out www.boroughspublishinggroup.com/submit and see if we can help you make your dreams come true.

Made in the USA
Columbia, SC
17 April 2021